THE RETURN OF THE RANCHER

MAX BRAND

Author Of Millions Of Books In Print!

"A good and gripping yarn with plenty of punch."
—*New York Times*

A writer of legendary genius, Max Brand has brought to his Westerns the raw frontier action and historical authenticity that have earned him the title of the world's most celebrated Western writer.

In *The Return Of The Rancher*, Jim Seton is released after serving a hellish five-year sentence for a crime he didn't commit. Now he's back in Claymore, and ready to take on the yellowbellies who framed him. The spineless sidewinders are coming at him with murder in their eyes, but Jim is ready to settle the score.

MAX BRAND

THE RETURN OF THE RANCHER

LEISURE BOOKS **NEW YORK CITY**

CHAPTER 1

When the stage left the town of Sage Valley on the last lap of the journey to Claymore, Jimmy Seton found that there was only one passenger with him in the coach. She was young, she was pretty, she was always smiling; but, though Seton liked a pretty face as well as the next man, he did not speak to her, because none of the smiles were for him.

Whether she looked at the ragged mountainsides that jumped up around them, or at the hardy patches of evergreens, or at the hell-nests of rocks which blazed in the sun, or at the spinning wheels, or turned to view the dust cloud which tossed up continually behind and sometimes overtook them, she was always smiling. Water does not bubble from a spring more continually than the smiles of this girl welled up on her lips.

It is pleasant to see a smiling face, but Seton began to be a little disturbed. He was young enough—he was not yet thirty, in fact—and, if he was no Adonis, at least he was born with a cheerful eye and a clean look. Still, to this bright-eyed little beauty he seemed no more than a mist, a phantom.

So he set himself to watching the backs of the driver and the guard. The driver was in shirtsleeves. His blue flannel shirt was powdered white with dust. The guard wore a vest, and the unfastened buckle of it was always bouncing up and down. It fascinated Seton and made him rather nervous. He admired that guard. He admired the brown-black to which his neck was burned; the ease with which the veteran gave to the joltings and the jars of the big vehicle on that rough road; the eternal vigilance which kept his head turning a bit from side to side, lest, out of the shrubbery or from one of the barricades of rocks, heads and shoulders of armed men might rise and leveled rifles cover the stage. Across his knees was a shotgun. Behind him, laid along the seat with a muzzle pointing out, was a fifteen-shot Winchester. He was a fighting man, and the type which Seton could appreciate. He thought with a certain awe of the way this fellow cruised above the dust cloud, above the leaping mud, winter and summer, along this same route.

They climbed slowly to the divide, and then lurched down the narrow ravine which widened beneath them into Claymore Valley. Claymore itself, at the mouth of the valley, was not yet in sight. This was a different country. The south winds, forced up along the valley and collected, dropped their rain in sufficient quantity to keep Claymore Valley green all through the year, except in September. The ground was more rolling, too. The olive-gray bleakness on the farther side of the divide, the naked rocks, the heat, the desolation were here replaced by a comfortable sense that man would find life pleasant in this valley.

Most of the way was now downhill, winding along the drop of the valley floor, so they went on at a good cantering pace, skidding and heeling like a ship on the corners, and squirting the dust far out to the side. All the tall grass and the flowering weeds along the way were already chalk-white from similar dustings.

A little runlet made a dark streak across the road. The driver jammed on his brake with foot and hand, but the wheels were still running fast when they struck the soft mud. They cut through it to hardpan and the stage crossed over with a tremendous jolt and groaning. It heeled so far that the girl cried out and leaped to her feet.

Seton caught her by the arm and jerked her back.

"Hang on, and you'll be all right," said he.

She turned squarely to him, at last, and she began to laugh. Those straight eyes of hers, and the childish laugh

6

which flowed and bubbled effortlessly from her lips pleased him still more. He grinned broadly back at her.

"I was silly," said she. "I was thinking of something else when we went crash."

"Yeah. You better watch the road," said Seton. "They have a bad spill, once in a while." He pointed back. "That last corner, a fellow turned himself over out of a buggy."

"Heavens! Was he hurt?"

"Hurt? Well, you can see for yourself. There's a fifty-foot drop from the edge of the road, and he fell the whole ways."

She closed her eyes with a shudder.

"He was killed, then?"

"Killed? He was all spread out. It looked like something had run a crusher over him. You going to stop off at Claymore?"

"Yes. I live there. Do you?"

"I used to live there. I'm going to try to live there again."

"Oh, you'll find it easy. Claymore's the finest town in the world."

"I used to think that way myself."

"You won't change your mind. My father says he'd rather be here than any other place he knows about, and he's traveled a lot."

"You live right in the town?"

"No. About a mile out. He's got a ranch."

"On what road?"

"On the valley road."

"A mile out? Used to be the Benson place, along about there."

"That's the very one."

"Go on!"

"That's the place. Father bought it."

"That used to be a mighty good-sized piece of land. Three-four thousand acres, I'd say."

"It hasn't shrunk much," said the girl.

"Well, it was worth a pile of money in the old days."

"Yes. Father paid forty an acre for it."

7

"Hold on. Forty an acre? Has there been gold or something struck on that—"

She did not wait for the last of his speech but answered the first part.

She nodded and smiled at him very complacently.

"Yes, we got the place very cheap. Douglas Walters happens to be a friend of ours," she added, with much pride.

He nodded in turn.

"Yeah?" said he.

"You know him?"

"You better believe I know him!"

"He's wonderful, isn't he?" said the girl.

In her enthusiasm, she had to lean a little toward her traveling companion and give him the full benefit of her smile.

He enjoyed this for half a second before he replied:

"I'll say I never knew anybody like Doug Walters."

"He's so big and handsome!" said the girl.

"He's handsome; and he's big," assented Seton, gravely.

He began to watch her with a narrower curiosity. She was flushed with happiness, and he began to guess why she was so continually smiling at nothing at all. There was a light inside her. She carried, it seemed, an unalterable warmth in her heart.

Perhaps Douglas Walters was the source of it.

"Doug helped you get the Benson place for forty dollars an acre, did he?"

"Yes. We never could have managed it otherwise, I suppose! But he knows just how to do everything!"

"Does he?" said Seton.

He had recourse to rolling a cigarette.

"I guess he's foreman for you now, then?"

"Yes, he runs everything for us. It's wonderful, really. He hires and fires and plans—Father isn't very practical. You know Douglas for a long time?" she added, as though she felt that she had been confiding too much in a stranger and wished to be reassured.

"Let me see," said Seton, reflectively. "I've known him about twenty-five years."

"Gracious!" said the girl.

She clasped her hands together and beamed at him with more friendship than ever.

"Twenty-five years!" she said. "What a lot!"

"Yes, it was quite a lot," said Seton, gravely. "But the last five years I haven't seen him."

"No? Not once?"

"No, I've been away."

"What a pity," said she. "He'll be frightfully excited when he hears that I came up on the stage with you, won't he?"

"I think maybe he'll be excited when he hears that I'm back," said Seton.

"Of course, he will. After five years?"

"Yes, it's quite a stretch."

"You haven't told me your name."

"I'm Jim Seton."

"I'm Mary Ash. Molly, I should say. Everybody calls me Molly—and you know Douglas so well. He'll be so glad to see you!"

The smile of Seton came and went, all in a flash.

"Well," he said, "he's going to see me, all right. How long have you folks been around these parts?"

"About three months, now."

"Three months, eh?"

"Yes. Father wasn't very well in the city. The doctors advised the country life for him. And we're so lucky that we found Douglas to take charge of everything."

"He can take charge of everything, all right," said Seton. "How'd your father meet him?"

"You'd laugh! It was in a poker game in the Sage Valley hotel. He won quite a lot from Daddy."

"Yeah. He generally wins at cards."

"But what a lucky thing that meeting was!"

"Was it?"

"Why, it saved my father's life."

"How come?"

"Afterward, two scoundrels attacked him in the street and demanded his money, but it seems that Douglas had seen

9

the two men acting in a suspicious way, and he had trailed Father—"

"He's a good hand on a trail. Like a cat," said Seton.

"Yes, he's wonderful! And when it came to the moment of trouble, he rushed in and scattered the pair of them. Heaven alone knows what might have happened, otherwise."

"Well," said Seton, "for one thing you mightn't have had the Benson place—at forty dollars an acre!"

"Oh, but we wouldn't have had Douglas, either, because after that he and Father talked, and they became great friends, and it simply led on to everything."

"Yeah, I'll bet it did," said Seton, and he looked down to the ring on her hand.

CHAPTER 2

She had not failed to notice the direction of his glance, and, looking up to him with misty eyes of happiness, she flushed deeply and by a silent implication allowed him to see that his surmise was correct. His old acquaintance with Douglas Walters removed all sense of constraint, it appeared. Her flush died away quickly; her bright glance remained contentedly upon Seton.

"*Where* have you been for five whole years?" said she.

"You mean, how could I stay away from Doug Walters that long?"

She seemed to see no irony in this remark.

"Yes. It's such a long time—when you were such great friends."

"Well, we knew each other pretty well," said he, "but the fact is that I wanted badly enough to see Walters again."

"Ah, but business kept you away?"

"Yes."

"What *is* your business, Mr. Seton?"

"Well, I'm what you'd call a common or garden cowpuncher. Good steady graft on a wild root, bearing about three hundred and sixty days out of the year, and five days off to play poker, and spend the harvest. That's been my regular calling, Miss Ash. But the last five years, I been mixed up in some government work."

"Oh," she said. "Then you're also a lawyer or contractor, or something?"

"I've had some dealings with the law," said Seton. "But this job of mine was mostly handwork."

"Handwork?" said the girl, bewildered.

"Yes, on a rock pile."

She blinked at him, and waited for an explanation.

"But it's a pretty good job, in a way, working for the government like that. They give you room and board free and plenty of protection."

"But I don't understand," said she.

"I'll tell you," said he. "Even the haircuts was free of charge where I've been staying, and they made 'em good and close, too!"

He took off his hat and displayed a short-cropped head, and at this she stared as at a page printed in an unknown tongue.

He said briefly: "I've been five years in the penitentiary." And he met her eye, squarely.

Her reaction made him laugh.

"Even Douglas couldn't help you?" she cried.

He grinned back at her.

"Even Douglas couldn't help me," he echoed. "They ran me up."

"But why?" she asked, horrified, it appeared, not because she was talking to an ex-convict, but because of the injustice which must have caused his sentence. "How did they dare to do such a thing?"

"Well," said he, "there was a lot of things on the mind of the sheriff and the judge and the jury. They figured that a little train-robbin' job was partly my work, besides a hand in a coupla killings." He smiled at her, broadly. "It gets people to feeling pretty hard, when they hear things like that!"

"Good heavens," said the girl. "How dreadful for them to suspect you of such things? How did they dare to?"

"Well, they pried a bullet out of one of the dead guards of that train, and they found out that it went pretty well with the sort of a gun that I was packing. And they found that I'd been missing from the ranch where I was working about the time that the robbery come along, and so they put one and two together and made a million out of it."

"Oh, poor fellow," said Molly Ash. And her eyes melted with sympathy and utter belief in him.

"What did Douglas say?" she asked.

"Near as I can recollect, he said I was lucky not to get hung."

"Hung?"

"Yes, but part of the evidence was kind of woozy, and, after five years, the governor decided that he'd pardon me. That's the only reason why I didn't spend the rest of my life behind the bars, in stripes. Good behavior got me out, and some pretty woozy testimony that had been used against me at the time of the trial."

"How glad all your friends will be!" said she.

His smile persisted, about the mouth, but vanished from his eyes.

"I've got no friends, Miss Ash," said he.

"What in the world do you mean?" she cried.

"Dead men have got no friends," said he.

"Dead men? But you're not—why, what do you mean?"

"Out of sight, out of mind; out of mind is the same as dead."

"Oh, but people never would forget a man like you!" said she.

"Wouldn't they? Well, you see that I'm heading right back

for the old stamping ground, and I'll soon have a chance to see how much they remember about me."

"Douglas," she said, "would never forget you."

His smile went out entirely.

"No," he said. "I reckon that Doug Walters will never forget me."

"Of course he won't. There'll be others, too. Of course I know that you feel bitter, having been injured the way you've been, but you'll find that things are better than you think."

"What makes you feel that I've been injured?" he asked.

"What makes me feel it? That's a question, I must say! Why, I can see in your face that you wouldn't hurt a fly, Mr. Seton!"

She beamed at him, again, as she spoke. Seton rubbed his knuckles across his chin, and then smiled down at the hard palm of his hand.

"Well," he said, "that shows how deceivin' appearances can be, because I was at that train robbery, all right."

"Oh!" she gasped.

Then she went on: "But *I* understand! You were there because you had some terrible, controlling motive. I know exactly how it was. You had a sick mother, or someone dear to you—and you *had* to get money for them. Wasn't that it?"

Seton laughed heartily.

"Shall I tell you why I was there?" he asked.

"Yes. Do tell me—if you wish to."

"I'll tell you, all right. I was there because I was five years younger than I am now."

She stared before her, at the windings of the road.

"I can't make out what that has to do with it," said she.

"Well, it's the truth, however. I was so young that I didn't know a thing. And I wanted to find out. So I found out, all right. I found out that fire burns and water is wet and bullets kill, and all of those things."

She drew herself back a little, at this.

"You don't really mean that you actually killed a man?"

He shook his head. There was a trace of wonder in his tone.

"No," he said, "I didn't kill a man. Never in my life."

"Well, no matter what you've done, you've been frightfully punished," she declared. "My heart aches for you, Mr. Seton. And Douglas will be so *delighted* when I tell him about—"

"No, don't tell him, please."

"But why not?"

"I'll tell you how it is. You know how long I've known him?"

"Oh, yes. Of course I know that."

"Well, I want to surprise him. He doesn't know that I'm out of prison. Nobody does. It doesn't make much difference, but I'd certainly like to surprise him. I'd like to see the expression on his face when he lays eyes on me without knowing that I'm expected to arrive in these parts."

She clapped her hands together.

"Ah, yes, yes!" said she. "Don't I know what you mean? Of course I do! You want to see dear old Douglas almost faint with pleasure and astonishment."

"Yes," said the ex-convict, without a trace of a smile, "I want to see him almost faint. I half expect that he will, for that matter. I hope that you'll be by to see it."

"I'd love to. Old friends—what's dearer and nearer in the world than they are?"

"Yeah, It's a good old world," said Seton, his mouth twisting a little.

"Isn't it?" said the girl.

She leaned back in the seat and half closed her eyes.

"Ah," she said, "but when I think of it—and the happiness there is, and the truth and the kindness—"

"Yeah, there's a lot of that!"

"And the charity and the gentleness—"

"Yeah. Tons of it. I've seen tons of it, passing by."

"Have you? Well, I often wonder *how* there can be really unhappy, worried, troubled, poor people who don't seem to know how to make both ends meet. All they have to do is to go to the right place and ask for help."

"Do they?" said he.

"Why, of course. Oh, you mean that proud people wouldn't do that? That's the pity. If people wouldn't be so proud. It turns men into steel. I've seen Douglas, even, be proud and haughty, to other men—the cowpunchers who work under him, you know. Not that he means it, but he can't help being a little proud."

"No," said the other. "He never could help that. It's the way he's made, I reckon."

"How beautifully you understand him!" said Molly Ash. "Ah, but there's nothing like old friends! I have some friends, Mr. Seton, that I love so much, the tears just rush into my eyes, sometimes, when I think of them. Such dear friends. And you know the grand things about having close friends?"

"I know some things about having close friends," said he. "Which grand thing do you mean?"

"I mean that, if you have dear friends, you know what they need and what you can do for them. They don't have to ask. You just know. Isn't that the beautiful part of it? You can read their minds, and tell what they're hungry for."

"Hungry," said he. "Yeah, I've noticed that friends are kind of hungry, all right."

"How happy Douglas will be!" she repeated. "You know what you ought to do?"

"What should I do?" said he.

"You ought to get off the stage right at the gate of our place and walk up with me. We can leave our grips down by the gate and send somebody down for them, afterward. That's what you ought to do. You know, *I'm* coming back by surprise, too. They don't expect me so soon. And dear old Douglas, won't he almost drop dead when he sees the two of us together?"

Seton seemed to be studying the future.

"As a matter of fact," said he, "I expect that he just about *will* drop dead. And if you don't mind, I *will* get off at your gate."

CHAPTER 3

They could see the town of Claymore, presently. It lay just at the mouth of the valley which pointed like a dagger at the heart of Mexico.

"On clear days," said the girl, "we can look from our top windows right down through the gap, and see the valley of the Rio Grande. It's rather odd to look out at an idea like Mexico from one's window. Don't you think so?"

"I'll tell you what's odder," said he.

"What's that?"

"To be not only looking at an idea like Mexico, but to be right inside of it."

"Oh, you've been there, have you?"

"Yeah, I've been there, all right."

"Well, it must be very strange and wonderful."

"You've said it," declared Seton. "That's what it is. It's strange and wonderful."

"And beautiful, isn't it?" said she.

"Beautiful?" he said, deliberating. "Yeah. It's beautiful, all right."

"How long were you there?"

"Centuries—"

"What?"

"Yeah, thousands of years, it seems like to me."

"My goodness, Mr. Seton, what do you mean?"

"Well, you know how long a day can be when you're young."

"Yes. Like a summer afternoon with nothing to do?"

"That's it. Time sort of dragged for me, when I was in Mexico."

"But why did you go there, then?"

"Well, I wasn't invited. I just went."

"Oh, did you?"

"Yes. Some people they up and suggested that I ought to go to Mexico."

"But I don't understand. Why did they suggest it?"

"I've kind of wondered about that, myself."

"Didn't they give any reasons?"

"Yes. They thought that I'd find it a lot more healthy down there."

"I've heard that the mountain air *is* wonderfully good for one; it's so dry."

"Come to think of it, they *did* mention the air. They thought the Mexican air would be a lot better for me."

"Yes, it's so wonderfully dry."

"Dry? Well, Miss Ash, I found Mexico pretty wet."

"Wet? Oh, but you mean the coastal plain, then?"

"No, it was kind of wet all over," said Seton. "Wherever I went, it was wet."

"Isn't that odd!" said she. "I've always heard—but then, perhaps it was an unseasonal period of rain?"

"Yeah. I saw some unseasonal rain, all right," said he. "It rained pretty hard on me a couple or three times down there."

"Yes, one has to keep a slicker along, I've heard."

"Slicker? Slickers wouldn't keep out the kind of a rain that I saw, down there."

"Terrible hailstorms, I suppose?"

"Hail? Hail's no word for it. Hail's close to the word, though."

"What word?" said she.

He did not seem to hear.

"Hospitable lot, those Mexicans," he said.

"Yes, yes!" she replied. "Sometimes one hears unpleasant things about Mexico, but *I* know some very splendid ladies and gentlemen from Mexico."

"Yeah, I'll bet you do," said he.

17

"And I'm so delighted to hear you speak so warmly about Mexico."

"Yeah. You don't know how warmly I can speak about Mexico," said he.

"And the hospitality—the beautiful hospitality that one finds here in the great West. I suppose it's the same thing down there, or even more so?"

"I'll tell you how hospitable they are."

"Oh, yes. *Do* tell me."

"They were so hospitable to me that they would hardly let me go."

"Dear Mr. Seton, were they really? How it warms my heart to hear about it."

"It warmed me up a good deal, too," said he. "Warmed me up to the sweating point."

"Making excuses to get away from their kindness?"

"That's exactly it. I made all kinds of excuses."

"And they wouldn't believe you?"

"No, they just wouldn't. They were set on having me, and that was all there was to it. Have me they would."

"Oh, I've had some difficulties of the same sort since I came West," said she. "Do you know, some of our big-hearted friends, they've pressed me so to stay on longer that to get away I've actually now and then had to tell a fib, Mr. Seton?"

"You don't mean it!" said Seton. "Well, come to think of it, I had to do the same thing right down there in Mexico."

"Did you?"

"You bet I did. But the fibs didn't work at all."

"No?"

"No, they didn't."

"How your business must have suffered, then!"

"Yeah. Matter of fact, it was pretty near impossible for me to get any business done. My business suffered, and I suffered, too."

"Ah, but such kind, gentle people! One can forgive too much kindness, can't one? And too much attention!"

"Can one?" said Seton. "I dunno. I've had attentions paid to me down there in Mexico that I can't forget."

18

"Ah, I'll wager that you have. They just forced things on you, I suppose."

"You bet they forced things on me. I had to steal away."

"Did you, really?"

"Yeah. I really did."

"It must have been terrible."

"You don't know how terrible it was, a couple or three times when I had to slip away, down there. They even followed me."

"How extraordinary."

"Yeah. It was extraordinary, all right. It nearly flabbergasted me."

"I know," she said cheerfully. "Up in the mountains, in places where they don't often have visitors."

"Yeah. And down in the plains, too. It didn't seem to make much difference to them."

"Well, they hadn't seen a man like you, I imagine."

"There's a lot of truth in that, if I do say it myself. They hadn't seen many men like me, I guess."

"Your ways were different, I suppose."

"I'll tell you something, Miss Ash."

"Yes, do tell me."

"Well, they found my ways so different that they just couldn't get used to them. That was one of the reasons why they followed me around."

"How charming and annoying they must have been!"

"More annoying, I'd say."

"And they finally made you tired of them?"

"Tired? You got no idea how tired I got of Mexicans."

"And their open houses, and their pressing invitations, and all?"

"You bet you. Every town that I went through had a house open to me, and the men of the town didn't seem to have anything better to do than to try to get into the house."

"Oh, dear," said Molly Ash. "How frightfully embarrassing."

"I'll tell a man. Embarrassing was hardly the word for it. I used to sweat getting away from them, sometimes."

19

"But really, you must have been a very famous man for them to make so much fuss about you!"

"Well, I don't want to blow my own horn," said Seton, "but you know how it is. Sometimes you get known, a couple or three little things that you do, and don't think much of yourself."

"I know."

"You even hope that other people won't find out about 'em."

"Exactly!" said the girl, delighted.

"Well, I found myself getting pretty well known, that way, all through the north of Mexico."

"Did you ever go down to Mexico City?"

"Yes, I even went down there."

"It must have been grand, there. I've heard so much about it. Did you see some of the important people?"

"I'll tell you how it was. I just slipped into the town incognito, so to speak. But they found out that I was there, all right!"

"Did they? And then they tried to look you up?"

"You bet they tried. Speaking of important people, some of the most important people in Mexico were just busting themselves to get hold of me."

"Were they really? How delightful!"

"Well, I didn't feel that way about it. The work that I'd come to do down there, I wanted to do in the dark, as you might say."

"And did they find you?"

"Well, finally one of the big officials comes out with a reward for anybody who can locate me—that was after I'd been working there only a couple of weeks."

"How silly—and beautiful!"

"I thought it was more silly, for my part."

"And did they find you, at last?"

"No. I decided that I'd better move along. So I did."

"Oh, and they didn't get you?"

"No, Miss Ash. They didn't get me. There was a pretty close call, but I had a good horse, and away I went."

"Why, Mr. Seton, what a recluse you must be!"

"Sort of, at times. I generally like to be quiet and do things my own way."

"I know. I often feel that way. I just want to stay quietly in my room. It's quite wonderful, the way I feel that I understand you, Mr. Seton, all the way through."

"Do you?"

"Yes. It's just as though there were a sort of a sympathy between us. Though I suppose it's just because we both know dear old Douglas. But I *do* feel that I understand you well."

He leaned toward her. His voice became deep.

"Do you know, Miss Ash, that I feel no one in the world ever has understood me the way you do!"

CHAPTER 4

They drew near the gate of the ranch and there the stage stopped. The two got down. The driver waved to them. The guard grunted and made a movement with his hand, and the stage rolled away. They watched it, for a moment, until the dust cloud which its wheels turned up gradually obscured it, and they had only dim glimpses of the heavy body rocking on the springs. Then they turned to the gate.

It was a heavy affair of five strong bars, and it sagged down from its main post. While Seton slid back the bolt shaft and dragged the gate open over the rut which had been worn in the ground, an inquisitive colt in the pasture near by came and hung his head over the fence.

Seton looked up to find that the girl was rubbing the nose of the colt and the latter snorting at her hand, half delighted and half terrified, and a little mischievous, too.

"Isn't he a darling?" said the girl, in her confiding manner.

"He looks kind of darling in a pasture, maybe," said Seton. "He's got a bucking eye in his head, though, if I ever saw one. Look out!"

The colt had wheeled, and with a flourish of its heels in the general direction of the girl's head, it cantered away, whinnying, across the pasture. Other grazing horses lifted their shaggy heads to stare at the newcomers.

Seton looked at them, at the hills beyond, dotted with cattle, at the mountains still farther away, some of them with white heads of snow.

"It's pretty good," said he.

"Isn't it all beautiful? But you know the place, of course. We'll just leave the two suitcases down here, Mr. Seton, and one of the men will come down for them. Oh, no. Don't try to carry them. I can see that yours is heavy, but mine is really just like lead. Such a lot of books in it!"

Seton picked up the cases and carried them inside the gate, which he shut after them. He picked up the grips again, and went on. No matter how heavy the suitcases were, he carried them with an easy swing, and his arms were not pulled straight by the burden.

"How strong you are!" said the girl. "How beautiful it is to be so strong!"

"You swing a sledge hammer for five years and it puts on stuff that you never had before," said Seton.

"I suppose it did," said she. "I suppose that I ought to try it."

"Yeah. You try it. Pick out a good little old fourteen-pound sledge and swing that for eight hours a day. It'll do you a lot of good. D'you ride those mustangs?"

He jerked his head toward the horses in the field.

"I've tried," said Molly Ash, "but I don't seem to have a very good balance in the saddle. They get out from under me, somehow."

"Yeah. They get out from under you. They get out from under me, too, now and then. Have some bad falls?"

"I was rather bruised, for a time. And then I found a little pinto mare I could understand better, and since then she and I have had no trouble together."

"That's good," said he. "I guess that Doug Walters picked her out for you?"

"Oh, yes. He did. Of course he knows everything about horses. He seems to know about everything else, nearly, too."

"He bought her for you, eh?"

"Yes. He bought her. There she is, now!"

She pointed to a little slim-bodied mustang in a corner of the field, close by.

"Get her cheap?" asked Seton.

"Well, she cost a good deal; but, considering what she is, I don't suppose that she cost much."

"What is she, then?"

"Well, she's the very best sort of range blood," said the girl.

"Oh, is she? And what's the best kind of range blood?"

"I don't know. But Douglas knows all about those things."

"What did you pay?"

"Two hundred dollars."

"Hold on! Two hundred what?"

"Dollars. Why? Don't you like her?"

"Well, I've only seen about ten thousand that are as—well, she looks all right. She's easy gaited, anyway."

"How could you tell that?"

"Well, she has plenty of spring in the fetlock joint when she walks."

"I do wish that I could read horses like that!"

"I'd rather read their minds than their gaits. How old is she, did Doug Walters say?"

"She's five, is she?"

They were quite close to the corner where the mare was standing, and Seton paused for a moment and stared at the mare.

She's five, is she?"

"Yes. Just past."

"I should say she was just past," nodded Seton. "If she's five, I'm—"

He stopped himself.

23

"It'll never make her mad to call her five," said he.

"I don't know what you mean," said the girl.

"Oh, don't you mind me. I just sort of ramble along. You paid two hundred for the mare, did you?"

"Yes."

"To whom?"

"Why, to Douglas, of course. He'd had all the trouble of finding her, but he wouldn't take a penny of profit. But you know what sort of a man he is! Always thinking of others, and never a thought for his own interests."

"No?"

"No, never a one. Sometimes when I think about Douglas, it really makes my heart ache."

"I've had a good many aches, too," said Seton, "thinking about Doug Walters."

"Have you? He's wonderful, isn't he!"

"Yes. There's nobody else like him, that I've ever met."

They went up the deeply rutted lane, the girl keeping to the grass at the side of it, and Seton walking squarely in the middle of the road.

"Is he likely to be home, now?"

"Oh, yes. He's generally at the house."

"I thought that he was running the place for you."

"Oh, yes, he is."

"Does he run it by staying at the house?"

"You know—there's such a terrible lot of planning to do."

"Yeah?"

"Yes, and accounts, and things. He's generally in his office."

"Oh, he has an office, does he?"

"Yes. We've fixed up quite a nice room for him, looking south over the valley. It's such a pleasure to know that he's in rather pleasant surroundings when he's sitting there, thinking and working for us."

"Yeah. I'll bet that it makes a big difference to him. He don't have much of a chance to get out and ride the range with the rest of the boys, I guess?"

"Very little. That's the sad part."

"Sad for you folks, you mean?"

"Oh, no. Sad for him, because he yearns to be in the great outdoors and have the sky for a ceiling over his head."

"Does he say that?"

"Yes, I've often heard him say that. He really has the soul of a poet, you know."

"Yeah. I know all about that."

"There's a great sympathy between you two, isn't there?"

"You wouldn't believe the kind of a sympathy that there is between him and me," said Seton.

He walked on down the road with her, nodding his head a little.

"Your arms must be nearly pulled out of their sockets," said sympathetic little Miss Ash.

He did not answer. He reverted to the noble character of Douglas Walters.

"I guess he sort of yearns to get piled back into a saddle and ramp around on some of those mustangs," he said.

"That's it. To gallop with the wind in his face—that's what he loves, he always says."

"Well, maybe he'll have a chance to do a good deal of galloping, before long," said Seton. "Maybe he'll have a chance to enjoy a lot of riding, and fast riding, at that."

"What do you mean?"

"Well, it's getting along toward the soft time of the spring, when the ground is a lot safer to fall onto. I always like to break the young stock at that time of year. There's not so much dynamite in them, for one thing. Your father likes the Durham stock, I see?"

"Oh, Douglas picked out the cattle to stock the place for him."

Seton stopped and put down the suitcases.

"Oh, Mr. Seton! Really, you must be exhausted. Your face is quite red."

"I *feel* sort of red," said Seton.

He picked up the cases again, with a jerk.

"Let's go on," said he. "He picked out all of the stock, did he, and all of the horses. I suppose he built that new barn over there, too?"

"Oh, yes, he built that. He pointed out that we needed a big barn to hold winter feed."

"Why, they only have to do winter feeding in this valley about once in ten years, don't they?"

"But when the terrible famines come—"

"So he took and built that farm for your father, did he?"

"Yes. It's quite splendid inside."

"Yeah. It looks splendid, all right. I suppose Doug Walters handled all of the building contractors, and made the prices, and everything?"

"Yes. He saved us thousands of dollars, really—in the building."

"Did he say so?"

"Oh, yes. He showed Father how he had saved the money."

"He's a mighty intelligent man," said Seton.

"Yes, isn't he!"

"You bet he is," said Seton. "I used to think that he was only one in ten thousand, but I see that he's one in a million."

CHAPTER 5

They got to the ranch house. It wasn't much of a house. It was built of thin boards nailed on in irregular courses, warping here and there, and with plenty of gaps and cracks. Here and there, a patch of tar paper had been put over a particularly bad section of the wall.

There was a veranda running clear across the face of the house, the roof held up by skinny wooden pillars—mere three-by-fours. On this veranda sat half a dozen chairs, every one of them looking ready for the repair shop.

A windmill was spinning and clanking at the side of the house, and Seton could hear the water falling with a regular pulse and a musical reverberation into a big tank which must have been more than half empty at the time. A pipe from this tank supplied a watering trough in front of the house and near the long hitching rack.

All the trees, near by, had been cut down for firewood, by the lazy and improvident Bensons. There was nothing but the faint beginnings of a flower garden on one side and a flourishing vegetable garden on the other. To the right of the path extended the raw tangle of fencing which composed the corrals, and the great red-painted barn at the back of the fencing. There were two huge straw stacks near by, their tops blackened by the winter rains, their sides deeply cut by the hay saw which had worked out strips either for bedding or for food.

A little smooth-haired fox terrier came dashing out at them, and, from its path, chickens which had been scratching about in the garden fled away with clapping wings and rattling voices. He paid no attention to the stranger; he began to bounce up and down in front of his mistress.

"This is Spot," she said. "He doesn't like strangers, but he knows almost as much as a human being. There never was another dog like Spot, really!"

"He'll like me, I hope," said Seton, and, putting down the suitcases, he extended his hand.

Spot danced away like a prize fighter—like a prize fighter he sidled cautiously in, again. He sniffed at the extended hand. He leaped away as though a gun had been fired in his face.

"Oh, he'll never come to you," said the girl. "He—"

Suddenly Spot ran in and, crouching until his belly touched the ground, submitted to the patting, stroking hand of the stranger, while his vibrating tail knocked up a continual fountain of dust.

Molly Ash was amazed.

"I've never seen him do that before!" said she. "What a

27

wonderful way you must have with animals, Mr. Seton."

"I aim to get on with them as peaceful as possible," said Seton.

And he picked up the suitcases again, and went on toward the house, with the little terrier bumping his nose against his heels, so eager was he to learn more of this strange man.

The front screen door of the house was flung wide, with a screech. A white-headed, thin, meager little old man came hurrying out and reached his arms toward Molly Ash, and she, running forward, caught the old fellow in her arms.

By contrast, even the frail girl, for the moment, seemed robust and strong. And big Seton, putting the suitcases down on the edge of the veranda, stood by to watch them. Then he turned his eyes toward the corrals, the newly repaired fences, the cattle in the nearest fields.

Whatever the peculiarities of Mr. Douglas Walters, he seemed to have done a good job in putting the place in working order. With an experienced eye, Seton noted these things, and turned as his name was called.

He was introduced to Henry Ash, and took the thin, cold hand in his big grip, and met fairly the boyish, candid blue eye of the old man.

"But my girl tells me that you're an old friend of Douglas?" said he.

"I've known Doug Walters a long time," said Seton.

"Come right in and sit down," said Henry Ash. "It's very good to see you. Any friend of Walters' is free of this ranch, you may be sure. Molly, sit down here. Let me look at you. These have been long days, with you away from the place."

"I'm back for good," said she. "Have you brought on the garden, a lot?"

"The wistaria is sprouting leaves," he said. "It's going to make a great growth, and that mapelopsis at the back of the house is covered with red buds. I'll show them to you, pretty soon."

"I'm wild to see them. Who is that? A new man?"

She indicated a tall form which slouched slowly down the board walk that led from the back of the house to the corral

28

gate. The man was dressed in overalls, sagging outward at the knees from saddle friction and much wrinkling. He had on the usual high boots, with long heels, and glittering spurs.

"That's a new man," said Ash. "He's just come down from town. Seems that Douglas knows him."

"I thought he had rather a bad, dark face," said the girl.

"Douglas knows all about him."

"Oh, then he's all right, of course."

"Well, I think I've seen him myself," said Seton. "I'll go say hello to him, if you don't mind."

He stepped from the veranda and swung across the yard with a long, easy stride. At the corral gate he overtook the leisurely puncher just as the latter opened the gate by means of a resounding kick.

"Hello, Sparrow," said Seton.

The puncher whirled on his heel. The gate, reclosing by force of the weight attached to it, banged heavily against his side, but he did not seem to notice the blow. The cigarette which he had been making fell from his fingers, the tobacco, like a pale yellow dust, and the wheat-straw paper fluttering off in the breeze.

This he did not regard, either. The world had gone out for him. The only thing of importance that remained was the face of Seton, one might have said.

"Why, Sparrow," said the other, "a person might think that you didn't remember me."

"Is it you or your ghost?" croaked Sparrow.

"Feel me," said the other, and extended his hand.

Sparrow looked from the hand to the face of Seton, and shook his head.

"What in hell has happened?" he asked. "I thought that you was——"

"Having a long rest? I got rested up, Sparrow. I began to hanker after the outside, and so outside I came."

There was a gleam in the dark eye of the Sparrow.

"You're on the wing, are you?"

"That worries you, doesn't it?" suggested Seton, in his easy, good-natured voice. "You wouldn't like to think of me being a fugitive from the law again, would you? No, I understand the way you feel about me, Sparrow. It's touching, I tell you. It touches me to the quick. It touches me quicker, almost, than it touches you. But don't you worry. I'm carrying around with me something that I like better than a permanent royal flush. I've got the governor's pardon, Sparrow."

The Sparrow backed away a little, still looking the other up and down in a half bewildered way.

"It don't seem likely—" he said.

"No, it doesn't," said Seton, nodding and smiling; "considering the friends of mine who helped to put me away for a long rest, it doesn't seem likely that I'd get out again. I should have written to you about it, seeing that you helped me into the pen. I should have asked you if you didn't think that I'd rested long enough."

The Sparrow blinked rapidly.

"Look here," he said. "I dunno what's in your mind, but the fact is that I never had nothin' to do with the railroadin' of—"

Seton held up his hand, with a genial smile, and looked straight into those overbright, wavering eyes of the other.

"There you go!" he said. "There you go, talkin' down about yourself, makin' your share small. But I know how you tried to help me in there. I know how it used to worry you, seeing the way I was wearing myself out on the trail and the range. You could hardly stand it, Sparrow. It used to make your heart ache. And so you helped the others put me away. Why, you can't tell how grateful I am to you, Sparrow. The fact is that I have no words for telling it. But I'll never forget. Will you believe that?"

The Sparrow's thin lips were beginning to tremble. He moistened them with the tip of his tongue.

"Well, I dunno what you've got in mind, Seton," said he.

"I've got nothing in mind," replied Seton. "I just wanted to tell you that I expect to stay on at this place for quite a time. I ought to have a chance to see a lot of you."

The other turned a pale yellow-green.

"You're going to stay here?"

"Yes. I expect to. It looks like a good layout, to me."

"You dunno who else is here," said the Sparrow, with a savage lifting of his upper lip.

"Don't I? Well, I dunno. You don't mean my old partner, Doug Walters, do you?"

"You know that he's here, too?" said the Sparrow.

"Sure, I know it."

The eyes of the Sparrow wavered from side to side. Suddenly he turned on his heel and went out through the corral gate. The moment he had taken a step, he gave a convulsive start. He almost began to run, but checked himself and went on, stiffly erect, rigid from head to foot.

Seton looked after him for a moment. Then he went back to the two on the front veranda.

"Was it an old friend of yours?" asked the girl.

"I've known that fellow almost as long as I've known Doug Walters," said Seton. "I hoped that I'd see some more of him, here on the place, but he tells me that he's just had some bad news."

"Bad news?"

"Yes, and he'll have to pull his stakes and get going back to Claymore."

"That's rather odd," said the father, "seeing that he arrived here only the other day."

"He's a floater," said Seton. "You never can tell what sort of an idea a floater will get into his head. But now that he's gone, I begin to have a hope that old Doug will be able 'to make a place for me among his hired men."

"A place for you?" cried the girl, and struck her hands together. "Of *course* he'll make a place for you. How wonderful it will be for him to have you here."

CHAPTER 6

Douglas Walters was not in the house, but he was expected back soon. Mr. Henry Ash wanted to take Seton to a room and consider him as a guest at once, whether or not he took employment on the ranch. But Seton preferred to wait, he said, until he had had a talk with the foreman of the place.

"I don't want to stay unless I'm needed," said he.

And he persisted in his refusal.

So they sat out on the veranda, and felt the day lose its heat. Henry Ash and his daughter talked busily together about the ranch, about her recent visit, about the garden which the old man was making. Seton became the listener. Sometimes his lips pinched together a little. Sometimes a light glinted in his eyes, as when he said:

"You going to make a good profit on the ranch, Mr. Ash?"

"Oh, yes, we couldn't fail to, with a man like Douglas handling our affairs," said Henry Ash. "Not right away. A year or two of settling in is necessary. Douglas pointed out all of those things to us. Of course, one has to spend a good deal more than one expects in starting any new venture. I suppose that's the course of all financial experiments. Stocking a place, building barns, buying horses, saddles, harness—those things take time, naturally."

Seton nodded.

"What other places has Doug Walters run as foreman?" he asked.

"What others? What others has he mentioned, Molly?" said the old man, turning to his daughter.

"Why, I don't remember that he's mentioned any," she said, shaking her head.

"Kind of odd, isn't it?" suggested Seton, amiably.

They felt that it was a little odd, too, but their faith in their foreman was so implicit that no real doubt could linger in their minds. The name—Douglas Walters—was a rod of Aaron, for them; and, the instant it was used, a chorus of praise burst forth and innumerable anecdotes to illustrate his courage, his wit, his wisdom, his providence for the future. So Seton sat back and listened.

Presently a horseman came down the road, and, as quickly as his form could be separated from his dust cloud that rolled behind, the girl jumped up and ran down the path toward the gate, crying out:

"There's Douglas, now!"

"Don't let him know that I'm here," said Seton. "I want to surprise him, you know!"

She nodded cheerfully over her shoulder, laughing back, and went on toward the gate.

Henry Ash had risen, also, smiling broadly, and nodding his head in expectation.

"There's a man for you," said he. "There's a real man!"

He rode like a man, at least. Big, erect in the saddle, graceful, with the brim of his hat blowing back from his face, he swept closer to the gate. And Seton leaned forward in his chair, his jaw set hard, for a moment, and his eyes shining in a way that might have had great meaning for Henry Ash, if he had had eyes for anything other than the figure of the rider in the lane.

Then Seton rose and stepped back inside the doorway. There from the shadow he looked out and saw the rider bring his horse to a sliding, Western halt, saw him lean from the saddle, bringing his hat off with a flourish. Leaning far over the gate, he kissed the girl who stood inside it; then he cantered away to the corral and out of sight around the corner of the house.

Seton reached under the pit of his left shoulder and fingered the handles of a Colt which was slung there, thumbing the hammer fondly for a moment.

The girl came back up the path to the house, singing, her face happily flushed.

"Well, here he is! Did you see?" she called to her father.

"Ay, that was like Douglas!" said the old man.

"Wasn't it? *What* a rider he is!"

"I never saw his like," said the father.

"There's *no* one like him," she replied.

She began to laugh. Sheer joy bubbled from her throat, and Seton saw, for the first time, that she was something more than merely beautiful. He had been smiling at her for a long time, her childishness, her simplicity, her straightforward mildness. Now he stopped smiling, for the moment, at least. Since he had seen her father, he understood that the water flowed from a pure and single source. One might smile at the same qualities in the old man, also, but plainly he had had intelligence enough to make a fortune in his own field. And if, with his nature, he had made a fortune, what would he have made if he had been able to use the shrewdness of the ordinary business man? He invested in the world pure spirit and mind; he received back from it some few dollars, and a great deal of shoulder-shrugging, no doubt.

And what would be the case with Molly Ash?

These thoughts were interrupted by the arrival of the foreman. He came with a fine long stride around the corner of the house, knocking the dust of his journey from his big shoulders, and smiling at his employer and his daughter. It was a glorious presence that Douglas Walters possessed, a face noble in profile and classic in line. But the full face showed the eyes the least trifle too close together. He was swinging his hat in one hand, and this showed a finely formed head covered with closely curling hair the color of bronze.

He came up the steps with a single leap, and seated himself between the other two. Instantly they formed a single group, so close was the harmony of feeling among them.

He poured out a few questions to the girl. She waved her hand to stop him.

"I'll talk later about the trip and how nice everything and everybody was. Now I want to hear *you* talk!"

She lay back in her chair and feasted her eyes upon him with a blind fondness.

"What'll I talk about, Molly? Steers and horses and fences and the price of hay?"

"Anything," she said. "The last thing you've been doing."

"Well, I had to go into Claymore and fix up a little new loan for the ranch."

"Oh," said she. "Do we have to get loans, now?"

"Come, come," said her father. "You don't understand these things, Molly. Don't try to. I hardly understand them myself."

She nodded. Her face was perfectly placid and without suspicion, for all that Seton could see.

"I only wondered," she said. "When we came out West, it seemed to me that we had whole mountains of money."

Her father laughed, indulgently.

"You see how the girl is, Douglas. You'll have to teach her arithmetic and farming, one of these days. Why, you goose," he went on with a pretended severity, "do you think that we can buy tons of barbed wire with hundreds of cows and quantities of everything else—to say nothing of horses —without spending money almost like water?"

"Oh, no, I suppose not," said she.

"Of course not," said Henry Ash. "Well, Douglas, I don't suppose that you had any trouble getting what we wanted?"

"Oh, not a bit at the First National."

"But Hooker and Cross—haven't they handled all of our business and advanced all of the loans up to this time?"

The face of handsome Douglas Walters darkened decidedly at this. He leaned forward and shook a finger, as if at a child.

"I told you in the first place," he said—"I told you in the first place that old man Hooker was a crook!"

"Tut, tut, Douglas. That is a very hard thing to call a man!"

"How can I help it?" cried Walters, throwing up his big, powerful arms in a gesture of surrender. "How can I help calling a man like that a crook when I hear him actually questioning such a man, and such a gentleman as you are, Mr. Ash?"

"Well, well, well! What did he have to say about me?"

"I won't repeat it," said Douglas Walters. "I'll be eternally confounded if I'll repeat it to you. No, sir, when a creature like this here Hooker starts calling a gentleman like Henry Ash a counterfeit proposition—"

He checked himself.

"I shouldn't have said that," he said.

"Did he say that of me?" said the old man, utterly calm. "I hardly expected that of him, I must admit. But then, business men have business passions. Let it go. I don't even want his reasons."

"I'm glad you don't," said Douglas Walters. "And I'm glad that you didn't hear what I told him, when I let loose."

"Ah, I hope that you didn't say too much. He's a much older man than you are, my dear boy, and I dare say that he has had much to try him and to wear his temper thin, in the course of his life."

"He's old, but he has young ears—and a young tongue. The infernal scoundrel. Why—among other things he said that you were a fool to keep me on here as a foreman."

"No!" cried father and daughter in a single breath.

"How perfectly outrageous!" exclaimed the girl.

"That really was going very far," assented old Ash.

"Of course he doesn't want me here on the ranch," explained the foreman, gently. "The reason is that he'd like to gather the ranch into his own hands, and put it in leading-strings. Oh, he's done it before. He has a skinflint reputation all through the countryside. However, I went over to the First National at last."

"Did you get it there, without any trouble?"

"Oh, yes, no trouble at all."

"That's good. I don't understand Hooker and Cross, though. I thought better of them than that. And the First National handed the money right over?"

"Certainly they did. They have sense. They know which side their bread is buttered on, you'd better believe! And all they wanted was a little bonus."

"Ah? A bonus?" said Ash, in a tone of surprise.

"Oh, merest kind of a formality. I have the paper here. You scratch down your name and we get the money for the ranch."

"Bonus?" echoed the old man, frowning a little. "Ah, well, you know best, my boy. I certainly won't dispute your judgment."

"Of course not," said the girl. "That dreadful Mr. Hooker! And yet I always thought that he had a kind eye."

"A confounded old hypocrite, and you can take my word for it," answered the foreman.

"But there's something else for you to think about, Douglas," said the girl. "I have a happy surprise for you. Can you guess what it is?"

CHAPTER 7

"Surprise for me?" said big Douglas Walters. "What sort of surprise?"

"Why, a human surprise!" said she.

He puzzled a little, smiling, as though he was confident beforehand that nothing but pleasant surprises ever could come from her.

"All right," said he. "A human surprise, then. What's the human surprise, Molly?"

Seton pushed open the screen door and appeared in the entrance to the house, while Douglas Walters, turning in his chair, still smiling, looked over his shoulder and saw the stranger appearing.

One would have thought that a gun had been leveled at his head. Yes, and that the gun had fired a bullet through his head! For he slipped out of the chair to one knee and, twisting about, he threw up both hands high into the air.

"Great God!" cried Walters.

Both the girl and the old man had leaped to their feet at the sight of his consternation.

"Douglas! Douglas!" cried the girl. "But your old friend—"

"Why, hello, old man," said Seton, and advanced from the doorway with his hand outstretched. "I guess it's a surprise for you, isn't it?"

Walters staggered up to his feet.

"Surprise?" he said hoarsely. "You could of—"

Seton laughed cheerfully.

"Didn't expect me, old fellow, did you? I just dropped along to surprise you; met Miss Ash on the stage. Funny how things work out, isn't it?"

"Mighty funny," said Douglas Walters.

He began to laugh in a half choked style. He was breathing hard, and his face had lost its color. What had been natural healthy pink before was now purple. His lips were gray as ashes. His eyes stared. But he put out his hand, and the other grasped it.

"Why, Douglas," said Molly Ash, "one would almost think that you'd had a bad stroke, or something!"

"Well, it's because I mean such a lot to him, Miss Ash," said Seton.

He released the hand of the other and clapped the strong shoulder of Walters heavily.

"You have no idea what we mean to each other, has she, Doug?"

Walters stared at him. A flicker of a new intelligence gleamed in his eyes.

"No," he said, his voice coming back closer to its normal tone. "She has no idea."

Seton continued, talking smoothly to cover the confusion of the foreman:

"I should have let him know, before I dropped in on him, like this, right out of the middle of the sky. You've had in mind for a long time that I might get out of the pen, haven't you, Doug?"

Again there was that earnest glance of inquiry and wonder in the eye of Walters, and again the flash of growing understanding.

"I've had it in my mind ever since you went inside the prison gates, Jimmy."

"Oh, how delightful," said the girl. "Look, Daddy, how Douglas is almost overcome! Isn't it a great thing to see a man capable of such a feeling of friendship? If a man is capable of that he's capable of still greater—"

She stopped herself.

"Why, Douglas, I thought you were sick, for a moment," said Mr. Ash. "Sit down, boys. Sit down, both of you, and let's enjoy your happiness for a moment. Then we'll let you alone, together. But for a moment we want to warm ourselves at the same fire. You'll understand that?"

"I can't sit down," said Seton. "I'm a lot too excited about seeing old Doug Walters again and at last!"

"Well, it touches me to the heart," said Henry Ash, "to look at the pair of you. There's a pair of men, my dear child, you won't see duplicated the world over. Look at them! Of a height, of a weight—with the look that conquers the world. Both of them together, and so devoted. That's a picture to take to one's heart and never to forget."

"I'll never forget it, Father. How could I?" said she. And there were tears in her eyes as she spoke.

"In this world," said Henry Ash, "where there's so much misery, misunderstanding, hatred, doubt, difficulty, estrangement, woe and grief, all caused by men who are on the wrong sides of simple questions, you don't know what it means to me, Douglas, and you, Mr. Seton, to see two men who really understand each other."

"Well, sir," said Seton, smiling, "I guess we understand each other, all right. Don't we, Doug?"

Walters dragged a hand across a dripping forehead.

"Yeah. We understand each other, all right."

"Yes," said Seton, "there isn't an inch of either of our faces that the other fellow hasn't punched, one time or another."

"How terrible," said Molly.

"Tut, tut, dear," said the father. "That's the way boys are. As a youngster I was a little frail, but I've had my own boyish tussles. One is all the better for them."

"A lot better," said Seton. "You always feel better, particularly if you usually win, eh, Douglas?"

Douglas Walters did not reply. He tried to smile, but merely succeeded in producing a rather wry face.

"Yes," said Molly, laughing a little, "I suppose that Douglas was always an unconquerable sort of a fellow!"

She looked fondly upon him.

"Yes," said Seton, "he always would take a lot of conquering."

Walters made a gesture with both hands, to stop that part of the conversation as though for some reason it suddenly had become rather painful to him.

"How're you out? How'd you bust loose? We've had no word of a prison break!" said he. "How'd you get down here?"

"How'd I get out? Why, I walked out," said Seton.

He turned to Mr. Ash.

"I've told your daughter. I haven't told you, sir," he said, "that I've just spent five years in jail."

He set his jaw a little, and waited.

"My dear boy," said the good old man, gently, "God forgive me if I should pretend to judge any other man. Sometimes I think that only the highest spirits, the souls too keenly strung, are the ones which dare to commit crimes—crimes which may be simply excess of spirits, wild joy of joy, boiling over, and therefore disturbing simpler, quieter souls. No, no, my lad, I never should pretend to judge you!"

From the manner in which the eyes of young Seton grew wide, it seemed that he was seeing in the face or in the soul of Henry Ash a picture which enchanted and astounded him.

Suddenly he said:

"I believe you, sir!"

"Thank you," said simple Henry Ash.

"You walked right out!" said Walters, staring at the other. "That'd be your way—while the fool guards looked at you, right in the middle of the day, carrying an armful of wood, or something—walked right out and up the hill; and they didn't know what to make of it; they didn't get surprised, because you weren't running! Sure, that's the way you'd do it!"

"Ah, Seton," said the father. "Did you break jail, then?"

"No, that's what old Douglas thinks," said Seton, smiling again. You know how an old friend is. Always expecting a fellow to do impossible things. Matter of fact, there were other hands that turned the keys for me, Doug."

"Ah, you got a guard or two to bed, did you?"

The nostrils of Walters flared as he asked the question. His head lowered a little.

"The governor was the man who turned the keys and opened the locks for me, Doug."

"What?"

"I'm pardoned. Washed clean."

"It ain't possible!"

"Yes. It's possible. I've come all the way in daylight, by train and by stage. I'm pardoned, Doug, believe it or not!"

Walters drew in a great breath.

"Pardoned!" he exclaimed, and shook his head.

"Won't hardly believe it, old Douglas Walters," said Seton, fondly. "I guess that there was many a day when you hardly thought that I ever *would* get out of that prison, Doug. Isn't that right?"

Walters glared at him.

"Yes," he said. "I never thought that they'd *let* you get out. Never thought of that. But I sort of suspected that you might melt a hole in the concrete, sometime, you'd be so hot!"

"Sit down, sit down," said the father. "And tell us some more about yourself, Mr. Seton. Such a dear old friend of our Douglas, he must be our friend, too!"

"I think I want to be your friend," said Seton, slowly, solemnly. "I think it would make a lot of difference to me to be your friend."

Douglas Walters started with great violence. He looked at Seton, and he looked at Ash and the girl. Then he stared suddenly down at the floor, and his brow darkened.

"But I'll have to tell you," said Seton, "that I was put in prison because I was convicted of train robbery, and suspected of several manslaughters."

The face of Ash wrinkled with pain, and yet he shook his head.

"Youth, youth, youth!" he said. "Youth is nearly always cruel—unless there's a Molly in the case to soften hearts!"

He looked down at her with the tenderest love, and she looked back to his face, with a smile. The trust between them was more profound than words or worlds could measure.

"No matter what he was accused of," said Molly, "the governor decided that he had been punished enough. And that ends everything, doesn't it?"

"Great heavens, yes!" said the father. "Five years in prison? Five years of stripes and misery and low companionship? My boy, you've been through the fire, and I know that you've been purified, if any purging away was needed! And who of us has a clean slate? There are red marks against all of us, marks that we cannot have wiped away. There are few old men, my dear lad, who would not willingly go to prison, if by so doing they could square the eternal account. But we must go away and leave them together, Molly. They'll have a great deal to say to each other. We'll have the room made ready for you, James. We really cannot have last names between us, can we?"

Seton drew himself up a little, and bowed.

"Thank you," said he. "I accept with all my heart!"

CHAPTER 8

Now that they were left alone, these two "dear friends" looked silently at each other for a long moment.

"It's a pity that the girl can't see us, now," said Seton, at last. "She'd say that our hearts are too full for words, or something neat and to the point, like that."

The shadow of a grin twitched at the corners of the mouth of the foreman.

"I s'pose she would, as a matter of fact," said he.

"Oh, she would, all right," said Seton. "Shall we take a little walk over there in the corral—for fear some of that fullness should get out in noisy words?"

Big Douglas Walters hesitated one instant. Then he turned on his heel and led the way. The corral gate slammed behind them, and an old mule which stood asleep in the sun in a far corner of the enclosure jerked up its head and shook its ears as though angry at the interruption of its daydreams. The two men walked up and down. A cooling wind was coming out of the west, where the sun was dropping lower.

Big Walters, his head dropped, studied the planting of his own feet in the dust, putting them down slowly, and his frown never varied.

"Look up and smile, man," said Seton, "or they'll see you from the house and think that you're crying for joy and come out to comfort you."

Walters jerked up his head and halted.

"What's your play? What's your game?" he snapped.

"How do I know?" said Seton, smiling still. "I've just come

43

into the room, as you might say. I've just begun to look around and see what the stakes are."

Walters nodded, and his look grew uglier, still.

"You're going to horn in, are you?" he said.

"Horn in?" exclaimed Seton, with an air of injured innocence. "Why, I've been asked in. I've been invited to sit down. The hosts wouldn't leave me out of the game, seeing that I've known their dear Douglas so long."

At this, something seemed to snap in Walters.

"Damn you!" he said briefly.

"Tut, tut," said Seton. "To hear you, one would imagine that you thought we were still back in our boyhood days, ready to punch each other on the nose. Jimmy Seton, and the 'unconquerable Douglas!'"

He put an odd little emphasis upon this last remark, and the upper lip of Walters snarled back from his teeth, like the lip of a wolf.

"But we're grown men," said Seton, "and certainly, for my part, I'm not going to do anything that'll put me back behind the bars."

Walters grinned with satisfaction.

"You've had a taste of the whip," he said.

"Yes," admitted the other, "I've had a taste of the whip, all right. I've been opened up to the bone by every stroke of it, you might say. It would hurt you to think what I've suffered."

Walters stared at him, hopefully, but then, with a darkening face, he shook his head again.

"I don't believe a damned word of it," said he. "You've had some easy job as a trusty. You've wormed your way into the confidence of the warden. You've been a sneaking trusty and a stool pigeon. That's your style. You always were a confidence man, sizing up suckers, and then trimming them with their own knives."

"You've got a lot of faith in me," said Seton, brightly. "It gives me quite a kick to hear the way that you talk, old-timer. You'd believe that I could get out of hell itself, if I put my wits to it."

"Not the hell that you're going to land in, one day," declared the foreman.

"Well, we'll see about that," said Seton, "but first, I wanted to talk about the game that we're sitting in on."

"What game?" said the foreman. "I've got no game, here."

"Haven't you?"

"No, I've got no game. I'm running this square."

"With birds like the Sparrow to help you out?"

The other blinked.

"You've seen him?"

"I saw the little old Sparrow, hopping brightly around. I went out and chirped at him, and he seemed rather surprised to see me."

"I'll bet he was surprised," said Walters, eying his companion narrowly. "You mean that you saw the Sparrow and that neither of you went to your irons?"

"Not I!" said Seton, as though surprised.

"Have you lost your nerve, you damned four-flusher?" said Walters, stepping ominously close to Seton.

The latter did not retreat. His steady smile met the threat of Walters.

"I never pull a gun until I have to," said he. "And I'm like the rattlesnake. I give every man three warnings, Doug, my boy."

"You do, do you?" said Walters, some of his new hope disappearing from his face.

"Yes. And when I have to strike, I strike out of a shoulder holster. And nothing but a snake-fighting rat can jump fast enough to get away. I always was slick, Doug. I always was oily with a gun, but now I run on the finest kind of new ball-bearings."

"I don't believe it," said Walters. "You've been five years in the can. You've had no chance to practice."

"Haven't I? Then step on me and see. I've given you one warning before, old son. That's all I have to say on the subject." Even in speaking in this manner, his voice did not become harsh. "Now, to continue with the matter of this little game you're playing. I said that I saw the Sparrow, and that the Sparrow has gone away."

"The devil he has!"

"Oh, yes. When he saw me, he remembered some business that he left unfinished and quit cold."

"Did he leave? The yellow dog! His nerve has gone!"

"Yours may go, one of these days," said Seton, coldly. "Remember that, my boy. Yes, the Sparrow didn't tell me that he was going. He didn't say a word about it, in fact. But I have an idea you won't find him anywhere around."

"We'll see about that," said the other through his teeth.

"Of course we will. Let's go on to the main idea, now. You have a game. You've bled old man Ash until his meat is white."

"You lie," said Walters.

"I never lie," replied the calm voice of Seton. "I prevaricate, on occasion, but I never lied in my life. Not even when I was a kid. And you know it."

"What do you know?"

"I know that poor old Ash now has to borrow and pay a bonus for it!"

"You heard that, did you?" said Walters. "Well, you can't run a ranch on air."

Seton waved his hand.

"You bought this place for them at forty dollars an acre."

"That's what the Bensons asked. I was only an agent."

"That's a lie. The Bensons never saw the day, even in their prime, when they wouldn't have sold out at twenty-five. You put about half of that sales price into your own pocket."

Walters took a great breath. It looked, for a moment, as though he would hurl himself at the other. But the shadow of a second thought appeared in his eyes, and he drew back.

"There's not a soul in the world, including the Bensons and the Ashes, that ever could prove I did," said he.

"Of course not," said Seton, nodding. "I know about bonuses, and I know about other dodges, and commissions, and commissions on commissions, and buying good will, and all sorts of ways to raise the prices. All honest. Oh, yes. All honest, but the price goes up."

"Think your own thoughts. I ain't a damn bit interested in them."

46

"I'll try to make you interested, my lad."

"Will you?"

"After you got the ranch sold, so that all the cream was yours and the skimmed milk remained to the Ash crowd, you figured out that you could get a little more out of them. A good deal more. You could play the game two ways from the start. You buy the top kind of cows and horses. You stock the place to the hilt. It may be that this old ranch can be made to pay big. Well, if it can pay, you'll see that it comes to you—through Molly Ash."

Walters struck suddenly, with his doubled fist. He struck fast and he struck hard, but he hit only the empty air. Seton had stepped to the side a few inches, and the blow went over his shoulder. He did not attempt to hit back; and Walters did not try to get in another blow. He wore a stunned look and fell heavily back a pace as though he had received a powerful physical shock. Said Seton, continuing in a grave, steady manner, as though nothing had happened of a violent nature between them:

"Little Molly Ash is a girl to tie to. She knows that the sun rises and that the sun sets inside the head of her unconquerable Douglas. She knows that Douglas can do no wrong. She loves him devotedly. If there's a glimmer of light in her old father's mind, she puts her little hands over his eyes and darkens his thought for him, again. So, old-timer, you have the ranch, if it turns out a paying proposition. And it may. The prices of beef and horses may run up, one of these days. There may be enough to make it worth while for you to marry the girl, and take the whole profit. On the other hand, you don't want the place to get fat, for in case you might have to move on—for the sake of your health, say—you don't want a foolish big bank account going to waste. A little debt makes a healthful diet, in your idea. Am I right?"

"What should I say to a fool like you?" asked Walters. But he still wore that stunned, white look.

"On the other hand," said Seton, "you may, as I said, have to move along suddenly; and, in that case, what a pity that all these cattle and horses should be wasted! So you have some good boys on your pay list, boys like the Sparrow. They'll any day take orders from you and run this stock through the muddy little Rio Grande and over to a place where you can collect perfectly good Mexican money for them all. Half to you; half to the boys. What's simpler than that?"

"What's your game? What's your game?" gasped Walters.

"Oh, my game is just to stay here and look around, for a while."

"You've looked enough. I won't have you here."

"Yes, you will, though. You'll have me here. Not in the house. I don't want to see you around that girl, again, if I can help it. It makes me a little sick, Doug. So I'll bunk in the bunkhouse, and you can tell the Ashes that you've taken me on as a regular cowpuncher, getting orders from you, and that you think my place is with the rest of the hired men. You're playing no favorites—you!"

He laughed a little.

"Just send my grip out, old son. And don't monkey with the lock. I've got snakes inside."

He laughed again, and, turning on his heel, he left Walters. The latter remained fixed in place, but gradually the black fury cleared from his face, and an expression of sinister hope spread instead.

CHAPTER 9

The bunkhouse stood back from the corral a little distance. It had two hitching racks in front of it and was a long, low shed, built in the style of the house and patched together in exactly the same manner.

On the way to it, Seton passed a tall young Negro who was carrying a bucket of water, his left arm stretched straight out to balance the weight a little.

"Where you fetching the water, George?" he asked.

"You listen to that cantankerous doggone calf bawlin' over there," said George, hastily putting down the bucket. "The hardest weanin' calf that I ever seen in all my days. I'm gunna stop him or choke him with this here water."

"How long you been here, George?"

"Coupla years."

"You were here in the days of the Bensons, then?"

"Yeah. I was here. Mr. Walters kept me over for rousta-about around the place."

"You sleep in the bunkhouse, I suppose?"

"Yes. Who are you, boss?"

"I'm a new hand that Walters has just taken on."

The Negro nodded.

"You look like the kind he wants."

"What kind does he want, George?"

"My name's Dick. He wants 'em all wool and a yard wide." Dick grinned.

"Other hands be in at six?"

"Along about that."

"Leave that water be for a while, Dick, and come over and have a little chat with me at the bunkhouse. I want to find out about some things."

Dick walked on beside him, willingly enough, and Seton paused in the door of the bunkhouse. There were ten bunks built end to end all around the room. In the center of the room was a round stove at which cigarettes were thrown, for scores of small butts lay about it on the floor. On the walls was the usual drapery of saddles, bridles, old slickers, coats, hats covered with dust. Blanket rolls, battered suit-cases, boots and shoes appeared under the bunks. Of these, eight were apparently occupied. The furnishings were completed by a number of broken-down chairs and a few stools. And there was a long table, the ends of which were heaped with magazines, most of which were yellow with time. A history could have been written about that table, so many

49

names and initials had been carved in it, so many cigarette butts had burned its edges.

"There's only one good place for a man to sleep in this whole room," said Seton. "That's the bunk under the window, yonder."

Dick grinned.

"Yeah. And that's where Mr. Walters' main right-hand man sleeps."

"Who is Mr. Walters' main right-hand man, if you please?"

"Why, that's Jake Mooney."

"And who's Jake Mooney?"

The Negro looked suddenly at his questioner.

"You're jokin' me, boss!"

"I'm not joking you. I'm a long time away from this part of the country, Dick. Who's Jake Mooney?"

Thus put to it, Dick turned his gaze at the ceiling and appeared lost in reflection.

"Outside of Mr. Walters, maybe, Jake Mooney is about the most man that I ever seen," he declared at last.

"He's big, is he?"

"Why," said Dick, with a suddenly flashing grin, "he's so big that he's gotta change states, every now and then. Any one state is a good bit too small for him. It gets him kind of cramped."

Seton nodded.

"He's left a long trail behind him, I suppose?" said he.

"He's left a trail," said Dick. "You can follow the signs on it pretty easy, they say, because the marks is all red."

"That sounds mighty interesting. Is he a gun man?"

"He's one of them that don't care," said Dick, again thoughtful, hunting for words. "I've seen mighty clever gamblers that would work at poker or seven up or black jack or dice, or pretty near anything that you wanted to name. And that's the way with this here Jake Mooney when it comes to a fight. He ain't particular. A knife will do him, fine; a good club he likes, too; and he can use a gun in both hands."

"He's a two-gun man, is he?"

"Yeah. He's a two-gun man, boss."

"They only come once in ten years or so," said Seton.

"Well, he's one. I've seen him roll two cans at once, and keep 'em jumpin' fast. He can fan a gun with both hands. I never seen such shooting. Nobody else around here ever did, either."

"He sounds like a regular picture man," admitted Seton.

"Guns ain't his main hold, though."

"No? What else does he do better?"

"His bare fists is what he mostly prefers to use."

"He's good, is he?"

"Why, he can knock a log right out of the side of a house with one punch."

"And not hurt his hand?"

"He's all iron. You can't hurt iron."

"He ought to be in the ring, a fellow like that," said Seton.

"Why, he's been there, boss."

"Couldn't he make any money at that game?"

"He couldn't make any money. I'll tell you why. The first time that he got into a real big fight, the referee was crooked, and kept warning him; and so what does Jake Mooney do but turn around and chase the referee out of that ring and into the crowd. And the crowd, they got up and went for Mooney. And Mooney, he takes up a bench for a club and he cleans a way through that crowd and gets out of the building. And after that, he's debarred from the ring. There's too much fight in Mooney to be kept inside of a prize ring, I can tell you, boss."

"He sounds mighty interesting," said Seton. "How are the other boys?"

"There's Tom Innis sleeps there. He's a red-head and a Scotchman. He ain't big, but he's awful tough. Not even Jake Mooney likes to make trouble with that little gent, and his pale face. He looks too doggone poison mean to suit most folks in a fight."

"Scotchmen are likely to be bad in a fight, take 'em big or take 'em little."

"Larry Crane sleeps next to him. Larry is a mighty jolly

smilin' kind of fellow. He looks sort of plump and round and soft. But he ain't soft, mister. No, he ain't a bit soft. He's as hard as nails, all over. You can't punch no dents into him, I tell you. He's just so tough if he was dropped off a barn, he would bounce as high as the top of it agin."

"Larry sounds the right kind," agreed Seton. "Who's next?"

"The next is Pedro."

"Pedro who?"

"Pedro himself. Just Pedro. That's enough. He's half Moqui or something like that, and half hell-fire. He gives me chills and fever when he looks at me."

"Pedro sounds warm, too. What else is there in this collection?"

"Oh, they're all men. That's Chet Ray's bunk. He's a mighty fine rider, and he's got a bang-up mare of his own, boss. He's a mite younger than the rest, and he don't look like he's more'n a kid. But he *is* more. He's a lot more."

"That's for Chet Ray. Who are the rest?"

"Well, there's Digger Murphy, that has a kind of a greasy look, like he was sweating a little, all the time. He says that he's pretty sickly and he sure looks it. But he ain't sick when it comes to trouble. He don't give no warning, like a snake. He don't give no more warning than a slidin' shadow. And Lew Gainor, he makes up enough noise to fill the whole place. When he gets to bawlin' around and singin', it sounds like a whole army yellin'. He's big and noisy, but he never backs up for nobody, hardly. He's done things on the other side of the river that'd fill a book, I've heard."

"Yeah. I've heard of him," said Seton.

"Have you?"

"Yes, I used to hear a good deal about him, in the old days. I've been in Mexico myself, in a quiet kind of a way. Does that finish up the list, son, outside of yourself?"

"Oh, I don't count, hardly. I'm just the roustabout. I sleep over there in the corner, the farthest from the stove. Nobody else would want that bunk, so I've got it. But I guess that I ain't gunna stay here long in the bunkhouse."

"Why not?"

"Well, Doc Raymond is the last of the lot. He wouldn't be the last of any other lot. He's one of the slickest gamblers in the world, I should guess. There ain't a thing that he can't do with dice and cards. You'd be surprised!"

"I guess I would," said Seton. "And what's between Raymond and you?"

"He don't like to have colored folks around, boss. It sort of rides him to think of sleepin' in the same room with me. He's one of them proud white men, boss. But I don't mind. I'd just as soon go and sleep over in the granary, except that the rats is bad over there. But I'm peaceable, boss."

"You won't sleep in the granary," said Seton.

"Yeah, and Mr. Mooney, he'd kind of like to get me out, I guess, when he gets round to it. He finds me kind of in the way. I sort of stop the talk."

"You'll stay right in here," said Seton.

"Will I?" exclaimed Dick. "How come, mister?"

"Because _I_ don't mind colored folks. I like 'em. I know some of 'em that I've sworn by."

The face of Dick was stretched by a vast grin.

"I'll ask you to do one thing for me, Dick, though."

"What's that, boss?"

"It won't take you long. Just move those blankets off the bunk under the window, and put my outfit there."

Dick opened his mouth but did not answer. His jaw merely sagged lower.

"Why, mister, I said that was Jake Mooney's bunk!"

"Did you?" said Seton, cheerfully. "Well, just move his things away for me, and put them wherever you please. I'll tell Jake Mooney that I did the moving."

CHAPTER 10

Dick made the changes which were desired. But he lost a good deal of the shine and natural dark blossom of his face in so doing. He turned a sort of dirty gray and went around with his eyes popping out of his head.

"Mister Seton," he said, when he had brought out blankets from the house to make up the new bunk, together with Seton's suitcase, "they's gunna be a most awful fight. They's gunna be a fight that'll about wreck the place, I reckon. I wouldn't want to do you no wrong, Mr. Seton. You look like a gent that knowed what you was about and could take care of yourself mighty proper, and all of that, but I just wouldn't advise you to be around when that Jake Mooney comes in. He's the right-hand man of Mr. Walters, too!"

"No, no, Dick," said Seton. "He's not the right-hand man of Mr. Walters. *I'm* the right-hand man of Mr. Walters, and the straw-boss on this ranch. It certainly nearly broke Doug's heart to move Mooney down the line, but he did it. He'd known me such a long time, and he knew that I generally was top in the bunkhouse."

Dick listened, more amazed than ever, but when the noise of horsemen entered the corral, the young Negro was hardly able to stand, his expectation of trouble was so great.

"Maybe you got some kind of magic!" he exclaimed.

"That's exactly what I have," said Seton, smiling. "Just go out there and tell them that there's a new man come, will you? And that he's been upsetting the arrangements in the bunkhouse, will you? That'll get you out of danger, for one thing. Then you hump back here as fast as you can, to see the fun. It ought to be worth seeing."

And, with that, Seton lay down on the bunk which once had been occupied by the great Jake Mooney. He folded his hands under his head and, lying at ease, he crossed his legs and smiled gently at the ceiling above him.

Presently, with a jingle of spurs, into the doorway stepped another man.

"Why, hullo, Jake," said he. "How'd you get in here so quick?"

Seton turned his head, and he saw in the door of the bunkhouse a tall, slender, handsome boy. By Dick's description, he could recognize Chet Ray, who "looked like a kid, but was more than he looked." And Ray, as Seton turned his head, actually halted and then stepped back a little through the doorway. Then Seton could hear him calling out:

"Hullo, Jake. There's a stranger come in here and taken your bunk."

The voice of one coming up in great haste answered him.

"I've heard something about it from the nigger. I'm gunna take a look into this."

Other men came, swiftly. There was much jingling of spurs, much puffing and panting, much stamping on the steps at the bunkhouse door. But Seton failed to turn his head. He remained at ease upon the bunk, casually examining the pattern of cracks along the ceiling above him. Feet stamped suddenly across the floor.

"It's straight!" someone cried out. "He's got Jake's bunk."

A man strode to the side of the bunk and stared down into Seton's face.

The latter, with wild eyes, looked up at a black-headed, black-eyed man, a lean face, a jaw like a crag. He saw shoulders, too, rounded with mighty power.

"Who are ye?" asked Jake Mooney.

"I'm the new hand that Walters has just signed on," said Seton in his usual gentle voice.

"Walters signed you on, did he?"

"Yes. He took me on."

"If Walters took you on, d'you know who's likely to take you off?"

"Why, I don't know that I'll be taken off," said Seton.

"Maybe they's other things that you don't know!" suggested Mooney. "You don't know who this bunk belongs to, maybe?"

"Yes. It belongs to me," said Seton.

He had his hat on his head. He pushed back the brim of it a little now, to enable him to smile unimpeded into the face of the angry Mooney.

"Who did it belong to before you?" asked Mooney, turning a deeper and deeper crimson. But still he was controlling himself. He seemed to be enjoying the beautiful ripening and perfection of his own fury.

"It belonged to a fellow named Jake Mooney," said Seton.

"You knew his name, eh?"

"Yes. I heard his name from Dick. He thought I'd better not take this bunk."

"Did he?" gasped Mooney, his fury heightening.

"Yes, he did. He thought that Mooney might be rather annoyed."

"But you didn't think so, maybe?"

"I knew that I could persuade Mooney that I was doing the only right thing."

"You could persuade him, could you? Not if you could talk French, you couldn't persuade him!"

There was a sudden shout of mirth from the assembled semicircle. Two of the men were carrying the table to the side of the room. Plainly they were clearing a working space for "Walters' right-hand man."

Seton did not see them, except from the corner of his eye, vaguely. His attention remained centered upon Mooney, whose face was gradually turning from red to white. Not a cold white, but a vibrant thing, like the color of the intensest flame.

"You see," said Seton, "I simply will tell him that I have weak lungs and have to be near an open window."

"Hey?" shouted Mooney.

"I'll have to stay near the open window," said Seton.

56

"That's the only reason that I had to take Mooney's bunk. When he comes in, I'll explain it to him."

"Lemme tell you a thing about Mooney," said the big man.

"Go right ahead," said Seton, with genial interest. "I hear that he's a character."

"He's something more than a character. He's a fool-killer!" roared Mooney.

"Really?" said Seton. "Why, that's a good job. That takes a lot of trouble off of other people, I suppose."

"He eats fools alive!" yelled Mooney, as his passion reached its perfect height. "And I'm Mooney! Me! I'm Mooney, d'you hear?"

"Why, I hear you beautifully," said Seton. "It's my lungs that are weak, not my ears. But my poor lungs, they need lots of air, Mooney. Fresh air, I mean. Not your air, Mooney."

Mooney stood as one suspended between two ideas. He grasped at the words which he had just heard, but he could not believe them. Then a wild rouse of laughter and whooping from the crowd convinced him that he actually had heard and conceived the thing aright. This fellow was not a fool, really. He was simply the calmest and most audacious challenger that ever had tapped Mooney upon the shoulder of his fame.

"Stand up!" yelled Mooney. "I'm gunna bite you in two. Oh, God, stand up and lemme at you—you—"

"Not a bit of hurry," said Seton. "I'm having a good little rest here, enjoying the air, Mooney, and—"

Mooney reached for Seton's throat. He reached with both hands. In expectant joy, the eyes started in Mr. Mooney's head, and his lips grinned so wide that they showed a red pocket at either side.

Seton did not attempt to writhe away from the attack. He simply took his hands from under his head and caught Mooney by either wrist. The lunge of the latter was stopped. He tried to press in. The grip and the arm power of the prostrate man held him off.

Then a veritable groan of amazement came from the spectators. And Mooney heard it. He had been Achilles among them. He had been the hero of the host. Among many hard ones, he had been the hardest. And this unexpected resistance maddened him. Wonder opened his eyes only for a moment. Then hideous anger narrowed them again.

He flung himself back. That effort brought Seton lightly to his feet but did not free Mooney. They stood face to face, Mooney whiter than a sheet, every muscle in his face quivering and twitching so that he scarcely looked human.

"I'm going to kill you," said he, in a ghastly whisper. "I'm going to kill you!" he screamed at the pitch of his voice.

Right, left and right, he struggled back with his shoulder-weight, braced and strained with all his power. Seton held him one moment, then followed the struggler, stepped suddenly in, and, drawing Mooney off balance with a jerk, caught him across his hip and tumbled him at full length upon the floor.

With the weight of that impact, dust leaped up in ten thousand little geysers from the cracks in the floor. The stove stirred and jangled. And the boards creaked against their nails. It was a hard fall.

"He's got a broken neck," said Chet Ray. "His neck is broke at the shoulders. I saw where he landed."

It seemed as though that was what had happened, for the big fellow lay stretched out at full length for nearly half a minute, not moving a muscle. He was not badly hurt, however. He simply was collecting his wits and planning his next move. He had been taken by surprise, and he would not be taken by surprise again. When he stirred, it was to twist over and hitch himself up on hands and knees. And then off the floor he leaped in at Seton.

Whatever his failings, here and there, in others of his accomplishments, he never lost a fist fight. He could not lose. He had the weight, the skill, the training, the power to strike. He had the toughness of rawhide and the surface of chilled steel.

So he came in now like a bull, confident, foretasting victory, his guard lowered a little so that he could hit the harder when he got within range. There he was, at exactly the right distance for a full-arm drive that would clip the head off Seton's shoulders.

"There it goes!" yelled one of the watching men.

"God help him!" yipped young Dick, the Negro.

His heart was filled with sympathy for the rash new hand.

But, at the instant when the impact should have come, when big Mooney had gritted his teeth hardest to enjoy the taste of it, he found himself hitting through thinnest air.

A mere sway of the head, reserved until the last instant, had made him miss. At the same time, Mooney saw the shadowy loom of the blow that was coming for him. It was a thing that the eye could see, but the muscles of the body could not work fast enough to prevent.

Long ago, when he was in hard training, he had seen the same blows coming from master craftsmen with the gloves. The eye could see them, as the eye could see the dodging flight of a bat, but the body could not avoid them any more than the clumsy June bug can avoid the bat's mouth.

So came the gleam of Setson's hand, glancing over Mooney's shoulder. The fist jerked sharply down, and, just as Mooney's brain spelled out, "Right cross!" and as he strove vainly to pull away from the blow, it clicked against the point of his jaw like the stroke of a sledge hammer.

Darkness leaped cross the mind of Jake Mooney. He did not fall backward, but his joints gave way at the knees, at the hips, at the nape of the neck. He sagged face forward; and Seton, catching him under the pits of the arms, lifted him easily, changed hands, and carried the bulk of Mooney lightly across the room and laid him on the naked boards of a vacant bunk.

"Give him a bit of water across the face, Dick," said Seton. "He's had a shock."

CHAPTER 11

Nothing could have been more interesting than the reaction of the group to the defeat of their champion, Jake Mooney.

Some of them scowled at the stranger with an intense dislike; others appeared to be swallowing grins; and a few actually chuckled. Perhaps they were ones who had felt the force of Jake's strength on their own persons. At any rate, they gathered silently about the body of the fallen man, where he lay sprawling upon the bunk with all his muscles and the features of his face relaxed. He looked like a sodden Jake Mooney, now, a helpless bulk, a motionless and useless weight.

"We'd better leave him here alone," said Seton. "He'll be all right, but I think he'll like it better if he finds himself alone when he wakes up." And he led the way out of the bunkhouse.

As he stepped out from the shadows of the room, into the rosy sunset light, there was a sudden whoop from big Lew Gainor. He marched up to Seton and planted himself in front of him.

"What did you call yourself?" asked Gainor.

"Seton, Gainor," said the other. "Jimmy Seton is my name. There still must be some people around Claymore who remember me."

"There are some people around Claymore that seen you first in other parts," declared Gainor.

He turned his back on Seton and faced the others.

"You remember the yarn I was spinning the other night,

60

boys, when you said I was talkin' bunk, Tom Innis?"

"I remember the bunk pretty well, too," said Innis.

"What d'you remember best?"

"Well," said Innis, whose expression was a continuous snarl, "mostly I remember how he handed himself down from the third-story window on the big climbin' vine. Wistaria, I think you said it was."

"That was bunk, was it?"

"It was such bad bunk it wasn't hardly worth laughin' at," declared Innis.

Gainor hooked a thumb over his shoulder.

"Ask *him!*" he said shortly.

"Seton?"

"Ask him if he ever climbed three stories down a wistaria vine, Innis!"

He turned back and faced Seton.

"You tell 'em, Jimmy!" he urged. "Your name didn't seem to mean much to me, until I seen your face, and then it rung a bell."

He grinned expectantly.

"I don't remember," said Seton in his gentle voice. "There may have been a wistaria vine somewhere back there. I can't recall, very well."

"He can't recall, he says!" exclaimed Gainor, laughing. "Can you beat that? He says that he can't recall. You can't recall the two at the bottom of the vine, in the brush, that was shootin' at you as you swung down, can you?"

"I don't seem to," said Seton.

"You ain't likely to recollect how you let go all holts when you was still about twenty feet in the air and heaved yourself out into the air and landed right on top of one of them greasers. You don't recollect a doggone thing about that, do you?"

"Why," said Seton, "it seems to come back to me rather dimly, like a dream, in fact."

"I'll bet it's dim," said Gainor.

"Lucky that I hit him and broke my fall," said Seton.

"Yeah. I guess it was luck. You didn't aim at him on purpose. And after he rolled over, dead to the world, you didn't pick up his rifle and shoot the pants off of that other greaser, did you?"

He began to laugh uproariously, and the others came a little closer, but by slow degrees. Their eyes were beginning to light. They looked at Seton as a seasoned hunting pack— sure of itself, and every dog fitted securely into the hierarchy of power—looks at a new addition to the pack.

They were not, as yet, sure of this man, but they distinctly had their hopes of him. They began to smile. Their eyes were friendly as they watched the impassive, good-natured face of Seton. As for Dick, he stared at Seton as at a demigod. His heart was quite lost to the big man.

"Oh, I remember some of the old days," said Gainor. "I remember the time that I was down in Vera Cruz and a pair of thugs got me cornered and in comes—"

"I don't see how you remember so much," said Seton. "It's a wonderful thing the way that you remember, Gainor. It must sort of strain your brain a little, doesn't it?"

Gainor blinked.

"You ain't long on memory, eh?" said he.

"It's a terrible weakness of mine," said Seton, "but, pretty early in my life, I got in the habit of forgetting things. Maybe you don't know what I mean?"

"Oh," said Gainor, half sulkily, and yet half smiling, also, "I guess that I know what you mean."

"Cheese it!" said the boy, Chet Ray. "Here comes old Muzzle-loading Bill."

"Ay, it's Perry himself," said another.

"What's the sheriff want out here, now?" asked a third.

"He wants to talk to me," said Seton, and straightway he advanced to meet Douglas Walters, who was coming toward them accompanied by a tall, thin, bow-legged man. He was so bent at the knees that a small dog could have jumped between them as he walked along. He wore a gunbelt, and the gun sagged low along his thigh, the handles close to the grip of his fingers.

The cow punchers did not hold back. They came slowly forward to hear what was said between the two.

"There he is," Walters was heard saying. "There's your

man, Perry. You can recognize for yourself, now, I hope."

"Hello, Perry!" said Seton. "How's old Muzzle-loading Bill, anyway?"

The sheriff halted at a little distance and gave a hitch to his gunbelt, bringing it higher up on his left hip and thereby expertly altering the position of the gun against the opposite leg. His eyes, as still and as hard as the eyes of a bird, stared without winking at big Seton.

"You're out, are you?" said he.

"I take it very kind of you, sheriff," said Seton, "to ride all the way out here just in order to congratulate me."

"Do you take it kind?" said the other. "Maybe you won't take it quite so kind when I'm through telling you just *why* I came all the way out here?"

"Well, you tell me," said Seton. "I guess you're pretty good at making speeches since you went into politics."

"I don't want none of your lip," said the sheriff. "I've come out here to tell you to move along."

"Thanks," said Seton, while all the punchers came closer in to enjoy the forthcoming wrangle, "but I like it here. No matter what you've got to offer me, I'm enjoying things around here pretty well, Bill. I know the kind heart that you've got, and the way that you'd like to provide for an old friend—"

"You ain't a friend of mine," said the sheriff. "You never was a friend of mine, and you never will be. You're a low-down gun-fightin', man-killin' skunk, Seton, and I'm here to tell you to move on of your own free will, or else I'll move you into the jail, myself."

A smile against which Walters fought nevertheless persisted and triumphed over him. He grinned broadly, a grin that was remembered by some of the men later on. But was he enjoying the sheriff's speech or the foretaste of the answer that was to come?

"Tut, tut," said Seton, with wonderful calm in the face of that cold, grim denunciation. "You don't realize that I've been away for five years in school, getting me an education, do you? You don't know that I'm a changed man, sheriff. You think that I'm just a common bum. But I'm not a vagrant. Ask my old friend Doug Walters, there. Why, he's just insisted on giving me a job here, and I couldn't refuse him. Ask Doug Walters if he hasn't made me the straw-boss over this ranch, since Jake Mooney got tired of the job?"

The sheriff turned quickly toward Walters.

"Did you give him that job?" he asked.

Walters looked intently into the face of the other. It seemed as though he hardly breathed, for a moment, and then he said haltingly:

"Yes—I guess—he's the man—for the job."

The sheriff shrugged his shoulders impatiently.

"If you've got a pardon and a job," he said, "my teeth are pulled just now. But mind you, Seton, I'm watchin' you. If ever I hear that you've pulled a gun, I'll be out here and run you back behind the bars where you belong so fast that your head'll swim. You mind what I say. I don't like you. I never liked you. I'd trust a snake sooner. You're a gun man. You never can go straight. Now you see where you stand, and you can watch your step."

He turned on his heel and walked away.

CHAPTER 12

For five days, Seton spent sixteen hours out of every twenty-four on horseback. He used two horses each morning, and two horses each afternoon. And those which he used one day were not much good the next. He kept the spur in and the whip going, while he traveled over every inch of the ranch. By the end of the five days, he knew every hill, every mountainside, every hummock on the ranch. He knew every rill, every creek, every slough, every draw. He knew the places where the land was richest and the grass grew the darkest green. He knew the places which would make horse pasture and where the cows would have the lushest pickings. He staked out in his mind's eye the right calf pastures, and those where the grown cattle could do the rustling. He knew the trees of the place, and where the groves could be thinned for the benefit of the owner and some hard cash, as well as those which had suffered too much from hasty cutting and where the ax should not appear for two or three years, at least.

The farther he rode, the more he stared at the land, the more often he swung down from the saddle and pulled up grass and weeds to look at their roots, the more convinced he was that the soil was rich and the place a fortune. It only needed the right working, the right care, the right protection.

Protection, perhaps, it needed most of all, for it was sprawled like an octopus across the side of the little valley. It was not a ranch where one can stand on the roof of the ranch house and survey the entire estate. It was scattered, reaching arms up into the little valleys that wriggled into the heart of the uplands. And in those uplands was something more than rocks and trees. There were men, up yonder, who liked the rough country for something more than its beauty. There were hungry men, with one eye on Mexico and the blue, delightful freedom of its distances. They would like nothing better than to reach down into the hollow of the ravines and cut the throats of a few of the fat cattle that ranged there, wearing the brand which Henry Ash had patented. What prevented them? Why, the fear of Jake Mooney, and of Douglas Walters, and of the formidable band they had gathered under them.

The attitude of the outlaws who fringed the hills was brought close home to him the second day of his ranging across the place. He had left the land of the ranch and reached a bit into the hills, riding through dense shrubbery, and then through clearings, woodland, rocklands, also.

In one of those clearings, he came across a rider who had

65

dismounted. The horse was grazing, its forelegs spread as it reached for the short grass. It was a very good horse, with the right lines. It stood over plenty of ground, and it had shoulders worthy of a king's attention, but its ribs stuck out all over its sides, and its very quarters were shrunk by famine.

The rider kneeled on the ground, cleaning a rabbit. He was roughly dressed. On the seat of his trousers there was a patch made of sacking, and sewed on with sack thread. His coat was not adapted to mountain wear. It was a blue serge, frightfully spotted and streaked with grease. It was too small, and wrinkled over his back.

When he heard Seton's horse approaching, he reached for a gun, whirled to his feet, and showed a face covered with a half month's grizzly beard. He was not old. He was not past thirty, but he was prematurely streaked with gray.

He found himself already covered. Even then he did not give up the idea of fighting, for a moment. Beneath the beard, and shining in his eyes, one could see the impulse to strike, at work.

"Hello, partner," said Seton, behind his leveled Colt. "Sorry I busted in on you like this. Your front door was open, and I just walked in."

The other slowly straightened from his crouched position.

"Who are you?" he asked.

"Being in your house," said Seton, "I thought that I might as well ask that same question first."

"My name?" said the other. "I'm Tom Smith. Who are you?"

"I'm Bill Smith," said Seton. "Maybe we're cousins, or something like that."

The other grinned.

"Maybe we're even closer. Maybe we're brothers," said he.

"Maybe we are," said Seton. "What jail did you go to when you were a boy?"

Tom Smith tilted back his head and roared with laughter. There seemed to be as much relief as there was amusement in that laughter.

"I went to a lot," said he. "I got my first degree from Sing

Sing, and they took and made me a master of the art at Fulsom."

"They're hard boiled, up there at Fulsom," said Seton.

"Yeah. It's too far West. That's what's the matter with it."

"That's what's the matter with it," declared Seton. "How's things?"

"Oh, fair."

"Not many razors in your life, nowadays, I guess."

"No. I miss something more than razors, though."

"What's that?"

"Soap."

"Well," said Seton, "bite a chunk out of this."

He did not put up his revolver, but he reached into a saddlebag and took out a cake of yellow laundry soap which he threw, and the other caught with expert hands.

"By the Lord," said Tom Smith, "I'd rather have this than a hundred pounds of honeycomb."

"I know," said Seton. "The grease on the skin is not so very good."

Then he put up the revolver.

"You always pack it, do you?" said Tom Smith.

"It's good for a lot of things," remarked Seton. "If you lose your horse and get footsore, you can rub it on the inside of your socks and get a lot of relief, that way. If you have to, you can make a poultice out of it."

"You never made a mold out of it for running soup, I guess?" said Tom Smith.

"Mold?" said Seton. "Of course I don't know what you mean."

"Of course you don't," grinned Smith. "Who in hell are you, stranger?"

"I'm Bill Smith, cousin of yours."

"You're a cousin of mine, all right. What brought you up here?"

"I'm working on a place right near by."

"Hello!" said Tom Smith. "Are you one of the Mooney men—one of Doug Walters' fellows?"

"I'm not one of Mooney's men," said Seton. "He's one of mine."

"Hey, d'you mean that Mooney's stepped down?"

"He's stepped down for a while. He needed a little rest. He was getting a lot of responsibility."

"What kind of responsibility? Kicking the rest of the boys in the face, d'you mean?"

"Not so much that. It never made Jake cry to kick another man in the face. But he got pretty tired of having to dicker with you boys up here in the bush."

He had reached into the dark, in saying this, but Tom Smith answered:

"He's sent you up here to finish the bargain for him, has he?"

"I'm bargaining for Henry Ash and Doug Walters," said Seton.

"Walters *and* Ash?" said Tom Smith. "Has Walters up and married the little girl, finally?"

Tom Smith's knowledge of the affairs of the ranch intrigued the attention of Mr. Seton. He even stirred a little in the saddle.

".Not yet," said Seton.

"He's a fool if he does that," said Tom Smith. "Walters has herded the boys off the ranch about as long as they'll stand it. The Bensons, they were different. A gent always had a chance to get a set-down meal and a quart of coffee from the Bensons."

"The long riders," said Seton, "were the ones that ate the Bensons out of their ranch."

Smith shrugged his shoulders.

"Bill," said he, "just where d'you stand?"

"I don't stand. I sit," said Seton.

"That ain't so funny. When you see Walters again, you ask him how long he expects some of us to starve around here in the hills, will you?"

"I'll tell him that you said that."

"He's been stringing us along," said Tom Smith. "He's been handing out the hope that if we keep hands off, we'd sure have all the opportunity that we wanted for making a red-hot haul, before long. But it ain't worked out that way. And some of us are getting pretty hungry."

"Why don't you go south?" advised Seton. "There's plenty of picking south of the river."

"Not for this horse," said Tom Smith. "I get indigestion the first minute that I start to thinking about old Mexico. And Mexico starts to grinding her teeth when she thinks about me."

"You've been there before?"

"Three—five times, maybe. You tell Walters what we want, will you? I was talkin' to some of the boys only the other day. They're getting tired. They're getting fed up."

"Let them get fed up," said Seton. "So long as they don't start killing the Henry Ash beef."

"You'd as soon see us starve, I suppose?" said Tom Smith, fixing his eyes gloomily on the other.

Seton smiled on him.

"Don't be ugly, Tommy," said he. "Be friends. That's the only way for boys to act. What's the population back here in the brush, just now?"

"Three more came in last week. Walters can tell you how many there were before."

"You get some deer, up here?"

"About a meal of venison a week."

"Well, then," said Seton, "you can snipe rabbits through the head, and squirrels make good eating, too."

"*You* can eat all the squirrels," said Smith, angrily.

But Seton merely chuckled.

"What do you want for that horse?" he asked.

Smith stared at the thin sides of his mount.

"I'll take a thousand flat," said he.

"It's cheap at that," said Seton, "but I can't pay that much."

"Hold on. I'll make it eight hundred. I could use some cash. Eight hundred to you, Bill, because we're cousins!"

"I'll see what I can afford to do about it," said Seton, "and I'll see you later."

CHAPTER 13

When Seton took his way back to the Ash ranch, he had several new things to turn in his mind. They could not be altogether called new, because he had suspected the thing before. In the old days, he had known this countryside perfectly, and he could remember that there never had been a time when there were not scoundrels of various sorts hiding out in the hills which, in turn, ran into the mountains, and the mountains verged the valley toward Mexico.

He spent a part of the next three days in making quiet questionings which gradually revealed all that he needed to know. Not only was Tom Smith up there, but at least a dozen other fighting men of various sorts were hidden among the trees and the gullies of the bad lands; and all of them had dealings with Douglas Walters, or with his lieutenant, Jake Mooney. They were the hidden power by means of which Walters might be able to play the game in two ways, either of which would be disastrous to poor old Henry Ash.

How Seton could match them, he had no means of telling. He was fumbling very largely in the dark and looking for ways out. His position on the ranch was, from the first, very strange. He had forced Walters into making him the straw-boss, and by that very fact, he had gained the running of the actual operations. Walters was much too lazy to keep afield and take charge of the affairs of the place. He preferred to remain in his "office" at the ranch house, and to bamboozle Henry Ash with his pretended wisdom. As for the other hired hands, they were careful to obey the orders of Seton to the

70

letter. Young Chet Ray, at first, seemed to be disposed to take the new boss hardly more seriously than he had the old one, but he formed a new opinion, one day.

It was on the fourth afternoon of Seton's stay on the place that he found Chet, who was supposed to be riding range in a distant section of the ranch, engaged in the innocent amusement of throwing tin cans over his shoulder and high into the air. Then he whirled, drew a revolver and tried for the can as it fell. Sometimes he hit. Sometimes he missed. It was not perfect shooting, but it was very high-class marksmanship.

Seton waited until he had seen two scores out of six chances. At the seventh chance, he pulled his own revolver and knocked the can afar with a well-aimed shot.

Chet Ray looked at the new straw-boss, who had stepped around the corner of the barn, and then he measured the distance, with his eye, from which the bullet had been fired.

After that, he put up his own gun. That of Seton had mysteriously and smoothly disappeared inside his coat.

"Did you fan that shot?" asked Chet Ray.

"Well," said Seton, "it doesn't make much difference. It's the hole in the can that counts."

Ray nodded.

"But I've seen the callous on your thumb," he said. "Who are you, Seton? I've been hearing some yarns. Why don't you open up and let us know whether or not you're one of us?"

"Why don't you open up," said Seton, "and let me know whether or not you're with me? That seems about as important."

"If you're going to take it that way," said Chet Ray.

"Anyway," answered Seton, "I suppose that you've just about used up this supply of tin cans?"

"No, there's a lot more."

"But your ammunition must be about gone."

"No, I've got plenty left."

"Well, but then your arm's tired, and I guess your horse isn't. What about it?"

Chet Ray looked him in the eye. Then, without a word,

he went to his horse and rode off to do the work which had been assigned to him. There were no further attempts to shirk. The men were told off in the morning for various tasks. They spent the rest of the day doing them. But Seton could not tell whether they were working willingly, or whether they were simply waiting for a change in the game, just as those other ruffians in the hills were waiting.

His own part was complicated by the continued presence of big Jake Mooney. After his downfall in the bunkhouse, Seton had taken it for granted that the former tyrant of the ranch and right-hand man of Walters would not be able to digest his shame in the presence of the others. But he was wrong. To his astonishment, Jake Mooney remained at the ranch, received orders with a black, downward look, and went about his business like the other men.

He was in a murderous humor. That was plain. From one day's end to the next, he spoke to no one. The young Negro, Dick, said to Seton one day:

"If I was you, boss, I'd watch out for that man, that Jake Mooney. He sure looks like he wants to put his teeth into you."

"I'm too old to eat raw," answered Seton, lightly.

But he never had Mooney out of his mind, or, if he was present, out of his eye. At last he went to Walters.

"Doug," said he, "your old right bower, your friend Mooney, is still staying around here. How long d'you expect him to be with us?"

"Does he do his work?" said Walters.

"He seems to."

"Then he stays," said Walters. "Are you afraid of him?"

"I'm afraid of anybody who's my enemy," answered Seton with a surprising frankness. "I'm afraid of you, Doug, and of the sheriff, and of a lot of other people. I don't like to be hit. Do you?"

Walters, for answer, stared sullenly at his new assistant, and then turned on his heel and walked away. He made not three paces when another idea turned him about, and he approached Seton with the air of one about to charge home.

"I'll tell you one thing, Jimmy," said he.

"Thanks," said Seton.

"You don't need to sneer at me. There was a time when we were friends. Anyway, we've known each other for a long time. Now, for the sake of the old days, I'm gunna tell you something that ought to do you a pile of good."

"Thanks," said Seton, again.

"You've made a grandstand play, here. You got yourself mixed up in the Ash business, but if you've got a little sense, you'll pack your traps and get out of here, and get pronto."

"What's the hidden meaning, Doug?" asked the other. "Are you going to have me murdered in the dark of the moon, one of these nights?"

Walters, having parted his lips to answer this remark, swallowed the words and went off.

So Mooney stayed, and the work of the ranch went on, ostensibly under the direction of big Douglas Walters, but really according to the directions of Seton. And, every moment, he felt his affection for the land increasing. He saw little or nothing of Ash and Molly. Now and then he passed them, but he spent no time at the ranch house. His days in the saddle were so long and arduous that, when the night came, he was ready to tumble into his bed and fall instantly asleep. The fat fell away from his athletic body. Everything was burned off him except hardest muscle. There were three days of acute and more acute misery, the unaccustomed muscles protesting against all that was demanded of them; but, after this, he hardened, and settled into his riding strength, which is really in the thigh muscles and the stomach.

On the fifth day old Hooker, the banker, came jogging out to the ranch in his buckboard. He did not stop at the house. He looked up Seton, instead, after he had made a considerable tour of the property, on foot. He found Seton tailing a steer out of the soft mud and slime at the edge of a waterhole, and, when the job was completed, Seton looked up and saw the hawk face and the hard eye of the banker fixed upon him. Hooker looked like a crow. He had a long, skinny neck, a little head, a huge beak of a nose and tiny, glittering eyes set close to the base of it. There seemed hardly room for a

73

quart of blood in his withered body. But he was the most successful banker in the county.

"Hello, Jimmy Seton," said he. "Are you working for yourself or for Henry Ash?"

Seton wiped the mud from his hands and curiously gazed at the banker.

"What's the idea, Mr. Hooker?" he asked.

"Why, I heard that things was beginning to hum, out here at the Ash place. I heard that there was more work and less poker goin' on, and I come out here to see for myself."

"You can ask Ash and Walters about what's going on. I'm just a hired hand," replied Seton.

"Is that all that you are?" said the banker. "That's kind of amusin' to me, Jimmy Seton. You never done a lick of hired work in your life, up to the time you went to jail."

"I did five years of work there to make up," said the boy, "and accounts are about square between me and the world."

"There's a coupla dead men would like to have a word in about that," said the banker.

"You call them up and ask their idea, then."

Hooker chuckled.

"I don't believe a word you tell me," he said.

"What business is it of yours, what happens on the ranch?" asked the assistant foreman, aggressively. He never had liked Hooker. No one else ever had, to his knowledge.

"I've loaned money on this here land," said Hooker. "Besides, it's everybody's business in this valley to see that the Henry Ash place goes along well. The doctors, the cattle dealers, the druggist, the lawyers, the railroad, everybody in Claymore has got an interest in this here ranch. It's a big part of the roots of business that we live on. And now I find young Jimmy Seton out here hoein' the tree and bossin' the job."

"I didn't say that I was bossing the job."

Hooker raised a bony forefinger.

"There's some men can work at the bottom, and some men can work at the top," said he. "If you was a partner of mine, you'd have me dead or retired inside of about three weeks. No, no, my son. You're not the kind to work at the bottom.

That's why you never done honest work, much, when you were a younger boy!"

He shook his head in the attitude of one whose opinion cannot be altered.

Seton rode straight up to him and sat the saddle, looking squarely into his eyes.

"Why are you poking around here?" he asked.

"To see what I can see," said the banker.

"Have you seen it?"

"I'm seeing it now," replied Hooker, and looked straight and deep into the unflinching eyes of Jimmy Seton.

Then he turned and went striding away toward the road, whistling as he went, and leaving a very dumfounded young man in the saddle behind him.

CHAPTER 14

Young Seton watched Hooker go.

He could make nothing of the enigmatic remarks of the old fellow. He could feel the sting that was in the tail of some of them; but then, Hooker all his days had been celebrated for the sharpness of his tongue, and it would have been strange if he had interviewed a returned convict from prison without pouring some acid into his speech. The acid was there, but there was something more than acid. There had been, in the fixed, keen look of that old hawk something that Seton could not help feeling was hope and a sort of surprised respect.

However, he had much to do. He dismissed Hooker from his mind and set forward on his errand. He had gone out to look over the site of a possible reservoir. Usually, there was water running deep in the creeks and the sloughs of the valley, but every year or two a drought came and then, during August and perhaps during all of September, the waters shrank to little pools in the creek beds, and these in turn became muddy, then dried up, and left only a cake of green hard slime over the rocks. In such times, terrible suffering was endured by the cattle. If they were started early enough, they could be driven down to the big river for water; but the trip was long, the trouble was great, and, unless the measures were undertaken in time, there was sure to be a great number of casualties among the stock.

A reservoir was what was needed to hold a small portion of the surplus water during the rainy season. If one could be created, it would be better than a most expensive insurance policy, and it would give Henry Ash the possibility of becoming a public benefactor.

These reasons had forced him to look over the place in the hope of finding an ideal situation, and he went on this afternoon with some hope that he had thought of the right spot. He had a half hour of hard riding through the brush and among the boulders of the foothills, and then he came to the spot where Benson Creek gushed out from the upper mountains and clove through the foothills in a deep and narrow channel.

It seemed to have cut straight through the middle of the last hill, before it issued into the more gently rolling country. Here the walls were upward of a hundred feet high, and, sitting in the saddle on the verge of the cliff, he measured the width. It was not more than thirty feet from side to side. In places, the rock jutted out to less than twenty, and half obscured the rush of the waters beneath.

Suppose, then, that some heavy charges of blasting powder were sunk in the sides of the ravine, a vast mass would be dislodged by the explosion, and, falling into the stream bed, would block the ravine practically to its top. It would be a rough way of creating a dam. Perhaps some of the water would, eventually, work through the rubble of the fallen rock. But enough would be held back to fill the natural reservoir. This was a rudely circular basin among the hills with several long arms stretching well back. Tens of millions of gallons could be stocked here. And the water could be used when the right time came. The mind of the boy went forward, with a dizzy leap. If the dam turned out as he hoped it would, then a flume might be installed to carry the over-brimming water down a spillway, and, with it to run a water wheel, which would make most useful power, a good-sized mill could be made there on the spot. Claymore Valley had an urgent need of one.

This daydream was not all mere mental vaporing and bright illusion. He felt that there was a good, stiff backing of possibility about it, and his heart bounded at the prospect. This would be something to do. This would be the very cornerstone of the new building which he was striving to erect —Character! He had gone to prison without one. He had come out of prison determined to get one. In the building of that little dam he saw the possibility like a smiling face beside him. They would have new things to say of him, if he could conceive and execute such a project. No matter what they still felt about his past, he knew that in the West time is the greatest charity. It draws the veil over what men have been. All people are so forward fronted that they rarely care, in the real West, to look over their shoulders at their own past days or at those of other men.

From most dreams we have a sharp awakening. That of Seton came when his mustang, for some reason, tossed its head and started aside so violently that it almost unseated the rider. At the same instant a rifle exploded on the opposite side of the ravine, and a big-caliber bullet jerked the hat from Seton's head.

He had his revolver out almost before he had made sure of his seat in the saddle, again; and, across the ravine, exactly opposite, he saw through the brush the figure of a man kneeling, his rifle leveled, his propping elbow on his knee.

It was Jake Mooney. This was the reason why he had remained on the ranch. This was the thing against which even Douglas Walters could not help giving his enemy some vague warning. Seton thought of that in the same flash in which he tipped up the muzzle of the revolver and fired.

He was certain that he had missed. He had fired too low, he felt sure. He could almost swear that he knew where the bullet had struck on the broad head of a boulder, just in front of his target. But Jake Mooney dropped his rifle and, with a yell, started to his feet, both hands clapped together across his face. What had happened? He could guess, at least. The heavy bullet, striking the surface rock, had knocked a volley of sparks and rock splinters into the face of Mooney, blinding him. So he held fire. The man was his. It was point-blank range, and Mooney was in the palm of his hand. He held fire with a stern satisfaction. There had been cowardly murder attempted. The bullet hole in his own hat would be proof enough to satisfy the most exacting Western jury.

Then, as the revolver remained balanced in his hand, he saw Mooney stagger straight forward to the verge of the cliff, topple there, lose balance, and, with a frightful shriek, plunge over the verge, feet first.

Seton closed his eyes. It was ended, now.

No, the shouting continued, in a horrible, high key that tore at the center of his brain. He opened his eyes again. There was Jake Mooney, not crushed to death on the rocks at the bottom of the ravine, but holding with both frantic hands to a shrub which grew out of the wall half a dozen feet below the rim of the cañon. That was not all. The shrub was being torn out by the roots by the dragging weight of the man.

"Jake!" shouted Seton. "Reach to your right. There's an elbow of stone sticking out there. Reach to your right, Jake!"

Jake merely continued to screech for help. The roots were beginning to appear.

A shower of dirt and pebbles fell into the convulsed, up-turned face of Mooney. Then suddenly his yelling ceased. He had recovered his grip on himself to a degree. He was ready to die as a man should, perhaps. And again Seton yelled: "Reach to your right, Jake. There's a rock you can hold to!"

Mooney was now perceptibly sinking as the last of the

roots gave way. He reached to the right and luckily his hand, at the first grip, found the projecting rock. He transferred the grip of both hands to it just as the shrub which had supported him gave way and dropped into the void beneath.

There he hung, at the length of both his arms.

He sagged back his head over his shoulder and turned his bleeding blind face in the direction of Seton's voice.

"Seton," he said, and his tone was strangely subdued and quiet, "Seton, what can you do for me, for God's sake? I would of murdered you. I got no right to ask."

"I'll do what I can," said Seton. "But what *can* I do? Is there anything above you that you can catch hold on?"

"I'm blind," said Mooney. "I can only see black and red, and flashes of the sun. I'm blinded, Seton. I can't see to get a new handhold."

Even if he could, it was doubtful if he could have worked up the sheer face of the rock, though it was a mere six or seven feet to the top.

If Seton were on the other side—

He looked at the gap between the two walls of the ravine. It had seemed absurdly small, a moment before. It seemed a vast gulf, as this new idea came home to him.

He refused the risk. He shook his head at it. There was no reason, for the sake of a brute and murderer, why he should risk his own life, and the life of his horse. There was every reason against it. This was, in a way, a judgment of God, he tried to tell himself; but, as the swift arguments flowed up into his mind, he knew with a cold heart that he could not resist the impulse which had risen in him.

"Hold hard," he called suddenly. "Keep your grip, Jake. I'm going to try to jump the mustang across."

"You're going to what?" screamed Jake. "Are you laughin' at me, Seton? What did you say about the horse?"

"I'm going to try," said Seton, and straightway he wheeled the pony back to a little distance. Prickles of cold stabbed through his forehead to the brain. His heart raced. Then it stood still as he drove the spurs deep and raced the little mustang toward the gap. He thought the mustang would rise for the leap. He swayed forward, but at the last moment the bronco dodged to the side like a cat. Seton was jerked from the saddle, he hung by one arm and one leg right over the edge of the ravine, and saw the white face of the water beneath him; then the mustang swerved back over the safe land, and Seton pulled himself back into the saddle.

He heard the loud shout of poor Mooney from the ravine. "Seton! Seton! What happened? Where are you?"

"The damned horse balked," called Seton. "I—I—I'm trying again!"

He beat his fist against his face, but that did not warm his icy heart. His breath was gone and would not come back. And yet, in the midst of his terror, he knew that he could not abandon the helpless man, yonder, any more than he could have abandoned a brother of his own blood.

He drove in the spurs again. He whooped. He cut the tender flank of the pony with the quirt, and from a longer distance he drove the little half-wild animal at the lip of the danger.

Ten steps from the brink, he felt the mustang stiffen and slow. In went the spurs again. His yell would have roused a spirit from the grave, and it roused in the mustang the spirit of its gallant forefathers. Straight to the brink of the ravine it galloped, then rose and flung itself bravely forward for the other edge.

It would have made the leap easily enough, had it not been burdened by the weight of a heavy rider. As it was, Seton looked down and had a glimpse of the rushing, roaring water beneath. Then they struck not over the edge of the cliff, but on it.

He felt the pony give. He thought the back of the little horse had been broken. But still it clung, pawing frantically with its forelegs and thrusting down vainly with the rear legs to find a footing.

Seton flung himself out of the saddle and onto the safety of the rock.

CHAPTER 15

He gave his whole might to helping the brave little mustang, then. It clawed and fought like a cat to get up on the ledge. Its ears flattened. Its eyes glared with terror. But, whereas a common animal might have given up, paralyzed with fear, and slid off to death, the mustang struggled on.

Big Seton got a hold on the strong bit-straps of the bridle. Bracing his heels against the rim of the very boulder from the surface of which his bullet had glanced, he leaned his weight back. He went down until his shoulders were almost touching the rock. He pulled until a red mist mounted to his brain.

He seemed to be gaining nothing, helping the horse in no respect. But the horse understood that help was being given. The terrible panic went out of its eyes. Its ears pointed forward. Man, the master, the dictator and director, often was cruel but always was wise. The horse struggled with more intelligent direction, reached more deliberately for footholds, and in a moment got the toe of a rear hoof hooked on a small projection of rock. Instantly it was over the verge of the cliff with a lurch.

Seton, the strain suddenly released, fell flat on his back. The mustang went straight over him with a rush, but it put down its feet so carefully that he was uninjured.

A horrible, hoarse voice was bellowing from the bottom of the ravine, as it seemed to him—the voice of Jake Mooney, half drowned by the uproar of the water that dashed among the rocks below.

Seton got to his feet, his head a little dizzy from the vast effort which he had expended upon the mustang. He crawled to the edge of the ravine. All his nerves shrank from the empty fall to the bottom, to the white teeth of the water, there. And he saw, immediately beneath him, the contorted face of Mooney. Thin streaks of blood showed on the skin. The mouth gaped. The throat seemed swelled with further shouting, but not a sound came from it. Most significant of all was the shuddering of the arms. While he looked, he saw the hands give a dreadful fraction of an inch.

"Steady! Steady!" cried Seton.

He leaped to his feet, his brain clear again. The mustang had not run. It remained facing toward the gulf across which it had just escaped, and, instead of trying to bolt away from the approaching rider, as it assuredly would have done that morning, it pricked its ears and softened its eyes at Seton.

He snatched the rope from beside the saddle, and cast the noose of it over the edge of the cliff.

It was almost too late. The eyes of Mooney, blindly rolling, were more dreadful than the sound of screaming from tortured crowds. His face was swollen. He had his teeth gripped hard together and the lips stretched away from the teeth in a vast grimace.

Seton drew up the noose over the right leg of Mooney, and allowed it to run tight when it was half way up the thigh. Then he dropped a pair of half-hitches over the nearest projecting rock edge that seemed strong enough to support the strain which would follow.

"Let go of the rock with one hand and grab the rope. The rope's on you now!" he called.

"D'you mean it?" gasped Mooney.

"Don't you feel the grip of the noose around your leg?"

"I feel a little something now. You mean it, Seton?"

"I mean it."

Desperate hope and fear seemed working together in the face of Mooney. He moved his head. It struck against the taut line of the rope, and then shifting his right hand quickly from the rock, he got it on the rope. His left hand slid from the rock. With both he was clinging to the lariat, sitting into the noose of it. His grip was so weak that he wound his arms around the rope to hold more securely to it.

Then Seton began to lift. He put his heels into a good deep notch a foot or so from the edge of the rock. He got a firm grip on the rope—how much simpler it would have been if the rope had been three times its actual diameter!—and then he heaved.

It was all that his best might could manage. There was well over two hundred pounds of burden on the end of the rope, and, even when he was standing at a fairly straight angle, he was still heaving the rope in over the corner of the cliff edge. That friction doubled the lift.

But he was strong, and he knew how to use his weight, his power. He used the arching muscles of his back, the shrugging muscles of his shoulders, the contracting biceps, the steel-hard, trembling power of his legs.

And he brought up the burden little by little. He had Mooney up three feet when he sat down and hitched the rope again.

He waited for the tremor, the numbness to pass out from his limbs. So he called: "Mooney! Mooney! Are you all right?"

There was a hoarse, shapeless cry in answer. No words were in it. There was· no apparent syllabification. It was simply a great roar, like the voice of an unreasoning beast.

After a minute or two, he stood up and resumed the struggle. There were two or three short pulls, and then he saw a pair of big hands grip at the edge of the rock. The weight that instant was diminished by more than half, and, in another breath, Mooney was over the verge and crawling on the flat of the top rock.

His whole body shook. He crawled on hands and flat elbows, as though there was no strength in his arms to support his body's weight. Then he slumped upon his face. He lay and quivered like a loose, helpless mass of jelly.

Seton, more than half disgusted, was tempted to mount the mustang and ride off. And then again, he changed his mind and told himself that he owed to society the apprehension of this murderer. It was not fair to save him and let him go free. The only just procedure was, having saved him, to bring him in and turn him over to the sheriff. For one thing, it would be a vast step in the direction of giving to himself a new character, which was the thing that he wanted to accomplish.

He set to work over Mooney. He massaged the trembling muscles of the arms and shoulders. Under the armpits, he dug his fingers deep, thumbing out the ligaments and the big, chunky contracting muscles. Mooney groaned a little.

Seton always carried a saddle flask for just such emergencies, and now he brought it and let Mooney empty half of the little flask at a gulp. Shortly after that, Jake could sit up. He put his back against a rock. His head lolled against the same support, and out of his bloodshot eyes he peered at his rescuer. The sight which had been temporarily blinded was returning. It was merely the stinging stone-dust driven up by the glancing bullet which had paralyzed the nerve of sight for a moment.

His big arms hung down; his hands lay palm upward upon the rock.

And he said nothing. Only his bleared eyes looked with gathering understanding upon Seton.

"Stay here and take things easy," said Seton. "I've got a hat on the other side of the ravine. I'll ride down to the ford and go back for it."

Mooney made not a single murmur in reply, so Seton mounted the mustang and rode down the sharp descent of the slope until he came to the ford, where the penned waters that shouted in the throat of the cañon were spread out in a shallow sheet. It still ran so fast that the surface water, striking the mustang at the knees, curled halfway up to elbows and stifles. Up the farther shore he rode to where the hat had fallen.

After he had stooped down and picked it up, he looked across to the farther side. Mooney sat exactly as he had been left, his arms falling loosely and his body all relaxed. Only the head, instead of lolling back against the rock, had tipped forward, and the chin was lying against his chest.

So Seton returned, revolving many strange ideas in his mind.

When he came again to Mooney, he saw that the big fellow was obviously somewhat recovered. He was wiping the water from his injured eyes, and the blood from his face, where several flying stone splinters had cut the skin. The tremor of his body had subsided, also; and, throughout, he was making the rapid recovery of a naturally very strong man.

He looked at his rescuer with the same half dumb and half wondering look that had been in his face before. Seton dismounted and came closer. The mustang followed like a dog behind him, regardless of its nearness to the edge of the cliff.

Mooney pointed a forefinger at the horse.

"What you done to old Blood and Bones?" he asked.

"Is that his name?"

"You don't know his name, even?"

"No."

"Well, he knows yours," said Mooney.

And he shifted his stare from the horse to the face of Seton. He began to nod, as though he were agreeing with a former conclusion which he had reached.

"What're you gunna do with me, Seton?" he asked.

"I ought to turn you over to the sheriff," said Seton.

"Yeah," said Mooney. "You ought to do that. You ought to of let me hang onto that rock till I slid off, too. *I* would of done that by you. I would of sat on the edge of the rock and laughed at you. But you don't do the same kind of things that I do, Seton."

He shook his head again, and appeared to be consulting an inner voice.

"It's getting on late," said Seton. "We ought to be starting back for the ranch, I guess."

"Yeah. It's getting late," said Mooney.

He stood up with a surprising show of strength and then slowly, carefully stretched himself.

"I guess I'm all right," said he.

"You look all right," said Seton. And he watched the other swing strongly up into the saddle on the tall, powerful horse which he was riding.

CHAPTER 16

The sun stood in the eye of the west, and the kind evening wind was up and about them as the two rode in toward the ranch house. Jake Mooney paid no heed to the riding. He kept his face turned straight ahead; the reins hung slack, and melancholy dimmed his eyes. They did not speak for a good while, but at last Seton said:

"Look here, Jake. I want to remind you of something. The time you get lowest down is the time when you begin to climb again. When you get to the bottom of the hill, you can't roll any farther."

Mooney seemed to need a full minute before the sense of the words came home to him, but still he looked blankly before him at the gold which rose in a wall along the west. The sun lay on top of a flat-headed hill and seemed to rest there for a long moment, without sinking any farther, but puffing out his red-gold cheeks. In the blue hollow of a ravine near them, a cow was lowing.

"I'm at the bottom of the hill," admitted Mooney, "but there's another drop under me. Compared with me, a monkey-faced Chink—"

He paused. It was hard to fill out the sentence.

"Partner," said Seton, "today never happened. It was something told in a story. It wasn't real. Forget about it, Jake."

"Forget about it?" murmured Jake.

He laughed in a way that was not good to hear.

"You're hard on yourself just now," said Seton, "but you'll get over that. Just remember that none of this happened.

Besides, what you did wasn't all out of your own head."

Mooney stiffened a little, and, though his head did not turn, it was easy to see that he had been stung to sharp attention by the last remark.

"What makes you say that?" he demanded.

"I judged by the fall of the cards that a crook had dealt you that layout," said Seton. "Am I wrong?"

Mooney, about to answer, shut his teeth with a click and shook his head.

"It was all my own idea," said he. "Who else would have any interest in a job like that? Who else would wanta get his hands dirty, even at long range, when it comes to a job like that?"

"Doug Walters would," said Seton, and watched the effect of this pointblank attack.

Mooney merely shrugged his shoulders.

"D'you want me to talk?" he said. "Or d'you want me to try to play square?"

Seton considered.

"A man who pays for murder doesn't deserve anything but a rope," he answered.

"What d'you think of a sneak that talks outside of school?" asked Mooney.

"You're right," answered Seton, instantly. "I shouldn't have asked. You're right, and I'm as wrong as they make them for putting the thing to you. I'm sorry, old-timer."

"Sorry?" said Mooney. He shrugged his shoulders again, with the same bitter laughter. "*You're* sorry?" said he.

"Well, forget it," said Seton.

"Yeah. I'd better try to forget it," agreed the big man.

He drew out a bandanna, and, though this was the cool of the day, he wiped glistening perspiration from his face.

"Shack along," he muttered, "and forget about it. Forget about it. That's easy, eh?"

"No, it's not easy," said Seton. "We've all got something to forget about."

"Have we?" said Mooney. "You mean that you've been to prison, eh? Why, man, I'd rather have a million years of prison behind me. I'd rather have a billion years of it. Prison —that's nothing!"

"I'll tell you what I can remember," said Seton. "When I was a big kid, tough as boiled owl meat, a new family came to Claymore out of the East. You never saw such tenderfeet, and there was a boy, about my age and size, who went to school and talked in a funny sort of a way. We all used to laugh at him, but I hated him because he had slick clothes to wear. He used to bring flowers in the morning and give them to the teacher. Well, I laid for the chance, and one day I slapped him across the face. He fought back. I mean to say, he tried to fight, but he didn't know anything. He sort of flopped his arms around, and that was all. I knew all about fist fighting—for a kid. I stood off and banged him. His face puffed up like a toad. He began to cry. I was glad to see the tears run down. I kept spatting my fists into the wet of the tears and the blood. I felt good. It was like eating and drinking, to me. I liked it. Finally he dropped and couldn't get up again. I didn't offer to pick him up. I went on home and still felt pretty good. But that night I began to think."

"Did you?" said Mooney.

He was fascinated.

"Yes. I began to think. It was hell. Lying there in the dark I had to think. I turned over on my face. I couldn't shut out the sight of the thing."

"Yeah," said Mooney, his voice hardly more than a gasp. "I know what you mean."

"No, you don't. You think you do, but you don't. You think you're pretty miserable, just now. But I was sick. No man can be as sick as a boy can. I couldn't sleep all night. The next morning I went to that kid's house. When his mother saw me at the door, she turned crimson and swelled up like that fat sun, yonder. I thought she was going to rise and float away, like a red toy balloon. But she didn't. She stayed right there on the ground and she gave me a dressing down. She had words, too, believe me. Most of the other mothers in Claymore wouldn't of had the vocabularies. But she'd been to school. They would have had to use a broom

88

handle on me, but a broom would just of been a weight and a waste, to her. She told me a lot about myself, Jake."

"Yeah. I'll bet she did."

"I had to stay there and take it. I'll tell you, honestly, that I felt pretty good as I listened to her. I mean to say that I *wanted* to do a little suffering—to make up. I stood there and she burned me up, and I took it. Then she wound up by asking how I dared to come near her house. I told her that I wanted to see the boy, and she let me come in."

"She was flabbergasted, I guess," said Jake.

"Yes, she was sort of flabbergasted, I guess. I went in and found the kid lying in bed. His face was all bandages. I stood there a minute. I felt weak, Jake. My knees were shaking under me. That mother gave a good look at me, and I imagine that she saw what I was going through, because she actually backed out and left me there alone with him."

"Did the kid dress you down, too?" said Mooney, still spurred by an eager curiosity.

"Yeah. What his mother had said to me was nothing to what the kid said."

"What did he say?"

"He told me that it was all right, and that he was ashamed because I felt that I had to come and apologize, and that he was only a girl, and no good at all. And that he wished he could die. He didn't blubber and cry, either. He said it out of the heart. To listen to him was worse than lying awake at night."

"I'll bet it was," said Mooney, in a tone of reverence. "I'll bet you sweated a good bit."

"It was pretty bad," agreed big Seton, with a sigh. "It was about the worst minute in my life."

"What did you say back to him?"

"Well, I had an idea. I said to him that, every day, after school, I'd box with him, and teach him everything I knew, and that I'd teach him to swim, too, and how to do high dives, and all that sort of thing. He was so bandaged up that he couldn't see me, but he stuck out his hand and reached for mine. You never saw such a hand. It was white and thin. I realized, as I took hold of it, that that was the hand that had been trying to punch me the day before. And that was another pretty bad minute for me, Jake."

"Ah, God, yes!" said Jake.

"Well, you see how it is. Everybody has something to forget."

"I guess you're right," said Jake. "I never looked at it like that, somehow. Listen, Jimmy. Where'd you get hold of these ideas?"

"I've been five years to a place where you have a chance to sit and think, you see?"

"I see," said Mooney. "I sort of understand what you mean, old-timer. You've had your hell."

"I've had my hell," said Seton. "I've had it on toast. I've had it done brown, and on toast, if you know what I mean."

"I know what you mean. I know now."

"So you forget about today."

Mooney said nothing, and suddenly Seton, for his own part, saw the meaning of that silence.

"I'll tell you something, Jake."

"All right, you tell me."

. "Look at me."

Jake looked, and, before his eyes, Seton lifted his right hand, solemnly.

"I'll never speak about this afternoon to a soul," said he.

Jake, who had been a rather sickly gray-green, suddenly flamed to the very eyes. But he made no answer. He rode on beside Seton in the same blind way, but he was straighter in the saddle, and Seton knew that the greater part of the dreadful burden had been lifted from Mooney's soul. He watched the man with a curious interest, like a doctor who had performed an operation on a man detestable to him. And he found, like the doctor, that the other no longer was detestable. Who can hate the man to whom he has rendered unbought services? Because he had given a little, he seemed able and willing to give a little more.

The ranch house rose before them. Then big Mooney stopped his horse.

"I can't ride in with you," he said.

"Why not?"

"Well, I wouldn't be any good to you, if I rode in with you. I'd better keep on hating you, Jimmy."

"I see what you mean. Thanks, Jake."

"Ah, God, don't thank me. There's only one thing I could do that would be worth thanks."

"What's that, old fellow?"

"Give you the only good advice—get out of Claymore Valley, and never come back here; because, if you stay, I don't care how smart you are, or what a fighter, or even with me and others for friends, they're too much for you. You don't know what you're up against. Jimmy; they'll kill you deader'n hell inside of three days!"

CHAPTER 17

That solemn warning did not fall lightly on the ears of Seton. It rang to his very soul, like the deep tone of a bell. There was the weight of utter surety in the caution. No shadow of doubt was in the staring eyes of big Jake Mooney. He meant what he said, and he glared at Seton to enforce his words.

But Seton could merely shake his head and ride on, slowly, toward the corral. There he unsaddled, turned the mustang loose, and walked slowly toward the barn to put up the saddle and bridle and blanket. All that was reasonable in his mind told him that Mooney was assuredly correct. They were too much for him. And Douglas Walters, as a brain or as a fighting hand, was in himself worthy of the best attention in the world.

Yet Seton could not give up the task which he had assigned to himself. Why, he could not tell. This dream, he felt, of rehabilitating himself before the eyes of the world, of stepping forth as an honest man, worthy of trust, believed in, loved faithfully—that was all very well. But it was a dream.

Perhaps the great pull was simply that this land was in Claymore Valley, where he had been raised as a boy. It laid hold upon him with a strong hand, and claimed something from him. Well, he would answer the call and give something back. He swore that he would! And as for the danger, each day would have to take care of itself!

When he reached the door of the barn, a horse neighed from the corral corner nearest to him. It was the mustang he had just turned loose. It ought to have been busy rolling and getting itself a drink at the long trough from which the water was forever dripping, forever making a black puddle on the lower side. In that puddle was always a duck or two, dipping its head to get at the food on the bottom of the pool. Chickens stalked and cackled around the edges of it, turning their foolish heads from side to side. And the margin was always stamped into round patterns by the hoofs of horses. Over yonder the mustang should be taking his ease; and, when the drinking was ended, since the bars connecting with the pasture were still down, it should have gone scampering into the green meadow, tossing its tail and holding its head low, and running aslant, like a puppy. But, instead of doing any of these expected things, it stood at the corner of the corral, having followed its late rider on the other side of the fence. And it neighed to him, and lifted its ugly head and shook it.

"By the lord Harry!" said Seton to himself.

He was amazed. Ordinarily there is more affection in a tangle of rattlers than there is in the Western bronco. The hand that touches them forgets not the whip, and they forget not their heels.

In the barn, Seton put up the saddle and other equipment. He went outside again and was even more amazed to find that the pony was standing in the same place. It whinnied at the sight of him.

"It's not true," said Seton. "You're a doggone liar and deceiver. You don't mean a word you're saying."

He walked up closer to the fence. There was nothing distinguished about this horse except the extreme ugliness of its Roman-nosed head, and the meager ewe-neck. Yet it had four good legs under it, and the rather tubby look of its belly might rather mean excess of bottom than excess of weight. Yes, there were good points about the animal. How good it was, in fact, one could not tell. It had the gait of a load of stones being dumped. It had the usual short, pounding canter. But he could remember, now, that it never had said no to him. No one would know the true value of that horse until it came to a matter of life and death. Perhaps it would blow up in ten miles. Perhaps it would gallop a hundred. He went up to the fence. The mustang whirled, flourished its heels— "You liar!" said the man—and then came straight up to him and nibbled playfully at the hand which he held out to it.

Seton was amazed more than before. The thing could not be, he told himself. As for the peril into which he had put the animal, and then helped to save it from the results— well, that was perhaps a key turned in the heart of the bronco. But who would have dreamed that the results could be so instant, and so great?

He rubbed the muzzle, the forehead of the pony, and stroked its neck, reaching through the bars. Then he went back toward the bunkhouse and, glancing over his shoulder, he saw that the mustang was pacing uneasily up and down inside the fence. Seton shook his head, but his heart was warmed more than he would have cared to admit.

Near the bunkhouse, Chet Ray met him, passing out toward the barn.

"They want you inside, Jimmy," said he.

He never had called Seton by his first name, before. It might be merely the impertinence of youth; not that it mattered greatly, but there was something about the look which the boy gave him that promised trouble to Seton, he felt. He did not pause, however.

For five days these fellows had been watching him, he

knew, waiting for him to hesitate, getting behind his back, whenever they could, trying in a thousand small ways to test his nerve, to gradually wear it out with continued friction. He thought that they had not made as yet any progress which would be perceptible to their own eyes; he hoped that he still could keep them at arm's length. The moment that he had to stop smiling, he had an idea that they would be in at his throat like so many wolves.

"They" were not at the ranch house.

Just inside the gate to the yard, he saw Sheriff Bill Perry standing with a stocky wedge of a fellow who wore a blue silk shirt and the gaudiest of bandannas around his throat. He almost faltered in his step as he saw the pair. He could tell beforehand that the sheriff wanted to see him, and no good was behind the errand, he was sure. But he made himself smile. That was the secret of diplomacy. Always to smile! And, smiling, he went through the gate and offered his hand to the sheriff. Bill Perry accepted the hand and gravely considered Seton.

He spoke while looking at Seton, but his words were addressed to the third man.

"Is this the fellow, Durham?"

"Sure it's him," said the stocky man. "Look at the face of him, to stand there and not bat an eye, with me right here! I got a mind to—"

"To do what?" asked the sheriff, rather irritably.

"To walk up and paste him on the jaw. He's got no gun on me, now."

"When you use this size man," said the sheriff, dryly, "you'd better trim him down a little before you take him on. If you didn't look out, maybe he'd put you in his pocket and forget all about you, Durham. But this is the man, is it?"

"Yes," said Durham, nodding confidently.

"You'll swear to that, eh?"

"Will I swear to it? Of course I'll swear to it."

The sheriff turned back to Seton.

"I'm arresting you in the name of the law," he said. "You know what I have to say. If you talk, now, your talk will be used against you."

Seton endured the shock for a moment in silence. He fought to keep his smile, and barely managed to keep it from going out like a candle.

"I'm just in from a long ride, Perry," said he. "Suppose that we go over and sit on the veranda for a while and talk the thing over."

"There's old Henry Ash and his girl, over there," said the sheriff.

"Well, that's all right," answered Seton. "I don't mind an audience. Do you—whatever your name is?"

And still he smiled, as he looked straight into the eyes of Durham. The latter bore the glance as well as he could, but his own eyes wavered a little.

"You can't face me down," said Durham. "Now I've got you, though, I wanta say that all I ask for is the money back. I ain't anxious to have you rot in jail, but I want the coin back, and I'm gunna have it or else run you up!"

"It's out of your hands, Durham," said the sheriff, firmly. "There's a case here for the law to take up."

"What *is* the case?" asked Seton.

"Attack with intent to kill, and highway robbery, young man. If they get you for this, Seton, you'll spend most of the rest of your life in stripes, I take it."

Seton nodded. The prison smell stifled him; his ears sickened with the prison murmur.

"Most of my life," he answered, quietly. "All of it, in fact. I couldn't live again in a prison, sheriff, and, if I'm tried before a jury in this county, I'm convicted before the trial begins. You know that."

"I gave you my warning," said the sheriff, harshly. "You preferred to laugh at me, and follow your own ways. Now you see what it's come to. And may every other thug and gun man in the world follow you along the same trail as fast as they can crowd onto it!"

He glared at Seton as he spoke. It was not, really, Seton was able to gather, a personal hatred. It was the deep detestation which the man felt for crime and for criminals.

"I'm not on the way to jail yet," said Seton. "Let's sit down on the veranda and talk the thing over a little. You'll be rather surprised to know that I never saw this fellow Durham before."

There was a loud, half-hysterical whoop of laughter from Durham.

"Listen to him!" he shouted. "Pretty soon he'll be saying that it's a frame. He'll be pulling some of the old, old gags, again. Let's run him in. Let's start now, sheriff."

"We'd better start along. It'll be about dark by the time we get into town, and I don't want to be out late with you, Seton."

"Are you afraid of catching cold?" asked the latter. "Well, Perry, if you insist, I'll have to go along with you. There's nothing else for it. I'll be walking up a gangplank, with hell at the other end. But I want to sit down and talk to you for a minute. Will you grant me that? I want to sit down and talk to you and this fellow Durham, here."

"What'll you gain by that, Seton?"

"I dunno. I'd just like to see what happens. Maybe something will come out of the ground, after all. Will you give me the chance?"

The sheriff hesitated. He looked at Seton, and the latter looked straight back at him. The sheriff sighed. Then he shrugged his shoulders.

"You're considerable of a man, Jimmy Seton," he admitted. "Ay, we'll go and sit down and talk to you."

CHAPTER 18

There already had been a whisper at the house, it seemed, for, when the trio rounded the corner of it, both Henry Ash and his daughter stood up. She came hurrying down the steps, white and staring, her hands clasped together as she went up to the sheriff.

"What can it be?" she asked. "What can it be, Sheriff Perry? There can't be anything against Mr. Seton. Why, he's Douglas Walters' dearest old friend!"

"Is he?" said the dry sheriff. "Well, we're gunna sit down and talk, and of course you'll find out what's what."

They went up on the veranda, all together. Old Henry Ash came and reached up and patted the shoulder of Seton.

"My poor lad," said he, "of course any backing I can give you—"

Seton was immensely touched.

"It's all right," said he. "If I come to trial, no backing in the world can keep the jury from finding me guilty. But so far I don't know exactly what I'm accused of."

They were all sitting down, now. Durham assumed a position of the most domineering confidence, his legs crossed, his trousers hitched up to show the brightly variegated pattern which was worked around the tops of his boots.

"This here is what happened," said he. "I step into Claymore day before yesterday. Am I right, sheriff?"

"Yes, you stepped into Claymore, all right."

"I get into a poker game with a fellow by name of Bushy Daniels and couple three other boys. Am I right?"

"You're right."

"I have a streak of luck," said Durham, his eyes glittering, "and I step out of that game with eleven hundred and fifty bucks. Is that right?"

"Tell your story," said the sheriff impatiently. "Seton is the man who wants to hear it. I don't. I've heard it once, and that's enough for me."

"I step out with eleven hundred and fifty bucks. I stepped in with a hundred and a quarter. What I mean, I had a streak of luck. Well, I have a little party that night. Good. I turn in that night later on. I get up yesterday morning and pay my bill. I count over my cash. I've got eleven hundred and twenty-two bucks. I step in at Tucker and Smith's grocery store. I spend two dollars on ammunition, thirty-two caliber longs. The clerk'll sure remember. I spend a dollar and a quarter on plug tobacco, and Bull Durham. Have the makings, sheriff—Mr. Ash?"

They shook their heads. Henry Ash was frowning with closest attention. His daughter was still white as stone in her fear and her pity for Seton. When his glance touched on her, once, her eye melted and softened upon him and she smiled a little, wan smile. After that he felt it was best to avoid her face.

"I buy some matches and things," said Durham. "I leave Claymore with eleven hundred and fifteen dollars and a quarter."

He snatched a silver coin from his pocket and spinning it into the air let it spat upon his open palm.

"That's all that I've got of it now!" said he.

"Go on," said Perry, "and please make it shorter!"

"I ride out," said Durham, "and I get going up the valley, and sort of lazy along. I feel pretty good. It's a fine haul. Nobody like an ordinary cowpuncher, like me, gets used to seeing eleven hundred bucks for an evening's work. Well, I get up into the hills right yonder, behind the ranch you've got, Mr. Ash, and all at once there's a gunshot, and the gun I'm wearing on my hip is shot right clean off. Here it is!"

He snatched it out from the holster. The weapon was badly battered and the handles of it were broken. He showed it to them, holding it high, like a torch that would shed light upon his cause.

"He's aimed for my heart or stomach, I suppose," said Durham, his voice quivering with emotion, "and he gets the gun, instead. There I am with nothing to fight with. He covers me. He comes out at me and I see, who? Him!"

He pointed his arm with a dramatic suddenness straight at big Seton.

"He cleans me out!" said Durham. "He takes my wad."

He leaped to his feet.

"He leaves me a quarter in the safe. That's all. He says to me: 'That'll buy you a beer.' Yeah, that's what he done. He rubs it in, the big haymaker! The dirty bum!"

As he finished, he continued standing, shaking his fist at Seton. And Seton, almost dreamily, eyed the hand. It was small, rather pale, and had a good clean look. Durham sat down, jerked his trousers up to the colored boot-tops, recrossed his legs, and, leaning back in the chair, looked around in a sort of savage triumph.

"I want that money back, Seton," he said. "That's what I want. Fork it over, and you'll hear no more from me!"

"You lie," said Seton calmly. "You've been hired to frame it up on me. Sheriff," he said to Bill Perry, "what do you think of this? A man says he has lost some money. He shows a broken gun. And with that for a proof, he accuses me of the crime—attempted murder, and highway robbery, eh? That's circumstantial evidence on a grand scale, isn't it?"

"It *can't* be right!" cried Molly Ash.

"Molly, be quiet, my dear," said her father.

He was watching with a grave, quiet eye, noncommittal and keen.

"You claim you never saw this man before?" said the sheriff.

"Never."

"Then what reason would he have for framing you?"

"There are people who want me out of this valley."

"Why?"

And suddenly Seton saw that he could not answer. What he knew was, outside of Mooney's attack, a nebulous thing that could not be explained. And about Mooney his lips were sealed. Even in that pinch of need, however, he did not regret the pledge of silence.

"I can't answer that," he said.

The sheriff smiled, and his smile was a sneer. There was no doubt as to his feelings in this matter. Durham cackled in open triumph.

"He don't know!" he said. "He can't answer. Why, it sounds like a crook on trial, already."

Seton faced him.

"Will you answer a few questions?"

"Yeah, a million," said Durham, complacently.

"I take it, sheriff," said Seton, "that the only ghost of a chance his case against me has is that his character is good and that I'm an ex-convict?"

The sheriff shrugged his shoulders.

"It depends on who the jury and judge wanta believe," said he.

"Durham," said Seton, "are you a cowpuncher?"

"Yeah. That's me."

"Been working lately?"

"Yeah."

"Where?"

"Down by El Paso."

"How long?"

"More'n six months."

"What doing?"

"Why, punching cows."

"Roping, and all that?"

"Sure. And fence riding, and fence building, and the whole thing."

"Will you shake hands with the sheriff?"

"What's that for? Sure I will."

He held out his hand, and the sheriff took it, with a faint frown of boredom.

"Tell me, Perry," said Seton. "Did you feel a callous?"

Durham jumped.

"You dirty crook! I wear gloves when I'm on the job!"

"Callouses make through gloves," said Seton coldly. "Particularly roping and fence building and the rest of the things you've been doing for six months. Or did you put cold cream on your hands every night when you went to bed?"

Durham twisted violently from side to side in his chair.

"Callouses! Tryin' to run me down on a thing like callouses! It's funny, ain't it?"

"No," said the sheriff. "It's not funny. If you've lied about one thing, you may have lied about the rest. No judge would listen to you."

"You've framed it between you!" shouted the other. "I've gone and laid a charge. I've been robbed. And then——"

Seton, who had been watching carefully, pointed to one of the boot-tops.

"What do you keep in there?" he asked.

"Where?" said Durham.

100

"There—where the edge of the boot has been opened up and sewed again several times. I can see the white of the new thread."

"Why, the thread give out and I sewed it up myself," said Durham, his voice suddenly weakening.

"The thread would never give out there. Not the thread of a good pair of handmade boots like you're wearing," said the sheriff.

"I'm gunna get out of here," said Durham. "You're a bunch of thugs workin' together—"

"Just one minute," said the sheriff. "Sit still, Durham. I'm beginning to get interested."

He leaned forward, felt at the indicated place, and, taking out a pocket knife, he snipped the threads. When he straightened again he held in his hand three little glittering pieces of metal, of different lengths and sizes. At these, he stared intently.

"Are you a watchmaker, Durham?" he asked grimly. "Make watches, as well as gamble and—punch cows?"

Durham had lost all color. He tried to speak. Every lie suddenly had run out of his mind like water when a dam is drawn.

"Have you ever been mugged?" asked the sheriff.

"Me? Mugged? Not on your life," said Durham, feebly. "I—I—"

His voice shook away for nothing.

"I'm gunna get out of here. You've framed it agin me!" he declared.

"Oh," said Molly, her voice thin and faint with a sick disgust. And she hurried into the house, her head bowed, overwhelmed by the patent cowardice and villainy which had been revealed to her. Even the sheriff seemed half sickened, also.

"You'll come back with me," said the sheriff. "I'm going to look you over. I got a little private picture gallery of my own, and maybe I've seen you before. Seton," he added, turning to the latter, "I was wrong. He was a fool to try such a thin game. I was a fool to listen. I was wrong. I hope that I'm always wrong, and that you're always right."

CHAPTER 19

In a sense, Seton felt that he had crossed perhaps the most perilous of all his dangers when he passed the sheriff on that day. There would be yet other troubles, of course. He was prepared for that. But, since the crude attempt of the so-called Durham to land him in jail on a trumped-up charge, the sheriff would not be so apt to listen to the first charge which was laid against him. A sense of decent shame would make the sheriff pause for a moment.

He wondered, in a way, why the sheriff should hate him so visibly, so patently. And yet he understood. It was not, really, a hatred of himself. It was a hatred of crime. Well, Seton felt that he had left the world of crime, but certainly he had not come to hate it and criminals. Instead, he had in his bones a continual urge and longing to get out into the fresh, wide pastures of adventure again where the taking is easy and the spending is still easier. But the sheriff was the man of the law. All people must be on his side, or against him. He would accept no compromise.

What had he gained from this hatred of crime? Why, a certain position in the community, a very small salary, on which he kept himself and his wife sufficiently miserable, and an opportunity to get himself killed, before many years had passed. His time was due now. It was only a wonder that he had lasted so long at the job. Seton had no hard feeling for the sheriff. Instead, to his amazement, a deep pity for the man began to well up in him. He looked on Bill Perry as a saint, a saint in chaps and rough language, but nevertheless one who would die for the sake of society. And what made a better definition of a saint?

For his own part, Seton was no saint. And yet he wondered why he remained there on the ranch, in daily peril of his life. For the sake of the cowpuncher's pay which he was receiving? Certainly not that. He hardly dared to delve down into his mind deep enough to find the sources of his attachment to the place. He went to a certain point, and there he always halted, like a horse at a shaky bridge.

Of course he knew that Douglas Walters was behind the affair of Durham. That man could have had no personal motive in lying about a person he never had seen, but Walters had a motive.

No one could be more embarrassed than Walters having on the ranch a man whom he had to present to Ash and Molly Ash as a dear friend, a man who was installed as straw-boss and real working head in charge of affairs. Every detail passed through the hands of Seton. Walters was a nominal head, and no more. Soon the others would begin to see it. Even Ash would guess, and the hired hands before him. Some of them undoubtedly already knew that Walters hated his supposed friend and assistant. Chet Ray was probably one of those who understood. Others would learn later. They would be taken into the confidence of Walters—at a price.

The moment that Durham was disposed of, Seton knew that he was living in a new and more rarefied atmosphere of danger. Ordinary expedients had failed—after all. Sheer physical force had not worked. Assassination had failed, also. And finally that most cowardly attempt on the part of Durham. Three times Walters had failed through his agents. Would he try his own hand, next? Or would he resort to other measures?

Seton had one comfort. It was the devotion of Dick, the Negro lad. He worshipped Jim Seton with a whole-hearted devotion; but, the day after the Durham fiasco, Dick disappeared. Seton was not surprised. He went to Walters and asked. He found Walters in the latter's office, and, when

Seton knocked at the door, he heard a faint scuffling sound and then a brisk voice bidding him to enter.

When he went in, Walters was revealed busily adding up a long column of figures in a ledger. He wore his sombrero. His rifle lay across the chair beside him. He had the air of one who has rushed in from outdoor duties and, dropping into this chair, been confined steadily to hard work ever since. He continued to write for a moment after Seton entered. Then he looked up. His dark eyes were as bright as glass, with a light behind the lens.

"What'll you have?" he asked.

"A minute of your time," said Seton.

"Close the door," said Walters.

Seton closed it behind him. He walked over beside the window and stood there where the light would fall more into the face of the foreman, as the latter turned to talk to him and watch him. It was not only a handsome but an intelligent face, this one of Walters'. The big, nobly built forehead was not there for nothing, nor the cool probe of the eyes, nor their luminosity. The man had a brain, he had courage, he had strength and skill. And yet Seton hated him. He had hated Walters from the first day, as a boy, when he laid eyes on him. They had fought together fifty times, and always he had won. But, if once he lost, he never would live to regret the defeat. He had had that feeling from the first, a loathing, a horror, and an inexplicable dread of this man.

Walters leaned back in his chair and, so doing, exposed in his lap the magazine which he had been reading. He pushed the ledger away from him. He extended his legs across a corner of the desk and rested his shoulders against the wall. Then he rolled a cigarette and lighted it.

All this time he knew that Seton was watching him. His air was that of one who despises and rather enjoys criticism.

"What're you here for?" asked Walters.

Seton continued to watch him for a time. He did not feel like speaking, at once. Suddenly he had realized the hopelessness of the thing he had come to achieve. And yet it might not altogether be hopeless.

"Walters," he said, "I've come to make a truce."

There was a flash of savage pleasure in the face of Walters.

"You're getting scared, eh?" said he.

Seton considered. Then he answered, honestly: "Yes, I'm getting scared. I'm getting cold, I'm so scared."

Walters made a little gesture, palm up.

"I told you," he said. "You can't buck me."

Seton nodded.

"Perhaps I can't. I dunno. But I'm not through yet. You're a hard nut to crack, Walters. But I'm hard, too."

"We'll see about that," said the other, and he tilted back his head contentedly, and blew smoke towards the ceiling. So often beaten, so often defeated, what was there now remaining in that handsome head of his? It would have been worth much to Seton to know.

"Walters," said Seton, "you've tried at me three times. First it was Mooney. He couldn't turn the trick. None of the rest of them can. They know it. You know it."

Walters merely laughed.

"You've had a little luck. Don't let it go to your head," said he.

"I know," said Seton. "There are other ways. The other day up by the Benson Ravine a bullet came an inch from my head. That's one way."

He looked at Walters, and the other looked calmly back at him, then sneered openly.

"That's one way," admitted Douglas Walters.

Fury almost strangled Seton, for a moment, but he controlled the emotion.

"Durham's trick was another way, too," said he, "and there may be a lot of others."

"There *are* a lot of others," said Walters. "There's only one way out for you, and that's a trip."

"I won't make it," said Seton gravely, shaking his head. "I'll never make it."

"You're a dead one, then," answered Walters, cheerfully. "You've squeezed yourself into a job here. You've fitted yourself in so tight that only you yourself can get yourself out—unless a bullet does the trick for you."

"I'll never quit," repeated Seton. "What I wanted to point out to you is that we have certain things in common."

"What are they?" asked Walters, aggressively.

"Brains and strong hands," said Seton.

Walters shrugged his shoulders.

"What do you make of that?" he asked.

"That we might make a team."

"You're crazy. For what?"

"For that."

Seton pointed out of the window. They could see the high shoulders of the barn, and beyond it the green flash of the rolling country, the groves of trees, twinkling in the wind, and the rich spotting of cattle, here and there. It was a pleasant land, a beautiful land. It held out its arms and smiled back at them.

"Well?" said Walters.

"You've given the ranch some hard knocks," said Seton, "but I still have faith in it. We could work together, Doug. We're not friends, but I love the lay of this land. I'd hate to see it bought and sold with a dirty mortgage on it. I'd like to see it clean. I've ridden every inch of it, now, and I love it. There's a lot of it that ought to be under the plough. We could get water on five hundred acres of that plateau where nothing grows now but tumble weed. There are twenty things we could do. We could boost the worth of it to three times what it is today. And I'd like to have a hand!"

Walters tipped forward and brought his heels with a hard bang onto the floor.

"What would your share be?"

"My wages. That's all."

Wonder, for an instant, clouded the brightness of the eyes of Doug Walters.

"I believe that you mean it. I really believe that you mean it!"

"I do," said Seton.

"You're a fool," said Walters.

Suddenly he stood up and went close to Seton.

"Listen to me," he said softly. "It's on its last legs now. It's a sinking ship. That old crook of a Hooker, he has a flock of short loans on it. He's going to force a collection in a few days and old Ash won't know where he stands. That's all. It's not my fault. I've tried to do the best I could, but the luck was against me. Ash, he knows nothing about business—and this old ranch is a ranch no more. It's just one big mortgage, my son!"

Then, from something in the face of Seton, he fell back a step or two.

"You've horned in. Now you can horn out," he said, and pointed to the door.

"I've been five years in prison," said Seton, slowly. "It's a good thing for you that I have, Walters."

And he left the room.

CHAPTER 20

He was stunned when he got outside the house. He was stunned by two things. One was the knowledge of the disaster which was about to overtake the place. The other was the bland confidence of Walters in giving him this information. There was no generosity in Walters. If he revealed his hand, it was because he knew that it beat everything else at the table. If he allowed Seton to know this, it was because he was certain that Seton could not interfere. As for the rest of the affairs of Walters, he would probably use his thugs to run off the cattle, one of these nights. That would complete the ruin of Henry Ash. And as for the girl? Well, if Walters really cared a snap about her, he might marry her, in spite of the fact that he had bled her father to death. He was in an imperial position, was Walters, and he could do what he pleased.

"Jim Seton!" called a voice beside him.

He looked up. Molly Ash was there at the kitchen window, smiling and nodding at him.

"I hoped you'd stay in there and cheer up poor old Douglas!" said she. "He's working himself to death over those wretched accounts. Poor dear!"

Her smile went out, as he stared blankly at her.

"Is something troubling you?" she asked him.

Still he looked at her, his eyes gradually clearing.

"No," he said. "Nothing's the matter with me now."

"But that sun, and no hat on your head?"

He passed his hand across his head. He had forgotten about the sun, though it was the full heat of the afternoon, falling with a sensible weight.

"I'll tell you how it is," said he. "I'm trying to get this here hair to grow. The sun is mighty good for it. Like grass, you see."

"You'll be sunburned. That's what'll happen."

"I never could get sunburned," he told her.

"Why not?"

"I've got inoculated against it."

She laughed.

"What nonsense," said she.

"Yes, I got inoculated with some stuff that thickens the skin. You know how it is. With a good, thick epidermis, you can't get sunburned, hardly."

"Really?" said she.

"Of course."

"I never heard of such a thing!"

"Well, a lot of people have," said he. "A thick skin is a mighty useful thing. It sheds hot sunshine, and a lot of other trouble."

"I'll have to try it," said she.

"Don't you do it."

"Why not?"

"It wouldn't go with your complexion."

"There's no help for me, then?"

108

"Yes, stay in the shade."

"Jimmy Seton, I never know when you're laughing at me."

"I never laugh at friends of mine. I hope you're a friend of mine, Molly?"

"Of course I am," she said.

She leaned on the sill of the window, closer to him, to show her earnestness. Her hands were covered with flour; the sunshine made her hair almost unendurably brilliant.

"Even if you weren't the friend of Douglas, of course I'm your friend, Jim!"

"I think you mean it," said Seton.

"Ah, but I do."

She leaned still closer. Her eyes held gently upon his.

"I believe in second starts!" she said.

"You believe in believing, Molly," said he. "So do I. Anyway, I'm just beginning to."

He waved his hat to her and smiled, and went off down the walk to the corral, and there kicked open the gate and went through. Old Henry Ash was a goner, it seemed. Nothing could be done. With anyone other than Hooker, perhaps —yes. But Hooker had no heart, no bowels of mercy. He was made of adamant and of steel. Such men must be the favorites of the devil.

And then, pausing in the middle of the corral, he looked around the countryside and saw the green of it, the roll of the hills, the gleam of the grass; and it looked back at him like a beautiful human face and seemed to smile at him, as Molly Ash had smiled, just the moment before. It was worth a battle, this place. It was not his. He was only a hired soldier, but he felt an odd willingness to die in defense of the land and of—well, he would leave the rest of it unthought. It was the ground on which he dared not tread.

He roused to a sense of the oppressive heat of the sun that was beating on his shoulders. His head buzzed with the mist of its force. The back of his hand was beaded with sweat. That fellow Walters could sit in the shade and smile, the game securely in his hands. But perhaps something could be done out there in the heat of the sun, in the open. With this, a thought came to him.

It made him hurry to the corral, catch and saddle a horse. He mounted and got to the corral gate. But when he was about to open the gate, he told himself that he was an impulsive fool. With any other man, yes. But not with a damned adding machine like Hooker!

Yet he persisted. The first impulse drove him against his will through the gate, and then, at a rapid gallop, down the road to town. It was only a mile. He raced the whole way. He wanted to get there before the first pressure of the idea had taken its hand from his shoulder.

He passed by the Acton place, the little house sitting on its hilltop like a hat on a bald head; then the Summers' ranch with its two windmills clanking resonantly in unison; and next the outskirts of the town jumped away behind him. People looked at him out of windows. Old Mr. Tom Jennings—how very old the man was, now—looked up to him from the cabbages which he was hoeing in the patch beside his house. It seemed to the boy that he never had seen old Tom Jennings, except there in the patch, hoeing away at his cabbages. The little main business section was before him, now. There was one paved block of street. The shoes of the horse slid on it. And so he came to a stop before the face of the Hooker & Smith bank.

It looked more like a funeral parlor than a bank. It had a false front of wood, like a silly pompadour on a woman's head. It had two windows on the street, and a door, painted green, with an iron knocker on it.

"Iron," said the boy. "That stands for Hooker. Damn him, iron can be hammered—or bent."

You had to knock at the door, always, as though it were a private house. That was old Hooker's idea. He wanted no little checking accounts, that need a flock of cashiers and clerks and accountants, and pile up the overhead. He wanted only a chance to sit like a spider in the hollow of his web and draw in the fat business flies to a place where he could suck them dry at his leisure. That was his way. Sometimes no one went through that doorway for a month at a time. But when someone went in, it was to do big business. No one loved the old man, but they respected his business

110

acumen. The people to whom Hooker loaned money had received an asset, as a rule, or else a blow to the heart that would ruin their credit elsewhere.

If he took a long chance with a new concern, the new concern was apt to put out roots, grow great, and prosper. If he gave credit to an old concern, the old concern was probably just about on its last legs. Hooker was ready to take in the last of its life—and devour it, there in his old house with the green-painted front door.

"You go in happy, and you come out dead," someone had said of Hooker's place of business.

Men said that he was very rich. Certainly, he owned at one time or another many of the finest properties of the district; but he always sold them again, and always at a profit. Nothing circulated in him except hard cash, people were fond of saying.

And it was to see him that young Jim Seton had come, with the burden of his five years of prison still weighting down his shoulders. As he used the knocker, he almost laughed aloud.

Men said that Hooker never had shown mercy in his life. He never had refused to take advantage of an opportunity. He had exacted the pound of flesh nearest to the heart. And to *this* man Seton had come. Why? He himself could not have told. The blacksmith picks the hammer from the row along the wall. He can hardly tell why his hand has chosen that special tool.

The door opened.

A Negro stood in the shadowy mouth of the hallway, a Negro so old that his face seemed to be covered with dust. Ever since Jim Seton could remember, that Negro had stood there, and his face had been gray with time, and he never had smiled. There was nothing in him but grimness and contempt and disgust. That was the bitter food upon which his soul existed.

When he saw Seton, he started to close the door in his face.

"I'm not a kid any longer, George," said Seton.

The door opened again.

"What you-all want?" asked George, frowning terribly.

"Money," said Seton, smiling.

George started to speak. His mouth remained open. He was frozen with amazement.

"You-all come here for money?" he asked.

"Isn't this a bank, George?"

"A what?" said George, canting his head. Then he added, severely: "You get along with you-all. Don' you come here wastin' my time with your fool jokes."

"You go and tell Mr. Hooker that I'm here to see him."

"He ain't in," said George, sternly. "He's done stepped out."

"You're an old gray-headed liar," said the boy. "I hear him coughing in his office, right now."

George continued to frown.

"I'll go and see," said he, and shut the door in Seton's face.

The latter turned around. Except for the childishness of such a procedure, he would have remounted his horse and ridden away up the street without waiting for an answer, but it was only a moment before the door opened again, and George stood before him, more forbidding than ever.

"You wanta see Mr. Hooker?" said he.

"That's it. He's busy, I suppose?"

"I dunno how it is," said George, "but Mr. Hooker says that he's willin' to see you. Come in."

CHAPTER 21

The hall was narrow, with a high ceiling; and a worn matting was on the floor. There was an iron frame for sticks and umbrellas. In it was Hooker's own gnarled walking stick and his own umbrella, with a cover whose original black silk was faded to green by time. Folded as it was, nevertheless, the boy could see one of the patches for which it was famous. Surely it was this very umbrella, or its father, which had been famous in the days of his boyhood in Claymore.

George opened the door to the right that led into Hooker's sanctum. And there sat Hooker himself in his celebrated black coat with his tall black hat on his head, and his birdlike, unhuman face under the brim of it. He always kept his hat on. "No man is at home when he's doing business," said Hooker, on a day long ago.

He sat not at a desk but at a table. There was a small filing cabinet in a corner of the room, but the important file of documents was the brain of this man. As for cash, he kept not a scruple of it in the house, except what was in the pockets of George for household purposes. For when George was through tending the door, he went out with his hobbling step and his grim face to buy supplies for one day and came home and cooked them. There was only one hot meal a day in that house.

"The smell of food gives one indigestion," said Mr. Hooker. "Mental indigestion."

The furniture of his office consisted, therefore, of the

113

table, the filing cabinet, the chair in front of the table, and another chair beside it.

"Business can only be done with one man at a time," said Mr. Hooker.

There was no rug, not even a matting on the floor, not even a stove in the corner. When the cold, damp winter days came, Mr. Hooker put on woolen underwear.

There was one touch of grace—if it could be called so— in this room. It hung on the wall facing Hooker's chair. It was the enlarged photograph of a young woman, with little keen eyes set close to her nose, much chin and little mouth. She would have been easy to draw in profile. Even a child could have drawn her. Some said that she was Hooker's mother. Some said that she was his daughter. She could have been either the one or the other.

Now Hooker, when he saw the visitor, said in his harsh voice:

"George, shut the door. Young man, sit down here."

Seton sat down. Outside the window, the white heat of the day flooded the street, filled it with fire, and voices sounded in the distance, out of tune. To be in this shadowy room was like being in a dream, or a delirium, half awake.

"What do you want?" said Hooker.

"Money," said Seton, smiling, forcing the smile.

Hooker folded his hands together and rested them on the edge of the table.

"What do you want?" he repeated.

Seton stopped smiling.

There was no chance, but he would take what chance there was.

"You're going to clean out Henry Ash," he said.

He stopped. He saw that he had said a ridiculous thing. He was amazed to hear the crisp voice answer:

"I reckon I am."

"Why?" said Seton.

"Because he's a fool."

"He's not a fool," said Seton. "He's trusting."

"That's only another name for a fool. What do you want?"

"I want to stop you."

114

"Nobody can stop me."

"Yes, I can stop you."

"How can you stop me?"

"With money," said Seton.

The banker looked steadily at him, and did not smile.

"You came here for money," said he.

"Yes."

"But you've got enough money to pay Ash's debts?"

"Yes."

"Let me see it."

"Come out to Benson Creek and I'll show it to you."

"You've got a mine, I suppose?"

"Yes."

"Gold?"

"No, water."

"A water mine, eh?"

"Yes," said Seton.

Again the banker was silent. He raised his locked hands and lowered them again slowly to the table-edge.

"Go on," said he.

"Do you know Benson Cañon?"

"Yes."

"You know the mouth of it?"

"Yes."

"For five thousand dollars I can bottle up that valley. I can hold a quarter of a million dollars' worth of water behind the stopper."

The eye of Hooker glittered like the eyes of a bird.

"So can I," said he, "when I get the ranch in my hands."

Jimmy Seton's head went back. He was stunned by the simplicity of the thing, the height of his folly.

He stood up.

"I'm a fool," said he.

"Yes, you're a fool," said Hooker.

"So long, then, Mr. Hooker."

"Sit down."

He sat down. He was farther in a dream than ever. He had not realized how much his heart was wrapped up in the Henry Ash ranch.

"Why didn't Ash come begging for himself?" asked Hooker.

"Ash? He didn't send me."

"Who sent you?"

"I sent myself."

"Don't lie to me."

"I'm not lying. I sent myself. Henry Ash? You don't know him, because he'd never ask for help."

"I've heard that before. They all ask for help, in the finish. All that have women do," said Hooker.

His eyes looked past the shoulder of Seton and straight before him, at the photograph on the wall. He sneered.

This reference to women brought the mind of Seton back to Molly Ash, her hands covered with flour, as she had leaned out the kitchen window and smiled at him. He switched his thoughts away. They leaped back to her. Soon she would be doing work like that for hire. Her face would grow sallow, wrinkles would come at the corners of her eyes. For women who cry easily grow old young.

"Why do you sit there like a stone?" asked the banker. "Why don't you tell me what sent you in here? Ash sent you. That's who sent you. Tell me the truth."

Seton shook his head, to clear his thoughts.

"It's no good," he said to himself. "I'll tell you why I came. I came in here because I like the place."

"Why do you like it?"

"Because there's something kind about it. There's honest soil out there. It can grow grass. It can grow cattle. I can see herds sprouting out of the ground. I like that place. I love it, in fact. But I was a fool to come in here to you to save it."

"It won't be lost. *I'll* take it," said Hooker.

Seton dropped a hand on the corner of the table and leaned forward a little.

"You? Yes, you'll take it. You'll take it, all right."

"It'll be the same land when I have it, won't it? Young man, you've got ideas. I might keep you on as foreman."

"Listen!" said Seton.

"Well, I'm listening."

116

"Did you ever feed flies to a spider?"

"No. What do you mean?"

"Well, I fed flies to a spider once, when I was a boy. Once was enough. I'll never work for you!"

He stood up. He searched the hard, white face of Hooker, and saw no change in it.

"Sit down," said Hooker. "Who sent you in here?"

"I've told you. Nobody sent me. The place sent me."

"You lie. Don't lie to me. Don't be a fool. Who sent you? Somebody sent you!"

He looked past Seton toward the picture on the wall, and he sneered again.

"Nobody sent me," said Seton, and he stared not at the banker, but at the white flare of sun in the street. Life seemed a dreary thing. There was no chance in it.

"There's a woman in the Ash family," said Hooker.

The head of Seton jerked.

"She has nothing to do with it," said he.

"No!" said Hooker, and he kept looking at the picture on the wall, his bird-eyes brighter than ever, his sneer twisting at his mouth. "No, she had nothing to do with it. She just sent you in here to me—to beg!"

Seton rapped his knuckles on the table.

"It's not true," he said.

"She put her arms around her handsome boy and he couldn't help doing what she asked."

"Hooker," said Seton, "don't say any more!"

Still the banker would not look at him; he stared at the wall, and the homely picture which hung there.

"She sent you in to put your ideas on the floor in front of me so I could kick them away. Sent you in to get down on your knees and beg. She sent you in. Don't lie to me."

A sudden fury that took Seton by the throat made him afraid of himself. He turned and went to the door, but the voice of Hooker stopped him.

"Wait a minute. I might give Ash some more time."

"What!"

"I might finance the dam, too, later on. We'll see about that."

"Do you mean it?" said Seton, feeling his way blindly back to hope.

"Yes."

"Will you tell me why?"

"Because I'm a fool. Now get out of here. Because I'm a fool. That's why."

And Seton went stumbling down the ragged matting of the outer hall and found the outer door, and the dazzling day.

CHAPTER 22

He took his time getting back to the ranch. He had a right to take his time, he felt, if what Hooker had said to him had been truth, and not a thing out of a dream. For dreamlike that whole episode appeared to him. He wanted to have a chance to let the whole affair simmer down and reduce to clear, cold facts in his mind. So he took a zigzag course through the western Cutshaw Hills, and it was late in the afternoon when he got back to the ranch. He was in time to see a show. There was a big, bald-faced roan gelding which Douglas Walters had bought for his own string not long before. That mustang was five years old, mean as a maverick, and never had had a rope on. And this day Walters had chosen to have a go at him. Seton got back in the midst of the party, and it was a party worth seeing, one could be sure.

He elected to make the ride near the ranch house, and old Henry Ash and Molly Ash were at the fence to look on. Why should not Walters exhibit his prowess before them?

Why should he not show the entire world what he could do? For he certainly could do it!

He rode straight up. He never touched leather, and he scratched that pony fore and aft like any competition rider in a circus. Henry Ash shouted in his thin, screeching voice, and clapped his hands, and laughed. Molly Ash tried to appreciate the scene, also, but as soon as she stopped being frightened and sorry on account of Walters, she began to be frightened and sorry on account of Douglas Walters' horse.

Seton, at a glance, saw through the thing. There was no danger to Walters. The man was a master horseman, ·and, though that bronco was pitching as though he had taken lessons in·school, the man mastered him strongly and steadily.

After a few minutes, the mustang stopped bucking and screaming with his rage. He tried to bolt straight away, but Walters, with an iron hand, pulled him to the left so that he had to make a circle and wound up in the place where·he had started—the patch of hoof-scarred earth from which he had been bouncing at the blue of the sky.

When the roan realized that, he was beaten. He was intelligent enough to figure the thing out like a man. He had fought. He had run. He had dodged and twisted like a wildcat to get away from the human horror and the torment which was clinging to his back. Now he tried a moment of submission, and instantly he got his reward. The spurs no longer scratched him like animal claws, and the long lashes of the quirt no longer cut into his flank and across his shoulders.

He had dropped his head, despairing. Now he began to lift it. Walters was laughing.

"Kind of a tough baby, this one," said he. "But he knows papa, now."

"Oh, Douglas! How dreadful! How wonderful!" said Molly Ash. "You won't have to hurt the poor thing any more, will you?"

He looked suddenly aside at her, grinning.

"Only for about another month," he said. "Every morning, when he feels his oats working in him, he'll take to a spell of pitching. But when it's over, he'll be all right for the rest of the day. But you can't be easy with him until he's really broke. When you start with a hard hand, you have to finish it the same way."

Seton, who had ridden up unobserved, could not help nodding. He admired this fellow in spite of himself. He knew Douglas Walters to be a sneak, a faithless traitor, with a heart full of murder; but he knew that he was brave, resolute, intelligent. He looked at the man as one looks at a brilliant and magnificent horse too wicked to be trusted. Granted a new heart to Walters, he would have been worth half a dozen ordinary men. Take him as he was, he was worth nothing but a bullet through the head.

"Could a horse like that be trained by gentleness?" asked the girl.

"Sure he could," said the foreman. "All you gotta do is to spend three hours out of every day with him. Feed him apples and sugar, fifty cents' worth a day. Talk to him, pet him. And start with him young. Start with him when he's a colt. Then he'll grow up gentle and never make a buck when you finally slap a saddle on him. That is, he'll be all right unless he's got the real devil in him, as I reckon that this one has. In that case, the more kind you are to 'em young, the more devil they'll raise when they're old."

"That's wrong," said Seton.

They all turned to him, noticing him for the first time.

"Here's Bronco Jimmy come to say his piece," said Walters, with a sneer and a smile conjoined. "You say that I'm wrong, old son?"

"You're wrong, Doug," said Seton, seriously. "There never was a bad horse, except what men have made so."

"Sunday school bunk!" said the foreman. "That eight-legged devil you're riding on, now. You think that you could ever gentle the devil out of that Roman-nosed brain of his? Tell me that, Jimmy? Don't go on bluffing. Just tell me straight. Can you make that horse eat out of your hand?"

He turned to the Ashes.

"That's Blood and Bones," he explained. "Have to have a good hand to stay on the back of that devil."

He turned back to Seton.

"I suppose that one will come when you call him, Jimmy?"

Seton dismounted. He took a childish pleasure in trying to appear to good advantage before the Ash family. He saw the face of the girl brighten at once.

"I always have a faith in kindness," said she.

Yes, she would always have a faith in kindness, even when she had to do with the Doug Walters of the world.

He tied the reins to the pommel of the saddle.

"Give him a scare, Doug," said he.

Walters glowered at him for a moment in the most ugly fashion.

"If I give that thunderbolt a scare, he won't stop till he crashes into the side of the first hill, over there," he said. "But here goes."

And a scare he certainly gave to the pony, running it for fifty yards, whooping, swinging his hat. The roan was strong and fast, but the bay pony fairly left it behind. It was still streaking away after the foreman had reined in his newly broken horse, which now began to throw its head and prance a little, anxious to imitate the wild freedom of the bay mustang.

Then Seton called. He really hardly expected that Blood and Bones would pay much attention to him, but he raised his voice in a long call.

"Try again. Keep on hollerin'!" exclaimed Douglas Walters. "You're going to have a long walk on your hands for that fool play, Jimmy. Next time you wanta show off before the family, pick a Sunday and a tame hoss!"

Seton looked askance at him. Then he called again, with a whoop on the end of his cry, and the bay mustang was seen to raise its head and turn it to the side, and to shorten its racing gait to a long, easy canter.

"He hears you!" cried Molly Ash.

"He's just easing up a little to laugh at you, Jimmy," Walters assured him.

But Seton called a third time, and now Blood and Bones was seen to turn in a large arc. At the end of it, he faced his starting point and stood there a moment, his head and tail high. He whinnied, and then, without another call given, he came trotting in.

Molly Ash crowed as loudly as though it were her own triumph.

"What a wonderful way he has with horses!" she said to Douglas Walters. "Did you ever see anything like it? I think he has a wonderful way with people, too. I don't wonder that you love him, Douglas. I love him myself, already."

The look which Walters sent after Seton would not have been a pleasant one for the girl to see; but Seton had heard her words, and a little song ran through his blood and flashed, quicksilver like, through his brain. She almost loved him already? Ah, well, friendship like that is a thousand miles around the corner from real love, he told himself. There is no relation. Hate itself is nearer.

But here came Blood and Bones, whinnying softly, pricking his ears, with a light of kindly expectation in his little, red, ominous eyes.

Seton rubbed his nose for him, patted his neck, and swung into the saddle again. At this, the wonder which had been accumulating in Walters burst out in spite of himself. He did not want to praise Seton, but his astonishment simply boiled over. He could not stand against the pressure of it.

"By the lord Harry!" said he. "That bay devil used to be our show horse. You think he got that name of Blood and Bones by accident? He's had three men in hospital all at one time. We didn't keep him for use. We kept him to take down swelled heads. He's put some of the slickest riders in the West in the dust and put them there hard. He likes a savage rider as much as a dog likes to eat meat. And look at him now, turned into a sort of a family horse, a regular pet, by the Lord!"

He shook his head.

"It's genius—and a great, kind heart!" cried Molly Ash, flushing with delight in this obvious triumph of the thing in which she believed.

"It looks that way to me," smiled Henry Ash. "I like that boy. Prison or no prison, he's all right. His heart is right, Douglas. No wonder he's your friend!"

These remarks rubbed salt into the wounds of Walters' vanity.

"He's doped the horse, that's what he's done," said he.

"Dope?" said Henry Ash, mildly.

"Yeah. Something strange about it. Nobody could of done that with Blood and Bones, without using some sort of a trick."

Seton came up on the pony, showing no undue elation.

"Good old Bones!" he said, simply, and slapped the sweating neck of the bay.

"How did you do it?" asked Henry Ash. "How did you tame the man-killer?"

"Why," said Seton slowly, earnestly, "one day he had a chance to help me out, and he did it. And a little later, I had a chance to help him, and did it. And ever since then, he's understood me, fairly well. Look out, Molly, or he'll bite a chunk out of you. He's still pretty mean."

He would have reined away, but it was too late, for she had walked straight up to the nose of the horse, saying:

"Oh, I'm not a bit afraid. I know you've taught him gentleness and kindness, Jimmy!"

And she laid her hand on the forehead of the bay. Behold! He neither tossed his head nor bared his teeth, as he was apt to do, but merely pricked his ears and looked with calm, gentle eyes into the human gaze that met him!

CHAPTER 23

The delight of Molly Ash knew no bounds. She grew more familiar, with the voice of Seton constantly warning her. But she insisted on patting the shining neck of the gelding, and slapping his shoulder, and speaking little foolish phrases. And Blood and Bones most manifestly liked it! That was the amazing part of the affair.

"I want to ride him, some day, if you'll let me, Jimmy!" she declared.

"You let me hold the reins while you're on," said Seton, "and you can ride him."

"No, all by myself," she insisted.

"Oh, she'll do it," said Henry Ash. "There's a wild, stubborn streak in my girl. When it comes up to the surface, she's pretty well bound to have her own way. Oh, she'll ride Blood and Bones, one of these days."

Douglas Walters laughed loudly, but Seton did not laugh at all. Instead, he looked earnestly, quietly, into the girl's face. He was seeing in it something that he had not guessed at before—and this was the strength of which her father spoke. Yes, she was not all softness and half childish gentleness. There was a woman's strength in her, besides; and perhaps, if the strain came, a strength like a man's as well.

Then he rode off with Doug Walters toward the corral.

"Well, you made your grandstand," said Walters, sourly.

"What's the matter, Doug," said Seton. "Are you afraid that I'll get too friendly with the Ash family?"

"I saw your line," said Walters, more bitterly still. "You wanted to make me out the big overbearing brute and horse torturer. That was it."

"You talk like a baby," said Seton. "You played that hand yourself and invited me to sit in on the cut."

Walters made no reply. His jaw was set like a rock.

"Another thing, Doug," said Seton.

"Go on, then."

"I've just heard that Hooker's changed his mind."

"Changed his mind? About what? He never changes his mind."

"You're wrong. He's changed his mind."

"You mean about the ranch, here?"

"Yes."

"The short loans?"

"Yes, that's what I mean."

124

"You're a fool!" said Walters. "Whoever told you that was making a fool of you. Why, Hooker's getting ready to take over the whole caboodle."

Seton shook his head.

"He won't."

"Who told you that?"

"He did."

Walters gasped. He literally was agape.

"You mean that you went in and saw him?"

"Yes."

"By the Lord!" breathed Walters.

His amazement still mastered him.

"Who the devil are you, Seton?" he asked.

"I'm Jim Seton."

"You're the devil, you mean, if you could dent Hooker. You mean that you're the devil himself."

"No, Doug. I'm simply an honest man, or reasonably so, I hope."

"Damn the Sunday school rot!" said Walters. "Talk sense to me. You mean that Hooker actually is giving more time?"

"Yes. I mean that."

"He told you so his own self?"

"That's what I mean."

"The sky's gonna drop on me in another minute," gasped Walters. "You'll be telling me that he wants to give us some more loans, in a little while."

"That's what I mean to say, too."

"Hey?"

"Yes, that's what I mean to say."

"Now, Jimmy, it's a fool line of talk that you're throwing my way. We couldn't get another bean out of him if we fell on our knees in a row. I tried him. How much will he give? On what?"

"An idea of mine."

"Hold on," said Walters. "You mean to tell me that he's investing money in ideas?"

"Yes, and in men."

"I'm trying not to get sore. I'm trying to listen to you," said Walters.

"Listen some more, then, Doug. Before I went to town, today, I made a proposition to you. I asked you if you'd work with me, hand in glove, and try to pull the place out of the ruck. Well, I had nothing to offer you then but talk. Now I have something better. I have Hooker behind me, to offer. What do you say?"

Walters stared at the ground.

"Say it over. Say it slow," said he.

"I say," he repeated, "that we ought to make one man out of this. You and I together, because we've got the hand power, I know, and I think that we've got the brain power, too. We'll pull together in one team. I don't ask rewards. You can have those, outside of a decent salary split for me. My heart's in the job. Now, then, we've been enemies in the past. We started as kids. I've hated you and you've hated me. I say, let's cross that out. Forget everything that went before this minute. Let's shake hands and go straight ahead, and show the world our dust!"

Walters jerked about in the saddle. His head went back, his hand flew out, his face was transformed. Meanness, jealousy, craft disappeared in a fine flare of open-hearted enthusiasm and belief.

"Together, we could open the world like an oyster!" he cried.

But as Seton, amazed and delighted, reached out to take the proffered hand, Walters drew his slowly back, and the light went out of his face.

"No," he said. "No, I can't do it."

"Why not, Doug?" pressed Seton.

"I've got calls on me," said Walters, sullenly.

"You've tied to some crooks, maybe," said Seton. "Well, we'll work it out together. Side by side, do you hear? We'll talk the whole thing over. If it's cash, we'll rake up what we can for them. If it's trouble, I'll take my half and try to carry it. Or I'll take two-thirds, for that matter."

"What's driving you on?" said Walters, surprised, and even more suspicious.

"I've told you before. I'm not going to explain any more.

126

Look at me, Doug, and you can't help believing me. I swear to you that I'm putting all my cards face up on the table."

Walters stirred with an obvious impulse toward assent, but then, slowly, he shook his head.

"Will you tell me why not?" asked Seton.

"Yes," said the other. "I'll tell you why not. You're too damn deep for me. That's why. I don't know what line or what lingo you use. But I know that I can't follow you. You've twisted Jake Mooney off his perch. Well, a fast hand and a strong back could do that. You've dodged a bullet that should have bashed your brains out. You've doped Blood and Bones, there, so that he's like a tame house cat. You've come here and made yourself a place in spite of me. And finally you hypnotized Hooker. Well, I don't understand any of those things, and I don't intend to have anything to do with things that I don't understand. Savvy?"

"I don't savvy," said Seton. "All I savvy is that I'm offering you a partnership where you have everything to gain and nothing to lose."

"You lie!" said Walters, suddenly going savage and talking through locked teeth. "I have everything to lose. I've been the top dog and the lead horse around here. Nothing started except what I started. Everything stopped when I held up my hand. You've taken that away from me."

"I'm under your orders. What I do, you get the credit for."

"Not by a damn sight, and you know it. You're putting your shoulder to the wheel, and they're forgetting me. I've been first, and you're trying to make me second. You've always made me second. I was the king pin boy in Claymore until you came along. You made me second. I've always been second to you. And by God, I'll be second no more. I'm going to stand by myself, and I'm going to stand on top— or else smash everything!"

He pointed a stiff forefinger at the other, like the barrel of a gun.

"I'm going to smash you, Seton. I'm going to smash you flat."

And he wheeled his horse and rode off.

127

Seton went thoughtfully on. He had made the last attempt; and now, if he remained at the ranch, it was the crossing of the Rubicon for him. It was entering into an open state of war. For Walters had declared his hand; there was no doubt of what was in his mind, by this time. The exquisite poison of jealousy was running in his veins, and would not out.

Yes, he had crossed the Rubicon, and every breath that Seton drew on the ranch, from that moment, would be taken in deadly peril.

CHAPTER 24

He gave the bay gelding a good grooming, and then he hung up saddle and bridle and went in to the supper table. It was a vague ceremony to him. Usually, he was amused by the awkward attempts of the rough punchers to make conversation with Molly Ash, and their clumsy efforts to win her smiles their way. But as a rule, big Douglas Walters was the lodestone toward which her gentle eyes were turned. They took that for granted. They sunned themselves in her presence.

Tonight, however, she would not be amused. Her smiles were faintest shadows, and her attention was fixed upon Seton. She told the whole crowd how she had seen him handle the bay gelding, that terrible Blood and Bones. They thought she was joking, at first. They turned to Walters for confirmation, and he sourly nodded his head, with a bit of a twisted smile, as though he could tell them, if he chose, a thing or two about that exhibition. But what knifed him to the heart was that the girl had not even mentioned his own handsome feat with the roan mustang, that wild young thunderbolt. He followed the direction of her eyes. It was always towards Seton. And the soul of the foreman stirred in him.

Who was Seton, after all? Was he a whit taller? No, not so tall.

Was he heavier and stronger? No, except in a devilish craft of hand which was like enchantment working against normal men.

Was he as handsome? No, no one could name him in the same breath with Douglas Walters.

What had he, then? What was the force which riveted the attention of the girl?

He remembered, then, what Seton had said not long before—something about the force of an honest man. At this, Walters started, and exclaimed beneath his breath.

What was it? Why, he had bitten his tongue. That was all. It was nothing.

But he continued to watch the girl and Seton. Ah, a very crafty fellow, that Seton. He did not take advantage of his opportunity to occupy the center of the stage by a display of asinine grins and loud talk. No, he sat there silently, with his head bowed, his face darkened by thought—the sneak, the hypocrite! He was playing a part. The part of the man with great emotions, great, far-reaching thoughts above the reach of the highest fingertips of such a girl as Molly Ash.

How thoroughly Walters detested him!

He made sure, now, of the reason why Jim Seton was striving so desperately to save the ranch. It was because of the girl, of course. He wanted Molly Ash. First, he would use a partnership with Walters in order to make the ranch safe from mortgage holders. As for the girl, he would brush Walters out of the way when the right time came. Had he not brushed him aside before? Yes, many a time—let him burn in hell for it!

The acid of jealousy began to scald the heart of Walters.

He had looked upon Molly Ash as a child, a mere baby. The ease with which he won her admiration had amused him, made him contemptuous. She was a lever by the means of which, and a small purchase, he moved the more important weight of Henry Ash. She was the blindfold by which he securely darkened the eyes of the kind old man. He had taken her as lightly as a handful of chaff.

But here was Jimmy Seton, that unique among men, taking the child seriously, offering his head to terrible danger, such as lurked for him on the Ash ranch, laboring without hope of a great reward, and all for the sake of Molly Ash —and some glimmering, distant hope of what might come of her!

At this, the foreman looked at Molly Ash with new eyes, and it seemed to him that he saw her five years older than she had been before. It was one thing to have her look with solicitude at him—a soft-eyed calf look, he had always felt it to be. It was another matter to see her glance in the same manner at another man. And that man was Seton. The spark leaped from heart to brain and from brain to heart.

She was worthy of high desire, or Seton would never have looked at her twice. Not high-flying Jimmy Seton! She was worthy of love, or Seton would not be sitting there at that table, sleeping in the bunkhouse, riding the range in danger of death.

If she was worthy of Seton's love, she was worthy of his. And suddenly Walters told himself that he loved her, that he could be happy with her, that happiness was not in the world for him, except as it came to him from the delicate slenderness of her hands.

"Poor Jimmy Seton!" said Molly Ash. "You have a headache, haven't you?"

He looked up at her, in haste.

"Yes, I've got something wrong in my head."

"Always was a wrong-headed cuss," said Chet Ray, impudently.

Walters watched carefully to see a dangerous glance of indignation directed from Seton to Ray, but instead, Seton looked at Ray with a smile.

"Yes," he said, "I generally am wrong. I suppose most all of us are. How about you, Ray?"

Ray grinned in turn. To be accepted on terms of something like equality by the dangerous man was a sufficient if a silent compliment from Seton. And Walters squirmed where he sat.

Whatever was to be done must be done quickly, he decided. Otherwise, before long, all of his men would begin to succumb to the peculiar magic of Seton.

What this magic was, he could not tell. He himself did not feel it; he felt only hate. But he knew that his punchers were feeling it, in spite of the way that Seton herded them steadily to their work. He had proof, also, that even Hooker, the man of iron, had been softened and molded by the influence of this man. We hate that which we do not know; and therefore the hatred of Walters for Seton was trebled instantly. The supper ended at last.

As for Seton, he paused in the door, stopped by the girl.

"You've got a bad headache, haven't you?" she repeated. "I have some bromo-seltzer. You'd better let me give you some of it."

"No," he answered, "that's not the trouble with my head. Bromo-seltzer wouldn't help it a bit. I've got to go and think something out."

"You're sure?"

"Yes. I'm sure."

He left the house and walked across the fields, aimlessly. It was after sunset, but not dark. A hoot owl skimmed past him, with its weird, hollow note. The sky was dull red, stained in the west the color of blood. The ground was already dark, in contrast, and he could feel the dampness of the grass through which he was walking. Dew was falling, and dew was good for the grass. Dew would keep it thriving almost without rain. And good grass meant fat cows. But in the midst of this train of thoughts, he looked suddenly up again to the red of the sky, and found in that color a greater sympathy.

Blood must be the solution to the riddle. Big Walters must die. And afterward, he would gather into his hands the reins by which he could guide the destiny of this ranch.

Everything called for the death of Walters. There was

the welfare of Henry Ash. There was the welfare of Molly. There was the welfare of the ranch itself.

As for Douglas Walters, the man was bad. If ever there were sheer evil in the world, it was to be found in Walters. Possibilities of good, likewise, of course, but chiefly the evil strain, the jealousy, the brutal disregard of others, the heavy and hard hand of the tyrant.

So he argued with himself.

He found the landscape beginning to be smudged and blurred over by the sooty finger of the evening, and then he turned back. He had ridden much that day. He had thought, felt, endured much. But he was not tired. An inexhaustible force of sheer life welled up in him. His step was light, his brain was clear and cold as a frosty morning, and he saw only one thing before him—Walters, dead.

A form loomed ahead of him. It took shape as a man. It waited in his path—a big man, with wide, bulky shoulders. Was it Walters himself, come out to meet his doom?

And Seton laughed, there in the quiet heart of the evening, savagely and quietly to himself. Now was the time, and he would make the best of it. There might be, for a reward, the hangman's rope, or the rest of his life in jail—but the gamble was worth while. He had ever played high.

So he stepped quickly ahead, only once passing his right hand inside his coat and feeling the handle of his revolver, as it hung under the pit of his left arm. He was ready. He trusted his speed of hand. He trusted his surety. He was to fight now—for more than life—

"Hullo. Is that you, Jimmy?"

It was the voice of Mooney out of the dusk. And a strange wave of relaxation and of regret passed together through the body of young Jim Seton.

"Yeah. I'm here, Jake. What you want?"

He came up to the other through the dusk of the evening.

"I want you," said Jake. "I gotta word to say to you."

They confronted each other, Seton almost as big as the other.

"What is it, Jake?"

132

"It comes out kind of hard, but I gotta say it. I been approached to try my hand at you agin, Jim."

"Murder, Jake?"

"Yeah. Murder."

"Who approached you?"

"I'm not sayin' that. But I was approached."

"How much?"

"That's what I guess I gotta tell you. I was offered fifteen hundred bucks, cold, to bump you off."

Seton whistled.

"That's a good stake, Jake."

"Yeah. It's a good stake. That's why I come to tell you."

He looked over his shoulder into the dusk, and the dimness seemed to comfort him.

"Other fellows wouldn't feel the way you seem to, Jake."

"You've said a whole mouthful," said Jake. "Other fellows wouldn't feel that way. That's what I come to tell you."

"Other fellows, and some of 'em pretty close by?"

Jake hesitated. His heavy breathing fascinated the ear of Seton.

"Yeah. Some of 'em pretty close by, that would listen to fifteen hundred bucks, like it was the voice of God Almighty. I know gents that would do a harder murder for a third of that."

"It might not be so easy," suggested Seton.

"Listen," said the other. "You don't get my drift. I mean, in the middle of the night, when you're sleepin' in the bunkhouse. Suppose that somebody was to reach a hand through the window and put a slug into you?"

"Yeah," said Seton. "Suppose that! It would be pretty easy, I guess."

"I guess it would. Seton, you skin out of here. You got nerve, but I hope that you ain't got nerve enough to be a fool."

"I won't be a fool. But I'll stay."

"The cards is stacked," said Jake, with a heavy certainty. "The cards is stacked, and you're gunna have trouble. I tell you that, that shouldn't talk."

"Jake, I'm grateful."

"Aw, hell, don't talk about gratitude to me. I know what you are. I know what you've done. I know that you're all right. Only—maybe I wouldn't come blabbing to you another time."

"I understand that."

"Maybe, another time, *I* would reach a hand through the window."

"I don't quite follow that, old fellow."

"Doncha? Listen to me and get this. Why are we here? Because we love Walters? No. Because he gives us bang-up pay? No. But because he knows us. He knows all 'bout us. He knows too much. He could slam every one of us into prison. We know it. He knows it. That's why we're here. And that's why you'd better get out!"

"He's going to bear down, now, is he?"

"I told him I wouldn't do the job. He damned me and told me that he'd fix me for it. I dunno if he will. But he's a man that's likely to. There ain't any heart in him."

The mournfulness in the ruffian's voice almost made Seton laugh. But laugh he did not, for the next moment his blood was cold enough.

CHAPTER 25

The impulse toward laughter died and his blood was cold enough, because he could look into the grim possibilities of the days immediately before him.

He waited for big Jake Mooney to get a sufficient head start, and went into the bunkhouse behind him. Four of the men were sitting by lantern light at a game of poker around the central table. Their moist faces gleamed as they turned their heads toward the straw boss; then they resumed their play, growling out their bets, sticking the butts of Bull Durham cigarettes around the edges of the table, breathing out clouds of smoke from mouth and nostrils.

Seton went straight to his bunk and turned in. It would be another hour and a half before the lights went out, and the last of the men went to sleep. During that interval he could fairly well depend upon safety in his bunk. So he set his mind like an alarm clock to waken the instant that the bunkhouse was dark. And, like a well-set organism, his subconscious brain reacted, rousing him promptly when the last lantern was blown out.

He sat up among his blankets in the blackness of the room, and looked out of the window. It was the dark of the moon; there were no stars, and he could see through the window nothing at all, yet he felt a danger reaching for him.

He slipped from his bunk and dressed rapidly, quietly, taking his boots in his hand when he prepared to leave the room. Two or three of the men were still coughing, turning in their blankets, not yet asleep. He waited for all noise to settle down before he rose. He carried with him his gunbelt, his slicker, and two warm blankets. Then he tiptoed softly across the room and went out of the door.

There he waited a moment. Now that he was outside, he could make out, by the light of the stars behind them, the dim drifting of the clouds. A dog was barking in the distance. The wet of the cool night air clung close to his skin and sent a chill into him with every breath he drew.

As he stood out there, he wondered how he had dared to spend so much time in the hopeless peril of the bunkhouse. He wondered, also, why Walters had not struck at him before as he lay there helpless, under the open window. Murder was a light thing for such a man as Walters. He should have acted before. Now, perhaps, there was something more than a fighting chance remaining to Seton.

He struck off for the nearest woods. When he reached them, the wind had cuffed from the face of the stars half of the clouds which obscured the sky. He lashed off a few branches with his hand ax, made a bed, laid down the slicker and the blankets on top of them. It would be a chilly place of repose, but he was accustomed to such sleeping. It was on the edge of the woods, and he sat up for a time, smoking in the dark, watching the changing pattern of the stars as the clouds swayed in and poured out again, driven by the wind. They were mysterious enough, those currents of the upper air, but not so strange as the forces which controlled his life, the dim and sightless powers which were commanding him.

Then he rolled himself in the blankets.

It might be that Walters or one of his emissaries had subtly followed him and would pistol him there in the half light, under the trees, as he lay asleep; but one must take chances in this world of ours. He closed his eyes, strictly ordered his thoughts for calm, and in another moment he was asleep.

He did not waken until the dawn gray was becoming tinged with pink. His face was wet and cold; his hair was wet; his eyelashes blinked chill against his skin; and his whole body was half numb with the damp cold.

He rose, bundled his blankets together, and went for the stream that plunged out of the hills a quarter of a mile behind the Ash barn. There he stripped and plunged into the icy snow-water. He remained in it half a minute, threshing vigorously with arms and legs. He came out breathing hard, his skin puckering into purple gooseflesh, his blood like running ice in his veins. Then he whipped the water from the surface of his body with the edge of his palm, swung his arms, raced up and down for a few moments until he was dry and his blood was hot; and, slipping into his clothes again, he took his pack across the hollow of his arm and went back to the bunkhouse.

When he walked in, the men were just rising, pulling on their boots, groaning, cursing range life. They looked up, agape, at their assistant foreman.

"Where you been, old-timer?" asked Chet Ray.

"Out to listen to the meadow larks singing," said Seton, calmly. "Hark at 'em now!"

They stared at him. No one laughed. As they stared, understanding came into the eyes of some of them, he thought.

At least, no more questions were asked and such indifference implied a certain hidden knowledge.

From that moment he was on his guard every instant. He never allowed men to come up behind him. He walked with an eye in the back of his head, as it were.

It seemed to him the longest day that he had spent on the ranch, and that night he did exactly as he had done before. He slept in the bunk until the lights went out. He waited until he was sure that the others were slumbering. Then he went off to the woods.

He went straight back toward the place where he had slept the night before, but, on this occasion, putting down his pack, he stalked the very spot where he had spent the other night. Like a cat he crawled up to it; and what had looked like the stump of a tree crowded against another standing trunk dissolved, presently, into the dull silhouette of a man.

He crept still closer. It seemed to him that there was a bar of iron in his mouth, and that he was biting hard against it, so fierce was his desire to attack the stranger there in the dark. He came so close that presently he could hear a whisper:

"He ain't gunna come here."

"He'll come here. He's gotta come here," whispered another. "He ain't such a fox as that. And even a fox will sleep two nights running in the same place."

They had been placed there to wait for him. Perhaps Walters had traced the trail of his straw boss through the dew-whitened grass of the early morning and found the spot where he had bunked for the night. Murder was in the air. Rank murder!

"Shut up, Slivvers. I heard something."

"Naw. That was the wind rubbin' a couple of branches together, Buck."

"I guess you're right. Why does Walters want him bumped off?"

"That's easy. He's gummin' up the deal for Walters, around here."

"Why don't Walters handle him?"

"You wanta know?"

"Yeah. That's why I asked."

"Because he's too much for Walters."

"You think so. But I've seen Walters in action. He ain't no cooin' dove, what I mean to say."

"He ain't no cooin' dove, all right, but this Seton, he's a damn hawk. You take it from me."

"I reckon that Walters could trim that jail bird."

"I reckon that he would if he could."

"What's Seton's play?"

"Nobody knows. A crook like him, you never can tell."

That was it. That was the mind of the whole world about him. Once a thief, always a thief. Once a crook, always a crook. Who could ever believe in his reform?

He wanted to see their faces. He had their names, but their faces would be better still, so he waited quite a time, hoping that at least one of them would light a cigarette. They did not do so, however. Finally Seton slid back through the darkness, resumed his pack, and went for a new sleeping place.

There were scores of little groves and patches of tall shrubbery spotted here and there around the ranch house. He selected one of the nearest, and in five minutes, despite what he had seen and heard, he was asleep again. Chances had to be taken, even every night, every minute of his life; and he was a beaten man, he knew, if he allowed his imagination to take hold upon him for a single moment.

In the morning, as before, he was back at the bunkhouse by the time the men were dressing. This time they showed no surprise at all when he entered. They felt, or pretended to feel, an absolute indifference as to his comings and goings. But now he felt certain that they knew and understood what was going on.

He waited until after breakfast. Then he gathered them together and made them a speech. Walters was not there. He almost wished that Walters had been attending. It would have given the affair a little touch of irony, pleasing to his spirit. Behind a near-by rock, he saw the quivering tips of the ears of a rabbit, afraid to dart for a more secure covert, since danger was so near and perhaps it was still unseen. He said:

"Boys, I wanta say a few words to you. A lot of you have been wondering why I'm here. I'll tell you. I'm not here for fun. I'm here on business."

He looked them in the face. Grimly, steadily, they all looked back at him. There was no retreat to be expected on their part.

"Some of you fellows," went on Seton, "think you have a grudge against me because I've kept you pretty hard at work since I hit the ranch. But that's not the reason that I have to keep from turning my back on you. Some of you are straight shooters. Some of you would murder me for five cents."

And still there was not a face that altered. All looked steadily back at him. They were a hard lot. They were even harder than he had suspected.

"You've given me my warnings, in one way or another," said Seton. "I'm going to give you mine. My nerves are on edge. I'm living like a hunted cur, and the first time I see a hand lifted, I'm not going to stop and ask questions. I'm going to put my teeth in that hand—and quick—like this!"

He hardly had known how to end his speech. He knew now, as he saw the rabbit take one bound from behind the rock and then rise on its hind legs, its foolish long ears rigidly erect.

"Like this!" said Seton, and the gun came out into his hand in a flash.

It exploded and he had the satisfaction of seeing eight hands leap for gun handles, and eight hands fail to draw. They looked around and saw the rabbit lying dead, its head shattered by the large-caliber bullet.

Seton was already walking toward the corral.

CHAPTER 26

Big Walters made a short tour around the ranch, that day, watching the cows. In the midst of that tour, he encountered Seton, who was coming up a draw whistling softly to himself.

"You made a fool play this morning," said Walters. "Those fellows are all laughing at you."

"No," said Seton. "They're not laughing at me. They're waiting. That's what they're doing."

"Waiting for what?"

"Waiting to see you show something. They begin to think that you're afraid of me."

"Bah!" said Walters. "They know me."

"Slivvers and Buck know you, too," suggested Seton.

"Slivvers and— What the devil do you mean?" asked Walters.

Seton watched him with an odd detachment. The man was turning gray. His face shone with sweat. His eyes turned into frozen point of lights, focused on Seton.

"Slivvers and Buck," said Seton. "They know you too, don't they?"

"What about them?" snapped Walters.

"Only that they think you're afraid of me."

"You lie," said the other.

"No, I don't lie. I'm telling you the truth, and it hurts you a little, old son. They think you're afraid of me."

"I don't know anything about 'em."

"Don't you? Then you try to remember back to yesterday, when you saw Slivvers and Buck and told them how much you'd pay for my head. Must have climbed to a couple of thousand, by this time, according to what they told me."

"They told you?" exclaimed Walters, his indignant rage getting the better of his discretion.

"I had a little chat with them," said Seton. "They were just laughing at you, Walters."

Reaching half into the dark, feeling his way, he was half amused and half excited to see the effect of his words upon the other.

"They'd never laugh at me," said Walters.

"You *do* know 'em, eh?"

"Oh, damn you and them both," said Walters, and pulled the head of his horse around.

He rode off to only a short distance and then turned suddenly in the saddle. Whatever he was about to say, Seton checked him.

"They were laughing at you. So am I, Doug. We're making a fool of you. So are the boys in the bunkhouse. Everybody sees through you now, you cheap imitation bad-man!"

Walters actually lowered his head and spurred his horse furiously out of sight around the shoulder of the next hill.

Seton was content. It might very well be, of course, that nothing would come out of this. On the other hand, he had a hope. If he could introduce an element of mutual distrust between Walters and the men who were employed or bribed by him, it could hardly fail to redound to the profit of the hunted man. So he watched Walters gallop away and smiled grimly to himself.

Then he followed. He kept at a good distance, so that he had only a brief glimpse of the other, from time to time in the rolling ground, for he thought, at first, that Walters might be riding straight for the hills to interview these scions of his and repeat to them what he had heard from Seton.

And what would the faces of the pair be like when they heard their conversation of the other night reported? He wanted to be there to see them. For more reason than that, he wanted to trail Walters the next time he left the ranch, for he was reasonably certain that Walters would now first review his assisting powers, and next try to probe the treason which he had heard about them. And Seton had to get knowledge of their plans, of their next steps. It was the only way he could ensure his life for the next few days.

But, above all, he clung to the hope of putting confusion and distrust into the ranks of the enemy. They were so many. He was so single in his strength. The only advantage he had over them was his singleness, as opposed to their sheer numbers and malignance. If once they began to question one another, then he might find a chance to detach from their numbers more than Jake Mooney—if Jake really was now detached.

When he was sure that Walters was heading back for the ranch, Seton went on about his day's work, which largely consisted in supervising the erection of a necessary line of fence which was to run for a full mile along a ridge. In one hollow which their fence divided, the feed was rich and good; but in rainy weather it was marshy, and the trampling of the cattle turned it into a bog and ruined the grass. The other hollow was not nearly so fertile and raised not a tithe as much grass, but it could be used as a holding pen, in a way, for the cows which were feeding in the lower district when the rains came. It was rather an expensive thing, but the fence would save quantities of labor and vaster quantities of grass.

When these things were all in mind, and the work pushing well forward for that day, Seton finally started back for the ranch house.

He found himself riding like an Indian in a hostile country, probing with his eyes every patch of shrubbery tall enough to secrete a man, every grove of trees in which an armed rider might be posted. For, though he had seen nearly all the hands of the ranch accounted for and engaged in the fence building, yet there remained the outlying ruffians who lurked in the hills and were closely in touch with Walters. Slivvers and Buck and their kind might be anywhere, headhunting on the ranch of Henry Ash. And the head they all wanted would surely be that of the assistant foreman.

He could not heave a sigh of relief when he came up to the corrals of the ranch house. In fact, that was the very site of his chief dangers, as he well knew, for there was Douglas Walters, and there the chief source of all the peril in which he rode.

He turned loose the horse he had been riding, and went to the horse pasture to spend a moment with the Roman-nosed bay, Blood and Bones. The bronco came to his whistle like a dog and followed him up and down the fence, pretending a savage fury in being unable to get through the barbed wire to him. There was a sense of humor in Blood and Bones. Every day Seton grew more fond of the mustang.

When, at last, he looked up from petting the little, ugly-headed animal, his eye fell upon a statuesque black mare moving at the farther corner of the field. He recognized it at once as Walters' favorite mount. Usually he saddled that mare when he was riding into Claymore for a festive occasion, or when he had some necessity for a great burst of speed, or vast endurance. She was a glorious creature, with the lines of a thoroughbred, seen from the side, and the quarters of a plough-horse looked at from behind.

Walters was fond of boasting that the mare could carry him at a steady canter for half a day at a time. Now Seton looked at the fine, long lines of the black and sighed a little. She would not, she could not have the racking gait of little Blood and Bones, and yet he wondered if all her beauty, her heart, her power would last as long as the pounding lope of Blood and Bones. Fifteen hundred dollars against fifty, and yet he was not so altogether sure that the fifteen hundred would win.

This idea left his mind. Another entered it. Why should the black mare be in the pasture now? For there was no fiesta in Claymore. There was no pressing need for a long ride, so far as the assistant foreman knew. Yet the black mare was never caught up except for some most important occasion.

What occasion could there be? What *was* important concerning Douglas Walters and his affairs?

Why, there was Mr. James Seton, of course, his ways and his manners and his means.

Yet no one needed a fast horse to find Seton. He was at

hand, at call upon the ranch. No, it was something doubt-
less to do with Seton, but it would lead in another direction,
far away from the ranch itself. Where? Why, far up into
those hills, no doubt, where the outlaws ganged, or lived
singly like lone wolves.

The explanation fitted perfectly into the mind of Seton.
He determined that he would watch the black mare like an
eagle, and he vowed to himself that, before that day—or that
night, at least—was ended, he would see Walters saddling the
mare and flying away on her across country.

The day ended. The supper was eaten in a dour silence
which even Molly Ash could not relieve. The men would not
talk to her. They would not look at her. Neither would they
look at Seton. Their minds were preoccupied, and Seton
could guess why. All that day they had taken and obeyed
orders without speaking back to him a single word.

Well, they could not cure him with a silent treatment. It
would take the barking of guns, he very well knew, to polish
off the conversation which he had started with them that
same morning!

CHAPTER 27

What had become a regular routine, he followed that night
up to a certain point. He went into the bunkhouse and fell
asleep when the poker game was in progress, as usual. But
when the lights went out, when the last of the restless were
asleep, he left the house with his pack, deposited the pack in
a clump of shrubbery, and then turned back to the horse
pasture.

He lay flat on the ground and stared across the field. He could see the dumpy profile of the bay, Blood and Bones. He could see the outline of the black mare, still exquisite against the stars.

Then he went to the saddle room of the barn. He did not take his own saddle. Instead, he picked out an old, discarded, worn-out affair, adjusted the stirrups to the right length, found two thin old saddle blankets, badly chafed in the center, and a bridle with a rusty bit; for a curious eye might look at his belongings that night, and his riding equipment must all be in place. Then he went back again to the verge of the horse pasture and hid himself in a low-growing tuft of laurel.

He waited a full half hour. The night chill was beginning to soak into his flesh as rain sinks into the ground. Finally he had what he wanted. He heard the sliding door of the barn pushed softly back. It grated again, gently, on its hinges, and a little later he saw a man coming around the corner of the building, carrying a bulk in his arms. It was Walters, he would bet his money.

The last doubt left him when he saw the shadowy form stalk the black mare. She had laid down. She bounded up when the stalker approached her. She was driven into a corner. The other horses in the pasture began to pitch to their feet and mill about; but, as the mare bolted out of the corner, from the hands of the man slid out a long filament of shadow that connected his hand with the neck of the mare.

She halted instantly. No Western horse will run against a rope. The first burning lesson is enough to last them the rest of their lives.

She was led, now, to the spot where the saddle and blanket and bridle had been left, swiftly equipped, and the man took her next to the gate, which was pushed open. That done, he mounted, and jogged off into the darkness, heading away toward the southern hills and mountains that fenced in Claymore Valley.

Then Seton started into action, feverishly, for already he might be hopelessly distanced and off the trail.

He snatched up bridle, blankets, saddle. He vaulted the fence, and, whistling softly as he stood within its rim, he had the infinite pleasure of seeing Blood and Bones come straight up to him. Blood and Bones, the terrible, reaching an open mouth to receive the bit, standing passively while the saddle was cinched upon him, only giving one pathetic groan as the knee of Seton dug into his ribs.

Seton did not wait to open the gate. In the game he played the winner would have to take chances; and a pony which could jump a twenty-foot cañon could surely leap a four-foot, ten-inch fence.

He rode the mustang straight up to the fence to let him be aware of it perfectly; then he made a short circle and charged back at it. He could see the ears of the gallant little horse flatten; then up shot Blood and Bones.

There was a twang like the strumming of a guitar string as the rearmost hoof of the mustang flicked against the top strand, and then they swooped down upon the open ground beyond.

By avoiding the gate, he had saved a precious half minute of time, perhaps, and now there was a good chance of overtaking the leader. So Seton rode on at brisk hand gallop, bending far to the side and down so that his eyes, closer to the ground, would have a better chance of looking up at whatever should break the skyline before them.

Straight on they went, but, after ten minutes of this pace, Seton halted. There was not a sound before them. What had halted him was the sudden, clumsy rising of a steer on a hummock just before them. The black mare and her rider were not in sight, not in hearing.

He looked back to the ranch. He could see nothing of it, but, by the contour of the hills beyond, he knew that it was a little to the right of the spot where it should have been, if he had followed truly out in the direction taken by the other rider in the beginning. So he swung to the right and galloped hard until he felt that he was again on the line. Then he faced again to the south.

Still there was neither sight nor sound. He hardly had expected them, however. The black mare, sweeping along on her long legs, would be reasonably sure to make such a pace, until she hit rough country, that the mustang would have to

race to keep up. Now further time had been lost by this ma-
neuver. The only chance of locating the other rider would
be to reach out into the dark, blindly.

Not altogether blindly, perhaps. Looking straight before
him, toward the south, he could see where the hills, raising
their heads against the stars, split away on either hand. In
the center of the cleavage was the hollow of the valley of
Benson Creek, he knew.

Then he struck his clenched first against his knee. He had
been a fool. Benson Valley offered the most open gate, the
easiest road to the heart of the upper country. He should
have guessed in the first place, from the direction in which
the other had started, that Benson Valley was the trail he
aimed at. So, gathering the reins, speaking through stiff,
angry lips to the pony, Seton steadied his course in that
direction.

There was one advantage, though a tardy one. There was
no part of the ranch that he knew more thoroughly. Besides,
he was well acquainted with the higher lands beyond the
limits of the ranch in this quarter, and he felt that he might
possibly have success if only his eyes and wits could be made
sharp enough.

Presently he was sending the pony through the higher
reaches of Benson Valley. The hill outlines to either side
grew more and more ragged. They were like the heads of
waves, some leaning forward, some leaning back, as though
a mad wind were whirling above them.

But there was no wind. There was no breath of air. It en-
abled him to hear every sound to a considerable distance.
It would also enable the other rider to hear the sounds of a
horse coming up behind him.

As well as he could, therefore, he avoided passing over
the hard surface of rocks which would give back the beat of
hoofs loudly. He lost time and distance by swinging from
side to side, to keep to the patches of earth, but here and
there he could not avoid allowing the pony's hoof to fall
upon rock so loudly that the noise echoed strongly up and
down the ravine. It was like a bell, an alarm bell beating in
the excited brain of Seton.

He had come to the head of the ravine, where the creek dwindled into a little affair that a man could step across in a single striding, and while he was pushing the mustang up the sharp slope, he looked up, without a real attempt to probe the distance, and saw directly above him a big horse, mounted by a big man, looming superhumanly large on the rim of the skyline.

Walters!

Who else could it be?

That sight caused a rush of fear and delight through him.

He was afraid because of the thousand perils into which he was riding. He was delighted, because he felt for the first time some assurance of eventual success.

From this time forward, he held his breath with every step the horse made. Then, coming to still rougher, steeper ground, he dismounted and took the reins of the mustang over the crook of his arm. It meant slower but more silent progress, for, going ahead in this fashion, he was able to pick out the ground more skillfully, avoid rocks, watch the terrain for stumbling places; and, above all, he could keep a closer outlook upon the skyline ahead of him, bending now and again, for that purpose, close to the ground.

He came to the head of the pass, with the hills rolling steeply up on either side of him—the cleft which he had had in mind when he first turned in this direction from the ranch.

After the first glimpse, he had had no sight of the rider he presumed to be Douglas Walters. The lack of a second view made him redouble his caution. A sharp instinct, like a whisper in his ear, told him that he was coming close to the place, whatever it might be. Though the starlight was strong, and his eyes now well accustomed to it, yet he went like a man walking in the total darkness of a room.

And so it was that he jumped aside as though he had seen a pointing gun when a spark of fire gleamed, before him and to the left, from the midst of a thicket.

It was a ray of firelight. There was the warm rosy-yellow color which could hardly have been cast off by any other thing. But, though he moved backward, forward, and from side to side, he could not see it again. The thing was gone. Perhaps the fire had been masked, in some manner.

In that direction he must now go forward, he knew. If he was right, where he had seen yonder glimpse of a fire, he would find at least one man, and Douglas Walters now with him. He must get close to them. He must overhear as much of their plans as possible.

Certainly he could not stalk them through brush with the mustang at his heels, clever and soft in going as Blood and Bones had showed himself to be. So he took the mustang into a clump of trees and tethered him there; and Blood and Bones, like a philosopher, hung his head and retired into his thoughts, or to regrets for his broken sleep, upon this night.

Seton went forward. He had thought of taking the rifle with him, at first, but he left the heavier gun behind, at the last moment. If there were action, it was apt to be at very close range, and for such purposes the speed of the revolver was likely to be better than the greater accuracy of the Winchester.

He came, after a moment, to a straggling growth of brush, out of which wind-stunted trees stood up, black and misshapen, their branches flying all one way, like tresses of disheveled hair in a strong wind.

It was difficult going, once he entered that wilderness. In the first place, it was almost impossible to keep on a straight line for the spot where he had marked the ray of what he took to be firelight. He had to rise, every few moments, and carefully study the landmarks before him and behind.

Furthermore, the ground was covered with fallen twigs, brittle as old cork. Getting upon his hands and knees, he literally felt his way among these obstacles, removing some of them, gently, going most cautiously over the others. He had been in similar places before this. It was not the first time that he had had to trust his life to the silence of his movements. And the practice infinitely helped him.

But it was a deadly and stealthy work, gliding snakelike, until he heard before him the sound of voices. At that, he paused, lying flat, one ear to the ground, all his faculties centered upon the listening. But the sounds went out, almost as they had begun, in an indistinct murmur.

When he made sure that the voices had paused, he started on again, almost in a panic for fear the slowness of his approach had caused him to miss the conversation which he wanted so much to overhear. He cursed, then, the excess of caution, as he felt it to be, and hurried without much regard to where hands and knees and trailing feet might fall. His heart was thundering in his breast. He had an insane desire to spring up and charge blindly ahead toward the spot from which he last had heard the sounds.

He mastered that impulse. And then, like the blow of a club, dazzling light burst out upon him in a wave, blinding, overwhelming him, after being so long used to straining his eyes among the most obscure shadows.

He should ordinarily, perhaps, have leaped to his feet, drawing a gun as he did so. But this time he merely flattened out like a worm in the presence of the danger.

He lay there immobile. He did not even reach for his Colt's revolver. He despised himself, but the stunning effect of the surprise still made him numb. And, every moment, he waited to hear jeering, derisive laughter, or to hear the crash of an exploding gun and feel, at the same instant, the weight of a leaden ball tearing through his heart.

They, certainly, would not hesitate to shoot a prostrate man—not if it was big Douglas Walters or any of his companions.

Yet there followed neither laughter nor the sound of a gun. There was merely a muttered oath, and a man saying:

"Hold on, there, Doug. You've gone and let the rock fall agin! Can't you watch out for nothin'?"

CHAPTER 28

Looking curiously about him, Seton saw at last what had happened. He had crawled through the brush into a small open space in the center. Here a fire was built, fenced around with rocks, so that the glare of it might not shine to any great distance. One of those boundary rocks had just fallen down and loosed the shaft of light which struck and dazzled him. A similar accident, before, must have been what he saw from the head of the pass. Against the pale upward glow of the fire, he could see the shadows of two dark forms, one of them a very big man, and the other much smaller.

"It's all right, Buck," said the voice of Walters, with no attempt at softening. "He's not on my heels all the time."

And Buck answered:

"The way you've been talking about him, I begun to think that he had a pair of wings and used 'em to foller you around the country. Begun to think that he even could trail down your thoughts, far as that goes!"

"Sometimes I have the same idea," admitted Walters. "But of course he can't. He's had a lot of luck. That's the only reason that he's pulled through so far."

"Luck and a brain," said Buck.

"And men that talk too much on my side," answered Walters, with a sudden anger. "Men that can't keep what they know to themselves."

Seton was working his way back with infinite precautions, and now he lay at ease, again, under the deeper shadows of the brush.

"What's your meaning by that?" asked Buck.

"I mean, that if I had men on my side, I'd be all right. I've got a lot of talking women; that's my trouble."

"Hold on," said Buck. "D'you ring me in on that side of the thing?"

"Ay, you!" exclaimed Walters. "You've done your share of talking."

"It ain't true," said Buck. "Who've I talked to?"

"Who? You've talked where it would hurt me most, and you know it."

"It ain't true," repeated Buck. "You name somebody that I've talked to."

"You've talked to Seton himself!"

Seton, in his place of covert, smiled a little. He could see the seed of his sowing beginning to sprout trouble in the opposite camp.

"I've talked to Seton?" cried Buck.

"Yes."

"You're crazy!" exclaimed Buck.

"Mind you, now," said Walters fiercely. "I'm holdin' myself hard. Don't you give me more than I can do."

"You're followin' the wrong steer and playin' the wrong game," declared Buck. "You know something?"

"What?"

"I never seen Seton in my life!"

There was an impatient exclamation from Walters.

"I tell you what," said he, "you talked to Seton. You and Slivvers both talked to him."

"Slivvers? Maybe that long-drawn-out drink of water done some talking, but I never did. I never seen Seton in my life."

"Now I'm gunna prove that you're a liar, Buck."

"That's gunna take a lot of provin', and a big man to prove it," said Buck angrily.

"Yeah. I'll give you the proof," said Walters, "and then you can do what you want about it. You went to him—you and Slivvers. I dunno when or how. But you went to him, and you told him that you were layin' for him. That I'd hired you."

"Now by the—" began Buck.

Finally he checked himself and exploded:

"Who told you this?"

"You wanta know?"

"You bet I wanta know."

"Seton his own self told me."

There was a muffled exclamation from Buck.

"It ain't no ways possible," said he. "I can't be hearin' right, at all. I can't believe my own ears!"

"You start right in and believe 'em now," suggested Walters. "I'll prove it, then."

"My head is kind of buzzing. How could you prove it?"

"He told me the right amount. He told me that I'd offered the pair of you fifteen hundred bucks."

There was a long whistle, apparently from Buck.

"He told you that!"

"He certainly did. Now tell me that I'm a liar. Or that Seton only guessed you two were after him, and then that he guessed the price."

"Hold on!" said Buck. "Suppose that the skunk sneaked up on Slivvers and me when we was watchin' over the place where he slept that first night?"

Walters muttered something and then added:

"Did you tell what price you were hired for?"

"No, we didn't. At least, I don't remember sayin' anything."

"You think back."

"I remember Slivvers sayin': 'We're gunna earn our money.' And then I said that he was a fox, that Seton, and that I didn't like the job, anyway. That's all that was said."

"If you didn't like the job, why'd you take it?"

"Because I'm ornery, I suppose, and a fool. And low. But I never went out for blood-money before, and I don't like the idea of it, right now."

"Buck, it's a poor line that you're stringing together for me."

"Lemme tell you something. I'll swear that I've told you the truth."

"I kind of half believe you," said Walters, mumbling the words to himself. He added: "It might be Slivvers."

153

"I wouldn't of thought it of Slivvers," said Buck. "He's got it in for Seton."

"Why? I thought he'd never seen Seton—like you?"

"He never seen him, but he had a girl six year back. When he comes to her town, after a trip, Seton has just passed through, and she's seen Seton, and can't see nothin' after him."

Walters chuckled.

"Yeah, he's that way," said he.

His chuckle died in a snarl.

"He's gunna eat lead for those tricks, too," said he.

"Yeah, he'll sure eat lead, if the Mexican will take the job."

"I've heard a lot about that greaser," said Walters.

"Hold on. He ain't a greaser," said Buck.

"He's a Mexican, ain't he?"

"Yeah. But he's something special. Ain't you heard about him?"

"Yeah, I've heard a lot of jobs that he's done."

"Well, you wait till you see him. He's all by himself."

"You know him?"

"Yeah. I know him. And I know a lot about him, too. He's different, he's a sort of a gentleman."

"A gentleman that can be hired to murder, eh?"

"Murder is a pretty heavy word to throw around so fast," said Buck. "I wouldn't do that. You wait till you lay eyes on him, and you'll understand. He's killed folks, here and there, but I reckon it's been more for fun than for the money."

"Playful, eh?"

"Well," was all that Buck could say, "you wait and see."

This talk troubled Seton, and called his mind back to a certain Mexican whom he had known in the other years. That man, indeed, could have been called a gentleman. He was, moreover, one who could actually have killed for the fun of the thing.

But he shook his head and would not believe that such bad luck could come to him as the addition of that famous and dangerous man to the already long list of his enemies.

Who had he as a friend? Only that strange eccentric of a man, Hooker, the banker. Or could he be called a friend, indeed?

"Buck," said Walters, "I'm sorry that I jumped down your throat. I see now that you meant what you said."

"Ay, I meant what I said. I'm no double-crosser. I never was. But I'm glad to get out of that job and shift it over to the Mexican."

"Tell me, Buck. Were you afraid?"

"Yeah," drawled Buck. "I was afraid, all right. I was damn afraid. So was Slivvers. That fellow is a fox. And he's a bear, too. And you gotta be afraid of a gent with the wits of a fox and the paw of a bear. I don't wonder that you want help agin him, your own self."

"I don't wanta go to the pen for killing him, for one thing," said Walters, in self-defense. "Not when I can hire the job done. Besides—yeah, he's a fighting man."

"Yeah, he's a fighting man, all right," said Buck. "I've been asking around about him. There ain't many up in the hills that know what he used to be, but those that do, they all say that he used to be lightning on ball bearings."

"I've seen him go through Claymore like a hot knife through butter," said Walters, thoughtfully. "I can remember a time when people used to get out their guns and do a little practicing around Claymore when they heard that young Seton was comin' back off the range. And usually there was a need for shooting, too, when he returned."

"But they never winged him, eh?"

"Oh, sure they winged him. I reckon he's spent about a year of his life in bed with knife wounds, or bullet wounds, or something."

"He learned by fighting."

"Yeah. He always was taking chances. He took one chance that landed him in the pen. That was all."

"How'd he get out?"

"Aw, some kind of a graft."

"He wasn't really reformed, like some of them say?"

"Say, it's easier to make a cactus grow no thorns than it is to make a gent like that Seton reform. Naw, he'll never

155

reform. He's deep. But he's as crooked as he's deep. I know him, all right!"

There was profound conviction in his voice, and Seton listened with wonder. No matter how detestable and dastardly the schemes of Walters against him might be, it appeared that at least the man was convinced he would be doing a good thing for society by wiping the ex-convict off the map of Claymore Valley.

"Hush!" said Buck, suddenly.

There was a whistle in the near distance, a thin thread of a silver sound. And then through the brush came a rider, the twigs crackling under the hoofs of his horse..

"It's him!" said Buck.

He came in rapidly, within the dim field of the firelight, and, dismounting, he raised his hat to the other two. He spoke something in greeting, but young Seton did not hear the words. His whole brain was obsessed and stunned by one overmastering fact. The face of this man was young, but his hair was purest snow-white.

It was the very man whom he had had in mind, the one of all the world whom he most dreaded.

CHAPTER 29

Into that thin field of the firelight, the Mexican came like a prince out of the pages of a fairy tale, for he was all gleaming with silver and with gold, from the band of his sombrero to the spurs on his heels. A most slender and graceful figure he made, with the exquisite head of his thoroughbred horse appearing raised above his shoulder to stare at the strangers like a child from the shelter of its parent's back. But what was most startling was the swarthy skin of that handsome, lean face, and the dark of the eyes and brows, and the dazzling contrast of the silver hair. He looked like a figure of eternal youth, or of age forever defied. His teeth flashed as he smiled at the pair.

Buck was saying in stumbling Mexican:

"This is Don Pedro El Blanco. This is Señor Walters."

Don Pedro shook hands with both. He looked hardly larger than a child, compared with the bulk of Walters; but, from the moment when one's eyes rested upon him, he appeared to grow in importance; there was such dignity, such pride in his bearing. Other men grew less, beside him, and he increased.

"I have to get back," said Walters. "If that slippery owl, that devil of a Seton misses me from the ranch, he'll guess that something is about to happen."

"Seton?" echoed the Mexican, and raised his brows a little in surprise and interest.

Walters went straight ahead.

"You've seen the cows of the Ash ranch, señor?"

"Yes," said El Blanco. "I have sent one of my men. He says that the stock are very fine. The horses, also."

"Hand picked," said Walters. "Now, then, if we drive those cows over the river, you could receive them?"

"With the greatest pleasure in the world."

"And get a good price for them?"

"The top market price, with just five per cent off," said the outlaw.

"How's that?"

"The agents with whom I deal," said the Mexican, "have found me a steady customer. They never attempt to cheat me. They know that if they cheat me once, my patronage is taken away from them. Therefore, when they make their sales, they turn over the full price to me. They only deduct five per cent commission for the selling. Is that reasonable?"

"Couldn't be better. Now, Don Pedro, what share do you want?"

"That's a matter I'd prefer to leave to you?"

"Say ten per cent?"

"Ten per cent?" echoed the outlaw, politely.

"Make it twenty, even, I don't want to split hairs."

"Fifteen would be ample, I should say. I never wish to rob my friends," said El Blanco.

"Fifteen, then, and everybody will be happy, I guess. Now, then, we guarantee to deliver those cows over the river, all in one big drive."

"Delightful!" said the other.

"But there's one thing that stands in the way."

"What is the thing? Let us remove it, señor."

"The thing's a man."

"Ah?"

"Yes. He's working on the Ash ranch. I don't know what his game is, except that it's against me. He's a crook. He's the deepest crook I ever met. And he's against me. If we try to make a drive and clean the place of its cows, he'll be sure to follow, see what's happening, and spoil the whole play."

"There is only one of him, and you have a good many men working for you—hand-picked men, like your horses and cattle, I believe?"

"I have some hand-picked men, but they don't wear gloves thick enough to grab ahold of that nettle."

"Ah, a dangerous man, señor?"

"Dangerous is a small word for him. He's the devil on wheels."

"However, there is only one of him," said the Mexican. "Who is he?"

"His name's James Seton."

Again the Mexican raised his brows.

"Tell me, señor. A big man, with a very quiet eye?"

"That's him."

"And a way with horses, and with women?"

"That's him exactly. D'you know him?"

El Blanco was lighting a cigarette.

"I used to know him," he said, after he had blown away a cloud of the smoke. "I used to know him very well. I used to know him when he was in my own country."

"Friend of yours, maybe?"

158

"Of all the men I've ever known," said the other, "he was least my friend. Now that you tell me he is the stumbling block, I should say that the man must decidedly be removed."

"Ay," said Walters, with a revolting eagerness. "That's it. Killed, Don Pedro. He ought to be killed."

"He ought to be killed. It should be arranged," said the Mexican. "But it is not quite so simple."

"There'll be a bonus in it for you," said Walters. "I'll tell you what, there'll be an extra percentage, if you want it. There'll be double the percentage, if you can handle him for us!"

"Percentage?" said El Blanco.

"Or if you want a bonus in hard cash, I'll pony up. I'll pay you anything you want, man—in reason."

"Percentage? Cash?" said El Blanco, apparently hurt. "You haven't understood, señor. Let me tell you a little story, and you will understand better."

"I'm listening. It's got to do with him, I suppose?"

"It has all to do with him and with me," said the outlaw. "There was a certain town in Mexico where there was a certain bank. It was not a great public bank. It was run by some very clever, hard men. They had their fingers on the public's throat. They sucked the blood out of the land. And when I heard about this, for patriotic reasons, I decided that their grasp ought to be loosened."

"Yeah. I follow that," said Walters.

"Even if it required guns to help in the loosening, do you see?"

"I see that. Go on, Don Pedro. It sounds great."

"I laid my plans carefully. I arranged with a certain clerk in the bank for a few details, and with a certain watchman certain other details. I won't bother you with all the particulars."

"You can't tell me too much. I like it."

"It happened that at that time I was much younger than I am today and that I was fool enough to put trust in one of my men—though he was not a gentleman. You two gentlemen will understand the point?"

"I follow your drift," said Walters. "Sail right ahead. What happened?"

"Well, then, the very day before the thing was to be done, it happened that this man of mine had trouble in a cantina with an American—a young American boy. He lost some money, in fact, to the man from the north of the river—"

"That American was Seton, I suppose?"

"That was his name."

"Things begin to thicken up," said Walters. "Go on!"

"They thickened up at once, in fact," said El Blanco. "My man followed Seton after the game, followed him out into the country, and devised a little trap into which Seton should ride. But Señor Seton has a certain instinct for trouble, it appears, and recognizes the face of it while it is still at a great distance."

"I know what you mean," said Walters. "The devil is always riding at his right hand."

"Or his good angel, perhaps," said the Mexican, more politely. He went on: "As it turned out, my man, who was the hunter, suddenly found himself the hunted. He was suddenly attacked. The hands of Señor Seton, as it appears, have the strength of shrinking hot iron. They mastered my poor fool of a man.

"Señor Seton then tried a little joke. It appears that he is not one who kills readily, for the sake of killing. But he pretended to be a hungry devil—a devil hungry for human blood, and he so worked on the fears of my man that the fool tried to buy him off. And what was the thing he offered to him? What was the bribe?"

"I can't guess."

"He told Señor Seton every word about the beautiful plan which I had made and built so carefully. He told him everything, and, that night, Señor Seton went alone. Do you understand me? He rode alone into that town. He went alone to the bank. There he approached the watchman; the watchman let him in; and an hour later there was a softly muffled explosion that blew off the door of one of the richest safes in Mexico."

"Ah!" said Walters, with a fierce, short intake of breath.

"A little later," said the bandit, "Señor Seton left the bank, and, as he did so, he raised the alarm which brought the police to the bank. There they found the empty safe, but Señor Seton was at a distance!"

"A good, slick job—damn him!" said Walters.

"That was not all. Among the moneys in the bank there was a large fund belonging to a hospital, and another belonging to an orphanage. A week later, while I was helping the police to hunt for the desperado through the hills around the town, Señor Seton rode quietly into the city again. Do you understand? Once more alone! And he brought to the door of the hospital exactly the sum which belonged to it, and to the orphanage exactly the sum belonging to *it!* You see, señor, how my hands were tied?"

"Of course I see," said Walters. "You mean that he got the people over on his side?"

"On his side? To this day, Señor Walters, there are places in Mexico where men would die for Señor Seton. That is the truth. I dared not show a strong hand against him. He was considered a great hero, and a greatly good man, although a little bit of a robber."

"But that didn't end it between the two of you, I'd say?" suggested the hopeful Walters.

"No, it did not end it. I followed Seton through Mexico. Wherever he turned, he found me and my men behind him. Once we overtook him. And then—"

His voice died away.

"And then?" exclaimed Walters, feverishly, in his excitement.

"And then, my friends, he and I fought together, alone. And he fell, shot almost to the death. His right arm was useless. But he fell near his horse, and then—"

"Tell me!" said Walters.

"Patience!" said the Mexican. "It is a thing I cannot speak of easily. I must have a moment to remember!"

CHAPTER 30

Walters, at this pause, made a wide gesture with both hands.

"Take your time—take your time!" he exclaimed. "Only, I'm gunna die of high temperature if it takes you long to tell me how he got away. Did he beg? Did he crawl? I didn't know, Don Pedro, that there was a single man in the world who could stand up to Seton and beat him fair and square!"

"It was a fair fight," said the outlaw. "We had met on a narrow trail on the round of a mountain's shoulder. We came upon one another by such surprise that neither of us moved, for a moment, and then I think our hands jumped for our guns at almost the same instant. I had my weapon out of the holster a fraction of a second before him. The mere wink of an eye sooner. He is older, now. Perhaps he is much faster, eh?"

"I don't know. Go on!" exclaimed Walters.

"Well, then, my bullet struck him inside the right shoulder, and the force of the stroke knocked him sprawling out of the saddle. I fired again as he was falling, and again as he landed, but the speed of the fall unsettled my aim a little. I must have missed, both times."

"Hard luck!" exclaimed Walters, tense with his excitement.

"And, as he fell, his gun fell with him. I saw him roll over on the rocks and pick up the gun with his left hand. Very brave, señor. Don't you find it so?"

"Brave be damned!" said Walters. "I hope his courage didn't make you go!"

"On the contrary," said the other, "I was trying every second to get at him again. As I said, I fired while he was still in the air, and again as he landed. So far he had not had a chance to fire at me at all, but now he scooped up his fallen gun with his left hand and made a snapshot at me."

He paused again, laughing a little, and nodding to himself in a reminiscent manner.

"That bullet should really have been the end of me, my friend. I should have died at that moment, because the course on which it flew went straight for my face. But my poor horse, at that moment—he was the father of this good mare which I am riding now—threw up his head at that very instant and received the ball between his eyes. He dropped dead beneath me, and pitched me to the side under the cover of some rocks.

"I was not stunned. But—"

"Good!" said Walters. "You stepped out and plastered him with a pound of lead, I hope—damn him!"

"I leaped out from behind the rocks, my friend, and crouched low to the ground, ready to shoot. But at the same instant there was a clattering of hoofs. Tell me what had happened?"

"I'll about die unless I find out pretty pronto," said Walters.

"Why, señor, that man Seton had been badly hurt by the bullet. He knew that he had only a fraction of a second to go before I would be at him. He knew, even if I kept away and still-hunted him, that by loss of blood he would soon be helpless. And he had to get away from that place."

"He got up and jumped into the saddle, I suppose, and rode off?"

"He had no time to rise, to grasp the pommel of the saddle, and to gallop away. He had only half of a second after the fall of my horse, and this is what he did.

"He must have seen that his horse had turned, and that its head was now pointing back up the trail, so he simply reached up with his left hand, do you see? He grasped the stirrup and with a word he started that horse galloping. Ha! That was the act of a man!"

"Hold on. I don't follow that!"

"I mean that he caught hold of the empty stirrup, and, as the horse cantered up the trail, he was dragging the loose body of his master beside him."

"By the Lord, who would of thought of that?"

"One man in a million. A man of steel. A fighting man. But Seton thought of it. I saw the horse galloping, and there was no man in the saddle. Then I had a glimpse of Seton stretched out there, dragging along the rough rocks of the trail which tore his clothes to ribbons and gouged away the flesh of his body. For afterwards I found that the trail was drenched with his blood, and it could not all have run down from his wounds. Ah, yes, a man of iron—to hold there in spite of that agony, which would have made ten thousand common slaves shriek with the pain. But he made not a sound, while the rocks tore him, and the hard hoofs of his horse pounded and battered beside him. One misstep, and he would have his brains dashed out as if by a club!"

"But you took a shot?" said Walters. "You didn't let that put you off, Don Pedro?"

"Put me off? Let such a devil as that get freely away from me? No, señor, not I. My blood is not milk and honey, I can tell you! I tried a fourth shot at him, and I hit him. Yes, I know that the bullet struck him—"

Seton, as he listened, instinctively put a hand down to the thigh of his left leg.

"And still he kept his hold?"

"Still, señor, most wonderful to say, he kept his hold upon the stirrup, and the horse jerked him out of view around the shoulder of the mountain. There I heard the sound of hoofbeats stop. I wondered at it."

"He can do anything with horses," agreed Walters. "But go on, Don Pedro. You ran forward to the shoulder of the mountain—the place where the trail turned on it—"

"Yes, and as I ran around the corner of the rock, turning the side of a great boulder, I saw that man before me. He had dragged himself up. By uttermost power he had pulled himself into the saddle. And there he sat, blood bursting from him, a terrible picture—"

"A beautiful picture!" said Walters. "I wish that I'd been there to see it!"

"You don't love him, señor. Neither do I. But I love his glorious courage. There he sat, as I have said, and as I rounded the corner of the rock, a bullet from his revolver—fired, mind you, from the left hand—took the hat from my head. A very good shot. But then, after all, I should have removed my hat anyway, to such a magnificent fighting man."

He paused to laugh, while Walters bit his lip in a frenzy of impatience.

"That bullet made me jump back into cover," went on El Blanco. "And then I heard the clattering of the hoofs begin again. I sprang back into the trail. I saw his head and shoulders bobbing up and down among the big boulders that bordered the trail. I fired my fifth bullet—my sixth—and the sixth bullet knocked him forward on his horse—"

"Three bullets in him, then!"

"Yes, three bullets," said El Blanco.

"He should of dropped. He must of dropped out of the saddle!"

"So you would think. So I thought, on that day. I reloaded my revolver as I ran forward. I could have sung, because I knew that I had beaten the finest fighting man I ever had met or heard of. I could have sung, also, because I was sure that he was mine, and that, after this, his name would have to be written under mine, by those who had been praising the great Señor Seton so highly all through the hill towns. Well, then, as I ran, I saw the marks of blood along the trail; but as yet I had no glimpse of him. Only once, far away, I saw him dipping over the rim of a steep-sided ravine.

"Well, he was so far away, that I saw it was no use running at full speed. For three days I trailed him. Then, for a week, my good men blocked every road, watched every house from which he could get help, guarded the ways to the towns. For a week they blocked them. I knew, then, that he had not gotten away, that he was there in the rocks. The lion was denned up, and I must find him. So, for three whole months, señor, I let the world stand still, while I hunted this glorious, this great man!"

His enthusiasm for the man he had tried to kill overcame El Blanco. He looked upward toward the stars, smiling, and his face was beautiful.

"You didn't give up for three months?" said big Walters, admiring that persistence, regretting that the prey eventually had escaped.

"I did not give up for three months. No, señor. I did not give up. I had twenty men. I offered them great rewards. They were all tigers. We searched the crannies of the rocks. We hunted as a snake hunts for a rat. No hole was too deep for us to crawl into. And then, on the exact day which ended the third month, he broke through us!"

"The devil he did! How did he manage it?"

"Consider," said the Mexican, softly. "How my heart leaps when I think of it! Consider that he had been wounded so that he must have lain at the very hand of death for whole days together. Consider that, when he grew a little stronger, he had to drag himself around, not daring to fire a gun, because the sound of it would have drawn his enemies down on him, like wolves upon a sick house-dog. What was his game? How did he exist? I cannot tell. A few berries. Roots which a pig would have despised. Sometimes birds, rabbits caught in little snares; for we found such snares, here and there, while we hunted through the ravines of that mountain. And always on the watch, night and day. Trying to get away from that cursed mountain, turned back constantly by my good men on guard, all of them with a thousand eyes —what a life—and for three months!"

He shook his head.

"Is it not beautiful, Señor Walters?"

"Beautiful? It would be beautiful if you had caught him in the end!"

"You'll hear about the way he went through us. Three of my best men keep guard. It is the bright moonlight night. There is so much moon that the stars are drowned. The sage-brush shines like tarnished old silver. Three of my men keep

166

guard in the mouth of a narrow ravine. They are all awake. Do you understand?

"Out of the ground before them, suddenly, arises a naked man. Oh, a few tattered rags, that was all. He leaps in at them. They see his long hair flying. They see the gaunt belly of him, like the belly of a greyhound. They see his ribs standing out, every one, like a death, with skin stretched hard across the ridges. But he leaps in at those three brave men of mine. One he knocks flat with a stroke of his fist, picks the gun from his nerveless hands, shoots the second man through the heart, and the third—how could I blame him?—turns and runs for his life, while Señor Seton takes the three horses and rides away, away through the moonlight, away from my hands, into safety.

"Have you considered it, señor? Is it not beautiful? Is it not perfect?"

And he took off his hat and stood bareheaded, smiling at the sacred stars above him.

CHAPTER 31

The excitement and the disgust of Walters were almost comic.

"He got away, then! He got clean away from you?"

"We played together for quite a time, he and I," said the bandit. "I never could tell whether I was hunting him or he was hunting me."

"He wanted another chance at you?"

"So it seemed. I used my men to find him. But he could not be found. And he used all his wits to find me, but in those days there was a good deal of hard riding to be done, because the truth of the matter is that the police were rather excited, and there were rewards offered. I went as far south as Mexico City to get out of the disturbance, and my friend Seton followed me, but an unlucky chance prevented us from meeting. Again, he did another splendid thing, which makes my heart swell when I think of it."

"What was that? It sounds like you loved that fellow Seton, to hear you talk about him!"

"In a way, I do. Of all the people I have met, he was the nearest to a real man, a magnificent man. Of course I loved him for such qualities. At the same time, I was hunting for his head. I offered a little private reward of money and glory to my own men. They tried for his head, also. But they always failed. The devil was in it. I had no luck. He still went free, and then he hunted for me with another trick. He had no followers to help him, so he set a trap into which I had to come."

"Why did you have to?"

"Because it was baited with my pride, and that is a thing which no man can resist."

"I dunno that I understand."

"You shall, however. He rode into Leon, one day, and there he posted a notice in the main plaza, written out in great letters, and hung up where everyone would have to see it. In that notice he declared that he had been hunting for me for a long time, that he wanted no reward for meeting me, and that he would be glad to see me for the sake of his personal pleasure. He appointed a day on which he swore that he would be present in that plaza, and asked me to appear there, also. Do you see, señor? Do you appreciate the beauty of the thought?"

"Well," said the other, "I'd like to know if the police wanted him as much as they wanted you?"

"More," said El Blanco, with a sigh of regret. "One can never understand the mind of the police. It is a sad thing that they will follow fashions, like women: and, simply because a criminal comes from a foreign land, he obtains the preference over the perfectly satisfactory products of the home country. They had placed upon his head a reward twice as high as they had placed upon mine, and they hunted him, therefore, with twice as many men. I grew jealous. I used to lie awake at night and curse the stupidity of the gendarmes!"

He broke off his narrative and laughed a little.

"It would be harder for him to get into Leon than it would for you?"

"Much harder. He was a stranger to the country—I had ten thousand friends to help me. But he swore that he would appear in the plaza on a certain day, and invited me to appear there, also.

"What could I do?"

"Put up another notice and tell him that he was bragging like a fool."

"You don't understand my heart," said El Blanco. "I could not do that. He had touched my pride, where it is nearest to my heart of hearts. I had to go, and, therefore, go I did."

"Hello! You met him again?"

"It was impossible. I did my best, with honesty, but the thing was impossible. The town was filled with the police. I struggled vainly to get through the cordon which they had thrown around it, and the police with which the place was crowded. And, as hard as I strove, I always found that there was a crowd in my way. It was exciting, but I could not do the thing. Three times I came back in three different disguises. Each time I was hunted away. I went off, finally, sure that, if I had failed to enter Leon, my enemy had failed, also. I was glad of that. It saved my name, I told myself. But I was wrong. For, just as the evening was ending, a man wrapped in a great cloak was seen to walk up to the sign which the great Señor Seton had placed in the plaza, and he was observed to write at the bottom of the sign. The curious crowd herded in, as the man in the cloak disappeared. They read a little message. It merely said: 'El Blanco, I have waited for you here all day. You have not come. What has kept you away from me, my friend? Was it the light of the day or the roughness of the roads?'

"That was the sign which he wrote."

"Hold on," said the other. "You mean to say that he wrote this out and that the police did not put hands on him before he could get away? What became of the crowds of police that you were talking about?"

"They were there," said the outlaw. "While he wrote, there was a gendarme on his horse not three strides from the notice, watching the crowd; and when he read the sign, he galloped after the American. And caught him!"

He stopped, shaking his head, and smiling.

"Caught him? Caught him?" exclaimed Walters. "But let him get away again?"

"How could he help it?" said El Blanco. "You see, my friend, when the gendarme arrived at the spot where the other was, Seton turned and shot him off his horse. The bullet went through the hip. Then Seton took the horse, which was a very good one, and galloped away on it."

"The devil he did! And the crowds of police could not stop him?"

"Twice they tried to. He rode through them, with his gun blazing. And afterward a host of them chased him, but the horse he had taken was very good, as I said before, and so he got cleanly away."

"It's a hard thing to believe!" said Walters.

"It was hard for the entire city to believe, I assure you. And the next morning, it was still harder, for the city wakened to find another sign written in the same manner as the other. It was again from Seton. He thanked the city of Leon for the good horses on which they mounted their police. He thanked them also for the excellent quality of the beds in the town, and he mentioned that he was sending to the hospital five hundred pesos for the brave but unlucky man whom he had shot the day before."

"Hold on. Did he send it?"

"Yes. That same evening, a muleteer came into Leon and brought the little purse of gold to the hospital for the policeman. He said that Seton had met him and given him a good reward for carrying the money, and had promised to cut his throat if the coins were not honestly delivered."

"It sounds like a fairy story," said Walters, with a growl.

"Does it not?" said the bandit. "And in Leon to this day people talk of Señor Seton as the prince of the fairies. A magician! A worker of wonders. There was more harm done to my name in those two days than in all my life before or after. People, when they mention me in certain parts of Mexico, laugh. And I, my friend, am a Mexican!"

He smiled, but, though his teeth flashed, there was no mirth in his face.

"That was the end between you and Seton, then?" asked Walters.

"It was nearly the end. He made one more great effort to meet me; but, on the night when he visited my camp in the mountains, unfortunately I was away. I had been called away on a little business trip which kept me a week.

"When I returned to my camp, I found there a note which had been left with one of the men who kept the camp for me. The second man had been killed during Seton's visit. He said in the note that he was sorry to miss me again, and that he hoped for better luck the next time. And he mentioned, in a postscript, that, since he had a long journey to make, he had not hesitated to borrow by best horses. He had taken two of them. They were worth, each of them, many hundreds of pesos."

"Well, you ground your teeth," said Walters. "But what did you do?"

"What could I do? I tried to pick up his trail. It was a week old, and crossed the Rio Grande; and, not very long after that, he went to prison for a five-year rest. But now I feel that he is about to end his riding and his shooting, my friend!"

He smiled again—the same bright, mirthless flash.

"What's your plan?" said Walters, in the manner of a practical man.

"I have a plan which cannot fail," said the Mexican. "To-morrow Señor Seton will be dead."

"Good!" said Walters. "But after what you've told me, it's pretty hard for me to believe!"

"You will see. There is one weakness in the armor of Seton."

"Well?"

"He loves his friends."

"How do you mean that?"

"I mean that he is one of those men who never betray, never forget, never try to read the changing minds and hearts of the men they love. That is a weakness. What a man is today, is a different self a month hence. But Señor Seton never can realize that. He would have been free and successful and rich at this moment, with no prison shadow in his past, if it had not been for that weakness."

"Go on," said Walters. "What's the plan?"

"I have among my men a famous robber, a great rider, an excellent fighter, a man full of blood and wit. His name is Gaspar Sental."

"That doesn't sound Mexican."

"He is only half Mexican. However, in the old days he was a friend of Seton. At least, Seton thought that he was. They had saved one another's lives. Seton would have given him the last drop of his blood. But he forgot a little thing which Gaspar Sental remembered."

"What was that?"

"He forgot that once they had been wrestling together like two friendly boys, and that, in the midst of the wrestling, Gaspar grew angry, and struck Seton with his fist, and Seton then crushed him in his arms and threw him senseless on the ground. Afterward, he recovered him, threw water in his face, gave him brandy, begged his pardon for using such brutal force. And Gaspar Sental smiled and said nothing. But he could not forget. He remembered. He was waiting and biding his time, but it was as hard to catch this Seton asleep as to catch a wildcat off guard. He slept with one eye open, and so the great opportunity never came to Sental. Now, then, tomorrow my Sental shall appear at your ranch. He will see Seton. Seton will open his arms, open his heart. When Sental leaves, Seton will ride a distance with him up the trail which he follows. Very well. On that trail will be the finest shot among my men. He is Juan Ortez, who speaks to his bullet before he fires, and the bullet never disobeys his command. Do you see? Seton rides to his death, happy and laughing in the company of his friend, and dies so suddenly that he has not a chance to regret the blindness of his trust in his fellow men."

CHAPTER 32

When Seton had heard this, he would have been glad to linger still further to hear future plans; but there was a difficulty which prevented him. At any moment, the most important part of the interview apparently having been ended, Walters might start back for the ranch, and it was highly important that Seton should get there ahead of him.

So he began to work his way back through the shrubbery along the course by which he had come to the fire. The retreat needed as many precautions as the approach, unless all that he had gained was to be thrown away. So, little by little, he worked out to the open ground.

The stars were brilliant; there was only one place of obscurity in the sky, where a south wind was bringing up a patch of clouds; and, regaining the place where he had left Blood and Bones, Seton mounted the mustang and went down through the pass to the valley of Benson Creek.

With a familiar trail before him, with the mustang refreshed and eager on the bit, he made excellent speed until he had regained the ranch. There, in all haste, he pulled off saddle and bridle, and rubbed down the pony quickly but thoroughly; for it was vastly important that Blood and Bones should in the morning show no signs of the labor which he had accomplished in the dark of the night.

When saddle and bridle had been hung up, he returned

the horse to the pasture field and retired to his clump of shrubbery. There he lay down on his blankets. He was not yet prepared to sleep, however. He kept on watch, and he had not long to wait, for he heard the noise of hoofs in the distance and then the sound of the barn door being pushed back on its slide. Next, the big black mare was turned into the pasture, and her rider lingered for a moment.

It was a critical time for Seton, for if any suspicion were in the mind of Walters, he would be sure to examine the condition of Blood and Bones, and the bronco was still, of course, dripping with sweat.

Walters, however, went off toward the house.

Still Seton waited. Another full hour he lay on the blankets, turning in his mind the interview which he had overheard, and retasting, out of the past, and half through the words of the Mexican, the adventures of that other day.

When the hour had ended, he went out to the pony again. The wind, by this time, had blown the horse dry, and a few wisps of hay served to rub off all probable signs of the sweating. The hay which he used for this purpose he carried back with him into the shrubbery, and finally he rolled into his blankets.

He could not sleep at once. There was still before him the bright image of the silver hair and the flashing teeth of El Blanco. There was still a jumping along his nerves, as he remembered the time of his great battle with the bandit, and the famous manhunt through the Mexican mountains. But at last, telling himself that no worry could solve the problems of the day to come, he closed his eyes, fought away trouble, and finally fell asleep.

When he wakened, the sun was already over the rim of the eastern horizon. Sounds of busy men reached him from the corral. He got up in haste, dressed, and went toward the house. Chet Ray saw him issue from the clump of shrubbery; and, at night, he whooped as a man does to encourage a pack of hunting dogs.

It annoyed Seton. It removed from him some of the necessary veil of mystery behind which he had been living. It made his sleeping out from the bunkhouse almost a silly thing. And he was aware, over his shoulder, of the continued laughter of Chet Ray, while he marched on to the bunkhouse, carrying his blankets.

There stood Douglas Walters, before it, his hands in his trousers pockets, his legs spread. He smiled broadly.

"How'd you sleep, son?" he asked.

Seton, with no answer, went on into the house.

What had Walters meant? What had he guessed? Was he merely referring to Seton's sleeping in the outdoors, or did he know something about that ride through the middle of the night?

Seton came out again, and, covertly glancing at the foreman of the ranch, he saw that the man's face had a bright, healthy color, and his eyes were perfectly clear. No one would have guessed, to look at him, that he had spent very few hours in his bed, the night before.

But there was in him, for that matter, a perfect well of strength, an inexhaustible source from which he could draw energy at will. In the old days, more than five years before, Seton had looked upon El Blanco as the greatest and most dangerous of fighting men, but if the pinch came, it might well be that Douglas Walters would prove the more formidable of the pair.

And they were both against him, sworn allies, now, working for the destruction of a single man, and each with a band of devoted followers at his back!

Panic, fear, weak self-distrust swept over Seton in waves. He should leave the Ash ranch. He should go at once to any other place in the world—the more distant the better. But here he must not remain. So he felt as he went in with the others to breakfast.

They had a ranch breakfast. It consisted of fried potatoes, thin steak, fried until it was gray in the center, porridge of oatmeal, watered canned milk to eat with it, buckwheat cakes, half an inch thick, and untold quantities of black coffee.

He absorbed his share of this provender, all the while staring at the table before him, uneasy, filled with his own

175

thoughts. That day, his former friend, Gaspar Sental, would come to visit him—with murder in his heart!

He saw Molly Ash for a moment after the breakfast was ended, as the men trooped slowly out, walking with the deliberation of laborers about to begin a long session of hard work. They rolled cigarettes. They put on their hats gingerly, as though the brims hurt their heads. They lounged against the slender wooden pillars which held up the roof of the back porch. They looked like people about to commence a holiday, with nothing in it to fill their hands or their minds. But their hands were full; and their minds were full, also.

As he looked them over, Molly Ash touched his arm.

"Are you sure that you're not making the men work a little too hard?" she asked, looking up to him with her wide, gentle eyes.

He stared down into them.

"Did Doug Walters suggest that to you?" he said.

She blushed.

"He's such a great friend of yours—he's so devoted to you —I don't suppose that he can open his mind and criticize you to your face, Jimmy."

"No," said Seton, "I don't suppose that he wants to open his mind to me."

"But you know—Jimmy—"

"Well?" said he.

"They do look rather tired," she said.

"So am I," he blurted out. "I'm tired—I'm sick—"

"Sick?" she exclaimed.

"Sick!" said he.

And he turned his back on her, and he walked with long strides down the boards toward the corral gate. He had a vast impulse, halfway to the gate, to turn and go back to her, and to apologize for his rudeness. But he would not let the impulse master him. There was a hollowness in his heart which only her voice could fill, and there was also a sense of distaste with existence which only she could have inspired.

He went out to catch a horse for the first half of his day's riding; and he said to himself, as the horses milled in the corral, and he dropped the noose of his rope over the head of a mouse-colored mare, mean as a devil and tough as iron, that Molly Ash was not worth so much thought, so much emotion. Who was Molly Ash, after all? A girl, a young girl, a silly girl. A weak creature, a foolish, untrained child so far as the affairs of the world went. He decided that he would throw away all thought of her. Let Douglas Walters have her, so far as that was concerned.

Viciously he pulled on the cinches. Viciously, the mustang swelled its belly to resist the strain. He flew into a passion. He set his knee into the ribs of the mare and pulled with all his might. The stomach of the mouse-colored mustang collapsed. She grunted; it was almost a groan. And at the same instant the strap burst under the pull.

Seton fell flat on his back, with a whack that knocked the wind out of him. The mare, startled, already alarmed and angry, jerked suddenly against the lead rope by which she was tied, and the rope—an old, half rotten thing, snapped. Away she went, galloping.

Seton got up with a groan and a curse. His wind was so far gone that he had to lean over, biting at the air. When he straightened again, he saw young Chet Ray, straight and supple as the stalk of a four-horse whip, resting his hands on his hips and rocking gently back and forth with his laughter.

Other men were there. Big Digger Murphy was at the side, coiling a rope, and he was laughing, also—half sneer and half laugh. Seton walked up to him.

"What are you laughing at?" he asked.

"Whatcha wanta know for?" asked Digger, his eyes blazing suddenly.

Seton knocked him flat.

Digger Murphy rolled over. He came to his feet with a gun in his hand. Before he could use it, Seton knocked him down again. He took the gun away.

He turned and walked to Chet Ray. There was no laughter in Ray's face. He had a hand inside his coat.

"You were laughing, too?" said Seton.

"Keep away from me!" said Chet Ray, white, his jaws set hard.

Seton stepped lightly in. The gun flashed, but the fist landed first, and Chet Ray sank loosely down into the dust, his head falling back on his shoulders, his face the blank mask of an idiot.

Seton left him lying where he fell.

He went to the corral fence and climbed to the second rail. There he turned and surveyed the crew, most of them going slowly through the motions of saddling their horses. Seton addressed them. He did not raise his voice. He did not need to.

"I know you," he said. "I know you all. You're curs. You've got your teeth bared. But you don't dare to show your faces to me. If you do—if I see a lip curl—if I hear a laugh—if a finger stirs—I'm going to take account of all of you. And the next time, it won't be with fists. It'll be something for your relatives and the girl back home to remember."

CHAPTER 33

He saw Lew Gainor biting his lip, staring fixedly. A dangerous man was Gainor, and now pressed almost more than his manhood would endure. But even Gainor made not a move to combat these insults. Even Gainor did not reach for a gun or speak a word. Slowly Seton looked around him.

Then, when only silence answered him, when he saw Chet Ray gradually picking himself out of the dust, he went after the mouse-colored mustang again, roped it, replaced the broken cinch strap, and rode out for the morning's work.

He gave the men instructions. His words rang harsh and clear in his own ears, like the words that might have been spoken by another man. No one said either yes or no. They went off in a sullen silence, and Seton was left to curse the hasty temper which had forced him on to that use of his hands. They had begun to endure his presence with some degree of indifference. Now most of them were willing to put a bullet through his back, he knew.

He was about to follow the men and ride out into the range when he saw Hooker drive up to the corral gate, sitting bunched over, lean and crooked in the seat of the buggy. He stopped the horse and let the reins hang until Seton opened the gate for him. Then he clucked to the horse and, without making any attempt to steer it, drove into the corral. One hub grated against a fence post, but the buggy came in unscathed.

"You might have taken a wheel off," pointed out Seton.

"I didn't, though," said the banker, dropping the reins still further, and looping them over the dashboard. He turned idly in the seat and allowed the gelding he was driving to ramble on toward the mossy watering trough, regardless of what might happen on the way. He talked to young Seton, hanging a foot over the side board of the buggy.

"Where's that Henry Ash?" he said.

"What do you want with him?" asked Seton.

"I wanta see him."

"Why, he's in the house. I suppose so, at least."

"Where's that big feller, Douglas Walters?"

"He's in the house."

"Why ain't he on a hoss?"

"Because he's doing accounts, I suppose."

"Working men that do accounts had oughta use lamplight for 'em," said the banker. He stepped down from the buggy, groaning as he stretched himself.

"I'm getting old," said Hooker.

"I'll put your horse in the barn," said Seton.

"You leave my hoss be," said the banker. "Let him look after himself. A hoss that ain't able to take care of the buggy

179

behind him, he ain't able to take care of the man that sits in the buggy. Come on with me."

"I have to get onto the range," said Seton. "I'm late the way it is."

"Why are you late?"

"I overslept."

"Drinkin' last night?"

"No."

"Cards?"

"No. My own business," said Seton, angrily.

"Your business or the business of the ranch?"

"I've said enough," answered Seton.

"Mad, ain't you?" said the banker.

"Yes. A little angry, perhaps."

"I'll make you madder, before you're through with me. It was ranch business that took you out last night. Now you come along with me."

"I didn't say I was out."

"You was, though."

"Who told you that?" snapped the boy, startled and surprised.

"A good fairy," said Hooker, and grinned. "But I won't tell on you. Just come along with me."

And Seton went.

There was a force behind the drawling words and the casual air of Hooker. He was a man of meaning, and for that reason he bent the wills of others around him. At the hitching rack, Seton left his horse and went in with Hooker toward the house.

Under the shade of the creamery veranda, there was discovered the imposing figure of Mr. Douglas Walters, a pile of papers on his knee, a pencil poised.

"Hullo, Walters," said the banker.

"Why, hello, Mr. Hooker," said Walters, rising. "I'm glad to see you."

He came down from the veranda with the lumbering stride of a horseman.

"No, you ain't glad to see me, but I'm glad to see you.

And the reason I'm glad will sure make you sweat," said Hooker. "Where's Henry Ash? Where's his gal, Molly?"

Walters looked from Hooker to Seton, and back again.

"What you want?" he asked sharply.

"Nothing that you can answer, young man. I want Henry Ash and his daughter. Hey, Henry Ash!"

He shouted the name out in a piercing, broken treble.

Molly Ash ran out on the back porch.

"Who called? Oh, how do you do, Mr. Hooker."

She stood on the porch and bowed to him; her face was very cold. There was not even a formal smile to light it.

"Hello, Molly," said Hooker. "I want to see you pa. I want to see you, too, and right pronto."

"I'll ask my father," said Molly.

"We'll be on the front veranda," said Hooker, as Molly disappeared into the house.

Then, as they went slowly around the corner of the building, he went on:

"Sassy and proud, ain't she? That's the way with the girls that have been raised tender and careful. They get sassy and they get proud. Sassy enough to suit you, Walters? Proud enough to suit you, eh?"

He halted and turned toward the foreman of the ranch. Walters glowered at him.

"I have nothing to say about Miss Ash," said Walters.

"He ain't got anything to say to me," said the banker, resuming his way. "He's another proud one. A proud man and a proud woman, they make a spoiled life. You'll make a spoiled life, young Walters. But part of your own life, I'm going to spoil today."

They got to the front of the house and went up onto the veranda as old Henry Ash and his daughter came through the door.

"How do you do, Mr. Hooker," said Ash, as grim as his daughter had been chilly.

"I'm better than you think," said Hooker.

He did not offer to shake hands.

"You've got a grouch against me, Ash?" said he.

"I've not said that," said Henry Ash.

181

He looked over the three men, and Douglas Walters said:

"Perhaps I'd better see Mr. Hooker for you, Mr. Ash."

"Perhaps you had," said Henry Ash. "I'm no hand at this sort of business."

He turned toward the door again, but the harsh voice of Hooker stopped him.

"You've left too much to this young man, already," said he.

Ash whirled about at him, angry. His gentility stopped the words which were on the verge of his tongue.

"May I ask what you mean by that?" asked Ash.

"You've left the buying of your ranch to him, the buying of your cattle to him, the building of your barns and corrals, the fence-repairing, and your daughter," answered Hooker.

Ash turned crimson.

He balled up his slender, bony hands into fists.

"My friend," said he, "I must ask you to—"

"Listen," said Hooker, "I'm older than you are. I can talk to you, Ash. How old are you?"

"Old enough, I hope, to understand ordinary courtesy," said Ash.

"I'm being polite," said Hooker. "I'm being more than polite. Some people would pay a fee for what I'm going to tell you."

"About what?" asked Henry Ash.

"About yourself, about your girl, about this fellow Walters, about James Seton, here."

"Ah, you brought out Mr. Hooker?" said Ash, turning his eye upon Seton.

"He didn't bring nothing," said the banker. "He didn't bring nothing but himself to your ranch, and the best day that you ever had, when he came here. Ash, will you open your ears and listen to some sense?"

"Mr. Hooker," said Ash, growing white instead of red, "I am in the position of a man who is host. I must listen to whatever you have to say, up to a certain point."

Hooker turned and pointed a finger at Walters.

"You've got some short term notes due, ain't you?" said Hooker.

"The ranch has," said Walters, slowly.

"Why don't I ask them notes to be paid?" asked Hooker.

"Because you know that the ranch is good for them," said Walters, brusquely.

"Bah!" said the banker.

He turned back on Ash.

"Why don't I ask them notes to be paid?"

"I don't know," said Ash, angrily. "They *shall* be paid, however. Why haven't they been paid, Douglas?"

"Because—because—present condition of money—" began Walters.

"Bah!" said the banker, again. "Because you can't raise the price of them. I could foreclose on you tomorrow. I could sell you out. I ought to have sold you out. I'm a fool for not doing it. Who would lend you money, now? Not even the fools in the First National! They've had enough, even at the robber's bonus that they bled you for, Walters, and which this old fool paid for and signed for!"

He pointed back at Ash with a long, bony forefinger.

"I guess we've stood about enough!" said Walters to Ash. "Shall I run him off the place, sir?"

"You won't run me off the place," broke in Hooker. "Henry Ash ain't the fool to think that I've come out here for the sake of hearing myself talk. He knows that I've got something to say. Ain't that the way you feel, Ash?"

"I'm hearing," said Ash, "the most extraordinary talk that I've ever listened to. I suppose that you have something to say and that I must listen."

"Listen, then," said Hooker. "I'll either give you some good sense or dyspepsia, and I don't much care which!"

CHAPTER 34

Seton had been growing more and more uneasy as the talk went on. The glances which Walters, the girl, and Henry Ash had thrown at him, as suspecting him of being an ally to this old man with the brutal tongue, had rather unnerved him, and now he said:

"I've got nothing to do with this. I'll be getting on."

"You'll stand right there where you are," said Hooker. "You've got more to do with this than anybody else, except me. Henry Ash, I could throw you into bankruptcy in five minutes. And then I could buy in this old place for a song. You wouldn't have enough left to give yourself twenty dollars a week the rest of your born days."

Henry Ash, no matter how high his spirit was, could hardly hear this without a shock. He looked wildly toward Walters, who composed himself and said, with assurance:

"That's all rot, and he knows it's rot, Mr. Ash. He's coming out here, today, to try to scare you into something."

"Why should I scare him?" asked the banker. "What good would it be to me? You're a sick man, Henry Ash. You're so sick that you're ready to die, and I'm the doctor for you. I'm the first one to *tell* you that you're sick. You're bankrupt and you don't know it! All I have to do is to turn in those notes and—"

"Walters," said Ash, "is it true that we can't meet those notes?"

"Oh, a little hustling about," said Walters, "and I have no doubt that I could raise the money, well enough."

"Not even with a bonus, you can't get the money out of the First National, Walters," said Hooker. "Look here, Ash. D'you think that it's chance or a joke that's caused the only two banks in Claymore to turn you down?"

"Will you kindly tell me what *is* the cause?" asked Henry Ash.

"I'll tell you why," said Hooker. "It's because you've got a thug, a crook, a thief workin' for you. That's the reason."

Henry Ash and Molly, with one flash of the eyes, looked straight at the ex-convict, but it was at Walters that Hooker pointed.

"And that's the man!" cried Hooker.

"You infernal old scoundrel—" said Walters.

"Steady, Doug!" said Seton through his teeth.

Walters faced him purple with rage, trembling with a desire to attack. Something held him back—the old knowledge of the many victories which this man of uncanny power had won over him in the old days—most of all, the memory of the blow he had attempted to strike on the day of Seton's arrival, and how his fist had foolishly struck the empty air, alone.

This test between the two of them could not pass unnoticed by the girl and Henry Ash. They stared, bewildered, at this apparent clash between the two "dearest friends in the world."

"Walters is the leaden anchor around your neck," went on Hooker. "He's the fellow who's drowning you. He made you pay sixty per cent more for the land than it ever was valued before. He made you pay thirty per cent more for your cattle and fifty per cent more for your horses."

"You lie!" shouted Walters.

"Aw, go down in Claymore and ask why Walters has so many more friends this year than he had the year before!" exclaimed Hooker. "Don't trust me, but go down to Claymore and ask, will you?"

"You can't have any effect upon me by slandering the man in whom I put the greatest, the most implicit trust," said Henry Ash.

"Can't I?" said Hooker.

185

He looked at Ash with a sneer.

"Oh," went on the banker, "it ain't care for you that makes me take the trouble to come out here and tell you that you're a fool. It ain't care about what happens to that baby-faced fool of a girl, either. It's because of something else. It's because of him that made me keep from presentin' the notes when they was due. It's him—it's the *really* best friend that you've got—it's Jimmy Seton, here, the gun man, the train robber, the yegg, the ex-convict—he's the man for me, and if you had an eye in your head, he'd be the man for you, Henry Ash—he'd be the man for you, Molly Ash!"

He jabbed his finger at each of them, in turn, as he said this. Henry Ash grew whiter than before. Molly became oppositely red.

"It's enough," said Ash, sternly. "You wish me to invite Douglas Walters to leave my house, I take it?"

"Yeah. That's what I wish."

"Mr. Hooker," said Ash. "I must tell you that Douglas Walters is engaged to marry my daughter."

This sentence, pronounced with much gravity, merely caused Hooker to break into loud, sneering laughter.

"He's engaged to bleed you white, and he's just about done it," said he. "It's only Seton that's saved you, this far. He's struck the only blows on your side! It's Seton that begged me off from collecting the notes."

"By heaven!" exclaimed Ash.

He turned to Seton.

"Did you go to him? Who commissioned you to go to him in my name?"

"He didn't," said the banker. "He went in his own. I reckon he didn't even tell you that he was going, eh?"

"Certainly not—" began Ash, angrily.

"Sure he wouldn't tell you," said Hooker. "But he comes in to me and shows me the lining of his brains, and that lining was good enough for me. Jimmy," he said sharply to Seton, "you leave this gang of fools and thugs and come with me. I'll give you an opening that'll make your hair stand on end. I'll give you a chance that'll be a *real* chance. You understand me?"

Seton looked straight at the older man. He was amazed. But there was a fire of sincerity in the eyes of the banker. Was it some clever game which Hooker was playing, some mere desire to detach him from the Ash ranch before closing iron hands upon the tidbit? No, he felt the burning sincerity of Hooker in every word, in every gesture of the old man.

"I stay here," said Seton, "as long as I can be used."

Hooker stamped noisily upon the floor of the veranda.

"I've got money—I've got thousands tied up in this place of yours, Ash," said he. "And every minute that young scoundrel of a Walters stays on the place, that money of mine is in danger. I ask you will you come to my bank with me this minute and sit at my own table, while I show you exactly what I know about the financial transactions of Mr. Douglas Walters regarding the Henry Ash ranch?"

Douglas Walters, with a sick, fixed smile upon his face, endured the outburst. His burning eyes fixed themselves upon Ash. And Molly Ash, pale, lips parted, looked at her father, also.

Henry Ash himself lifted his head from the thought which had bowed it.

"My trust in Mr. Walters," he said, "is as implicit as my trust in this right hand of mine."

And he raised his hand. It was thin, it was old, it shook. But the gesture was filled with a solemn dignity.

"Is that all?" asked Hooker.

"That's all, sir."

"A fool and his folly, they ain't soon parted," said Hooker. "I wanta give you one more chance. I ask you to come in with me and let me show you some writings, and young Walters, he can come along too and throw dust in your eyes as fast as he's able. Will that please you, as givin' him a square deal?"

"Mr. Hooker," said the rancher, "I dare say that we've talked enough to understand one another."

"Be damned to you for an old petrified fool!" shouted Hooker.

He turned about, without any other farewell, and started

187

for the gate. Halfway down the board walk, he turned suddenly about.

"I'm going to bust you, then!" he shouted. "I'll show you what Walters has done for you. I'll own this ranch myself inside of a week! That's what he's brought you to!"

Then he whirled about and went striding forward again, his legs bending greatly at the knees.

Seton, staring after him, watched the corral gate slam with a loud bang that knocked the dust off the neighboring pickets. Then he looked toward the others.

All three of them seemed stunned by the explosion which had just occurred so unexpectedly under their very feet, but the pride of the Ashes did not falter. They looked back toward him, and their eyes were as cold as glass. They looked toward Walters, and their faces softened into smiles.

"Douglas," said old Ash, "will you come inside with us? I presume, Mr. Seton, that your affairs will take you out on the range?"

"They will," said Seton gloomily, and he went out toward the corral and his waiting horse.

He could see that Hooker had failed to bring Ash to his senses. Instead, he merely had fortified Henry Ash in his trust in Walters. The outright and outrageous attack delivered by Hooker had defeated his own ends. So furious had it been that Ash would not ask Walters to defend himself; he would merely be concerned in showing the younger man that his trust in him was absolute.

And as for Seton? It was plain that the visit of Hooker had undone him in the eyes of the family. They had no faith in him, thenceforward. He was looked upon as the man who had encouraged the visit of Hooker, and, masking himself behind the older man, produced a sneaking effect by having his praises chanted by the other.

So, very gloomily and slowly, he went out to the corral, and found Hooker on the verge of leaving the place. He paused, pulling in on the reins, when he saw Seton.

"It didn't work, my boy," said he. "That old fool, he's got forty feet of bedrock between his ideas and common sense. But it ain't all wasted, what I've done today. Some of them blasts that I let off, they've cracked the strata right down to the foundation. But mark my word—if you stay on here at the ranch, you're in danger of your life from Walters. He ain't gunna waste much time, now that he knows that I'm behind you. Take my advice. Hop into the buggy here, beside me, and drive into Claymore. I'll make you a new life, and a big life, my boy!"

Seton looked back into those overbright, birdlike eyes, and shook his head.

"You're mighty kind," said he. "But I'll have to stay on here. It's my job."

"Who made it your job?" snapped the banker. "The girl, eh? The pretty, soft face—the soft eyes—the baby smile! Bah! Bah! Bah! You're a fool!"

And he drove on through the gate, growling.

Seton watched the buggy vanish in a cloud of dust of its own raising. He felt like one who sees a steamer depart for another continent, bearing with it the last human hope.

CHAPTER 35

Seton knew when Gaspar Sental would come.

It was just six o'clock, when the punchers came in off the range. It was just at six o'clock, when the men were tired and the air was filled with golden sunlight like pollen shaken from the innumerable flowers of the sky. It was at six o'clock, when the working day ended, though the day of the sun had not, for still the twilight was far away, and the disk of the sun was tinged with red, like metal shot with blood. Then Gaspar Sental came.

He found Seton in the bunkhouse, where the latter, slowly, painfully, was pulling off a pair of boots and getting into shoes. He was very tired. His body was tired from the night before. His heart was tired, because of the many pulls which drew it this way and that. His very soul was weary, for it seemed to him that after all to leave this life of burden and go back to the old life would be as it is to a boy when he sheds his clothes and casts away, like an old skin, school, parental authority, the grim future life of labor, all with the first chill tingle of the plunge in the pool on a hot summer's day. So easy would it be to cast off these new responsibilities and relapse into the old ways. But, as he pulled on the shoes, and laced them easily, carelessly, his eyes doing one thing while his hands did another, he saw the form of Gaspar Sental come through the doorway.

He was half French, he was half Spanish. He looked neither one nor the other. He was a biggish man, with pale eyes, and a soft voice, and a soft manner. He had a way with him, women said. Playful ways, lazy, dreamy, careless ways. When he laughed, it was as though he regretted the effort. And sometimes his smile took the place of words. He had very blond hair, which contrasted oddly with his Spanish speech. His ways were Spanish, also. He had dignity, with just a touch of weariness, and a smile to redeem the sense of tiredness. One could think of him sleeping twenty hours out of the twenty-four. Not that he was lazy, but because life offered little that really was amusing.

Gaspar Sental stood in the doorway of the bunkhouse; and, when Seton saw him, he got up and forgot all that he had heard the great El Blanco say the night before. He ran to meet Gaspar as a child runs to meet Santa Claus. He caught him by both hands. He wrung those hands. He laughed, and with his head tilted back, he looked down over Gaspar with an infinite delight. Still holding him by one hand, he swung around and faced the astonished group of cowpunchers.

"Boys," said he, "this is my old partner, my bunkie, the straightest man who ever pulled a gun; the truest man that ever dealt with a cold deck, the most honest man that ever

190

robbed on the highway. This is Gaspar Sental. I owe my life to him. He owes his life to me. This Gaspar Sental!"

Sental bowed to the speaker. Then he bowed to the punchers. Then he laughed a little, and by his laughter he made the entire speech a jest, a foolish by-play. He was heard to say, in delightful Castilian Spanish:

"My dear old friend—my dear, foolish fellow—my dear boy, you have not changed!"

"Why should I change?" said Seton. "What in the world is there to change a man when he sees his friend? There are not so many friends in the life of a man. Work a million tons of hard rock and you will have a few pounds of gold. Work a thousand billion pounds of stubborn humanity, and there remains what? Why, one friend, Sental, and you are he. Are you not?

He turned on Sental. His head was still back, as if in an ecstasy. He smiled. His hand was yet closed on the hand of the Mexican. And Sental smiled in return, lazily, showing his teeth a little, his eyes half closed. The man always had the look of one newly awakened, or about to return to the depths of slumber.

"There is only one friend," said he.

Seton took him outside.

There had to be room and air for his suspicion, for his talk, for the hideous thought which had been planted in his mind by the words of the great El Blanco the night before.

The sky was all gold. Gold fell upon the barn, upon the white dust of the corral, leaving in the hollows of hoofprints purple shadows. Gold fell upon the barn and dimmed the brilliance of its red, and upon the green of the fields, making them burn softly. The trees shimmered, also, in the distance.

"Ah, Gaspar," said Seton, "my friend, my dear, dear friend. How long it has been! How long it has been! What shall we do?"

"We shall smoke a cigarette," said Sental.

"We shall smoke a cigarette," said Seton, and offered the makings.

They were accepted. They smoked cigarettes, each lighting the other's. They smoked for a moment, facing each other, their arms interlocked, smiling as lovers smile.

"Gaspar!"

"Yes?"

"What has brought you here?"

Gaspar Sental gestured with his free hand.

"You have never been much of a sailor?"

"No, but what of that?"

"Then you don't know how the needle points to the pole."

"Was it only instinct, Gaspar?" asked Seton. And his heart ached as he spoke. It was better, ten thousand times, to suspect all the rest of the world, rather than to suspect Sental.

"I heard a little. About a man who was doing strange things in the Claymore Valley. So I came."

"You suspected that it was I, Gaspar?"

"Of course I suspected."

"Well, you will stay here with me, Gaspar?"

Sental shrugged.

"How can I stay?"

"And why not?"

"Well, they are after me. That is why."

"Still after you?"

"Yes."

"Who, the ladies, Gaspar?"

"No, but their friends, the police."

"Ah, ha!"

"Yeah. And ah ha, again!"

"Who the devil are they?"

"Well, certain Texas Rangers."

"Bad business."

"Very bad."

"And for what, Gaspar?"

"The good, quiet, stolid faces of these banks; you know that they were always too much for me."

"Yes. You always had to see what was behind them."

"Exactly. They are so smug."

"Yes, and stupid and strong looking, Sental."

"Yes, and they forget that the key by which the president enters may let in the thief, also."

"Did you go in by the president's key?"

"Well, I suppose that I did. At least, it opened the door."

"Where did you get it, Gaspar?"

"From his trousers pocket."

"You picked it?"

"Yes."

"On the street?"

"No, but while he was snoring."

"Good, very good!" said Seton.

"His wife wakened. 'Is everything all right, John?' said she. 'Everything is all right, if you'll let me sleep,' said he. So he slept, and I took the keys. These men of business have great burdens, my dear old friend."

"What was the burden of this poor bank president? His keys?"

"No. His wife. However, there were seventeen keys in that ring."

"You are a kind man, Gaspar, to take them away from him."

"Well, I suppose that he has duplicates for all of them."

"Yes, but one of them he will never need again."

"True. I could guess that. One of them he will never need again."

"And then you started south?"

"I had a longing for frijoles, suddenly."

"And tequila?"

"That, too. Only an old friend could have guessed that."

"Of course."

"Look at this, then!"

He took out a wallet and showed the contents. The inside was packed with a thick sheaf of bills.

"Hello!" said Seton.

"We shall spend it together," said Gaspar Sental.

"Where?"

"In Mexico—The Rangers are too close behind me, here."

"Well, then—but I cannot go to Mexico."

"Why?"

"I am working here."

"But any man can stop working."

"Not I, Sental!"

"Ah, there is a woman, at last? One who really matters?"

And suddenly Seton looked into his own heart and he said, very slowly and gravely:

"Yes, there is a woman; one who matters."

He looked straight into the eyes of Sental, and Gaspar Sental looked straight back into his. Was he, after all, a traitor?

"Listen to me!" said Sental. "You are coming away with me. This is no country for you. There is no joy in you. It is a dry land. The people in it are dry. But come away with me to my own country. Do you hear me, my dear friend, my old friend?"

"I must stay here."

"Can nothing move you? You see what money I show. I have more, also."

Seton hesitated a moment. Then he laughed.

"Do you know something, Gaspar?"

"Tell me, amigo!"

"I mean, do you know how you act about this money?"

"No, but tell me that."

"You act as if it were blood money—you're so anxious to spend it quickly, with a friend."

"Blood money," cried Gaspar Sental.

Then he laughed.

But between the words and the laugh, Seton had looked into his soul, and he saw there that which turned his heart sick.

"At least," said Sental, "ride up the road with me a little, and we'll talk it over."

Then Seton knew, for certain. He looked steadily into the face of his old companion. Each had meant life or death to the other.

"Yes," said he. "Let us go!"

CHAPTER 36

So they rode away from the ranch together, Sental and Seton. The light was yet more dusky with gold. Crimson and rose began to flow around the edges of the sky. And the tops of the mountain took the deepening light, flaming and smoking with it into the heavens.

"Tell me," said Sental. "What are you doing there at that ranch, herding men about?"

"Oh, I'm working, Gaspar."

"But that? A sheep dog's work, and once you were a wolf."

"I've had the whip," said Seton. "I've been disciplined and made quiet. Now any man can call to me, and I trot at his heel."

He shrugged his shoulders, while Sental, turning a little in the saddle, looked at him directly in the face, and with that flashing clearness which sometimes took the place of the usual dreamy glance.

"No," said Sental. "No, you have not changed very much. You are still a man, my friend. The prison has not taken that away from you."

"However, you can see for yourself. I am not able to go very far. I can only escort you a little distance on your way, and then I have to turn back."

"Do you? To the ranch?"

"Yes. There is always something to do. I am a working man."

"Don't be a slave-driver, and don't be a slave," said Sental.

"That is something you used to say yourself in the old days."

"Oh, I forget everything that happened in the old days, except my friends. Except men like Sental!"

"Thank you," said Sental. "But you'll ride with me until I camp for the night. It will not be far. You can sit by my fire for a little distance."

"No. I cannot ride that far."

"Really?"

"No."

"Then up to the top of that ridge, amigo, so that you can look over the rim into the country beyond and see a little of the way which I must ride without you."

"No, Gaspar. There where the grade comes to the top of the hill, do you mean?"

"Yes, there where the brush begins."

"No, I shall stop there in the hollow, at the little bridge."

"Tush! But I want you to go on with me, because I have something to say to you."

"Ah, no. Not that you wish to take me back to the old life, Gaspar?"

"As a matter of fact," said Sental, "I wish to start you on a new life."

"Do you think that you could take me far into it?"

"Yes, the whole way."

"How? By words?"

"No, but I have something to show you."

"Really?"

"Yes. Something as clear as heaven or hell."

Seton looked with a smile upon his old friend. Behind the smile there was an agony of sadness.

"Here I am at the bridge," said he, "and I must not go on."

"Come, come, you must ride up the hill with me," said Sental. "That is not like a friend."

"Shall I tell you something?"

"Tell me, then."

"The fact is, Gaspar, that the wind, the last few days, has eaten to my bones. My old wounds begin to ache, and I must get back and put on flannel like a sickly child."

He laid his hand on his left shoulder, as he spoke, and shook his head, making a wry face.

Their horses were halted, now, in the middle of the bridge. It was a crazy structure. As the horses moved, the timbers creaked and gave a perceptible, sickening tremor. Under the bridge the water flowed in a swift and solid mass, as if through a flume. It was the color of flame.

"Is that the place?" said Sental, curiously.

"Yes."

"Well, I remember," murmured Sental.

"You remember what, Gaspar?"

"The night when you received the bullet, there."

"You do? Let me see. Well, I've forgotten that."

"You really have forgotten?"

"Yes. It's not in my mind."

"Well, I'll tell you the picture. Then you may remember. A cantina, in the mountains. An open fire burning on a hearth in one corner. Half a dozen people playing cards Someone scraping away on a bad violin in the next room. I was *La Paloma*. The people were tired of the tune, and tired of the cards. Suddenly a door flies open and in pour five rurales. Real devils. Their guns are out. They are ready for killing. They are hungry to kill. And one man at that card table is the man they want the most. He rises and turns toward the door. You remember I was that man, amigo?"

"Now it all comes back to me," said Seton, shaking his head. "It had left my mind, like smoke and sparks up a chimney and into the dark."

"Well, you may forget, but I remember," said Sental, almost sadly. "I remember the blow of the bullet that grazed my skull. It was like the stroke of a club. I remember falling forward. The next thing, I was being dragged along by someone. I opened my eyes. The stars were above me, spinning and whirling. The night air was cool on my face. And something else was dripping and running warm upon it. It was your blood, amigo. You were dragging me down a narrow path to get to the horses in the farther corral. A bullet had torn through that shoulder of yours. With one hand and arm you were dragging me. Do you think that I could forget?"

"No," said Seton. "You're not a fellow to forget. Well, we were young, then."

"But we were friends," said Sental.

"Yes. We were friends. We always shall be friends, from that day until we die, shall we not, Gaspar?"

Sental looked down at the swiftly streaming river. "No," he said softly. "No—I hope not." Then, with a sigh, he added:

"You must come on with me a little way. I have something to tell you—something to show you, amigo."

"Ah," said Seton, "you don't know, old fellow, how I ache with the wounds. The scars are all on fire—like that water, there. I must go back. Here's my hand, Gaspar!"

But Sental did not extend his own.

"I won't say good-by," said he. "I won't shake hands, because I know that it cannot be long before we'll meet again. I trust in the future."

"Trust in the future, then. Good-by, Gaspar. I never forget. We shall see one another again."

"Yes, again."

And Gaspar Sental, taking off his hat, raised it high and then bowed to his companion. After that, he turned his horse and galloped at an easy canter up the road toward the crest of the hill.

Seton turned also, and, riding from the bridge, he passed at a jog trot under the shoulder of the next little hill. The instant that it hid him from view, instead of continuing on toward the ranch, he swerved to the left and spurred his horse to a racing gallop. Straight across the fields he went, and, reaching the creek at a point a quarter of a mile from the bridge where he had parted from Sental, he forded the stream, the active mustang on the run. Up the farther bank they struggled. Then he slipped the horse through a growth of trees that shrouded the upward slope, and, working rapidly, they presently came to the top of the crest which Sental already had pointed out as the spot to which he wished Seton to accompany him.

Seton pushed down into the hollow beyond, to the verge of the trail. The trees grew in close ranks on either hand, and, dismounting, he tethered the horse. Then he took up a position, rifle in hand, under the covert of a tall and dense growing shrub.

There he waited. It was now the full crimson of the sunset, a bad light for accurate shooting at a distance, but enough for a marksman at close range.

It was not long before he heard what he had expected to hear, and this was the noise of two horses going in unison down the trail toward him, coming from behind. He peered out. One was Sental, as he had known it would be. The other was a slight man with a very erect carriage and a pair of moustaches which bristled out from the sides of his face. He seemed older, by a good deal, than Sental, and he had the air of a soldier.

On this campaign, at least for the time being, his strategy had failed. They came by, riding very slowly, the heads of their horses almost touching.

"There will be another time," said he of the moustaches.

"No," said Sental. "It's the last time for me. A dirty business, and I'm finished with it, today."

"That will be something to tell El Blanco," said the other.

"Yes. I'll tell it to him myself."

"You might have tried something against Seton with your single hand. Were you afraid of him?"

Sental turned in the saddle and looked fixedly at his companion.

"Yes," said he, "I was afraid. Do you understand? I was afraid. What have you to say to that?"

The man of the moustaches shrugged his shoulders and then laughed.

"We were sent out to fight Seton, not one another," he pointed out.

At this moment, they were passing the shrub where Seton was posted. He waited until they were a few yards beyond him, and then he drew his bead on Sental's companion.

"Halt!" he called.

The two horses stopped, unchecked by the reins.

"Diablo!" cried Sental's companion through his teeth.

Sental himself merely sat straighter in the saddle. He

raised his head. He made no attempt to turn about or to attack.

"Juan Ortez," called Seton, "I have you inside the sights of my rifle as safely as a little toy inside a boy's hand. Do you hear?"

"Who in the name of the devil are you?"

"Tell him, Gaspar," called Seton.

"It is he. It is Seton," answered Sental.

"Ah, damn you for a traitor, then!" exclaimed Juan Ortez.

"Unbuckle your gun belt and let the guns fall to the road," commanded Seton.

And, slowly, reluctantly, the thing was done.

CHAPTER 37

The gun belt with the two holstered weapons having fallen into the road, Juan Ortez asked crisply:

"What else, Señor Seton?"

"This," said Seton. "That you keep your face turned down the road. That when I have finished speaking, you ride on. For when I see your full face again, my friend, I have an idea that there will be a bullet flying in the air somewhere between us."

There was an inarticulate snarl from Ortez, but he held his head rigidly turned to the front.

"I am going to set you free," said Seton. "I'm not one of those who lie in wait in the brush and try to shoot down people who are helpless from surprise. And besides, I can use you. I can use you as a messenger to El Blanco, who sent you here."

There was a start, and a loud exclamation from Ortez, very quickly stifled.

"Go back to El Blanco," said Seton, "and tell him that I appreciate the attentions which he has wished to show me. I appreciate them, and I honor the thought he is giving me. Tell him that there are still things for which I have to repay him, and this is only a small scratch added to the old score. Tell him, however, that only a fool would have selected my friend Gaspar Sental to conspire against me. I am surprised that El Blanco should have done such a thing. I fear that he has grown old, or careless. Tell him that I have laughed with Sental about this thing and that we will laugh again, together. Tell him that I am waiting for the day when I shall meet him, and we shall be able to exchange ideas, face to face. That is all. You are free, Ortez!"

Ortez hesitated one instant. He did not turn his head—not even toward his companion.

"It is true, then, Sental?" he said. "You have betrayed me? You have betrayed El Blanco? You are such a fool that you will take this man's part against all the rest?"

Sental, who did not answer for a moment, appeared to be gathering a great breath. Then he exclaimed in a loud voice:

"I've heard you, Ortez. You were willing to lie there in the brush and try to murder a man who is my best friend. You were willing to take the blood money of El Blanco. As for me, I despise you both. I would have broken your neck with my own hands, but my friend wished to keep you alive in order to send his message back to El Blanco. Take another message to him. Take it from me. Say that I, Gaspar Sental, have had enough of him. From this moment we are enemies. I shall take nothing from him but blood and give him nothing of mine except my blood. That is all. Now run, like the cur that you are. Get quickly out of my sight!"

The shoulders of Ortez heaved with the greatness of his rage.

"I remember it all. I remember everything," said he. "I shall give every word you have spoken to El Blanco. Then he will come for you with his own hands. Pah! I shall come with him. You—Sental—"

He choked with his fury.

"You have made a fool of me today; I shall make a dead man of you tomorrow!" ended Ortez; and, plunging the spurs into the flanks of his horse, he darted up the road at a mad gallop. At the bend, he turned one instant to show them his brandished fist; then the speed of the mustang jerked him out of sight among the trees.

Seton, in the meantime, walked out and picked up the fallen gun belt. He paid no heed to Sental, made no attempt to keep on guard against him. But he examined the handles of Ortez' weapons.

"According to the notches, he's killed five men with these two guns, Gaspar," said he.

"Ah, amigo!" exclaimed Sental. "You knew! All the while you knew that I was a dog."

"Hush," said Seton. "I don't know what you're saying."

"It was not your wounds that ached, when you paused there at the bridge," said the Mexican. "It was your heart that ached to see what a cur I had become."

"It did not, Gaspar. Talk no more of it."

"I *must* talk more. There was once a blow you gave me when we were playing foolishly with one another—"

Seton went to him and took the reins of Sental's horse in his grip.

"Listen to me!"

"Yes?" said Sental.

His face was working, the mouth twitching at the corners, the forehead corrugated with deepest agony.

"You spoke of the night when I dragged you down the trail, Gaspar. Now let me tell you—I remember nothing between us since that night."

"Do you mean it?"

"Here is my hand, Gaspar."

"I am not worthy to touch it. You should have shot me down!"

"And lost you? I am not such a fool! Besides, you're not likely to die of old age—now that El Blanco is trailing you as he was trailing me. Take my hand, Gaspar!"

And Sental took it. But first he removed his hat and placed

202

it on the horn of his saddle. Then he pulled out from his belt a little stiletto with a small guard below the grip. This he raised in his left hand. It looked like a little glittering cross against the blood red of the evening sky. His right hand gripped that of Seton. It was very melodramatic; it was done in silence, also. But there was something of grandeur and sacred resolution in the manner of Sental that removed the slightest suggestion of sham from his actions.

That silent hand clasp having ended, Sental restored the stiletto to its secret sheath and replaced the hat upon his head. But the strength seemed to have gone out of him. His head fell forward until his chin was almost on his breast.

"I must go back," said Seton.

"Yes," said Sental, "we must go back."

"Are you riding as far as the ranch with me?"

"Yes, I'm riding as far as the ranch."

Seton got his horse from among the trees. They started off together, and all the way to the ranch, while the color died from the sky and the little bright stars began to grow and twinkle, burning their way through, they spoke not a word to each other.

"Here's the place," said Seton, when they came to the ranch. "Good-by, Gaspar."

Sental lifted his head for the first time and looked about him like a man who has been dreaming.

"Here is the place. Ay!" said he.

And he turned his horse in toward the gate.

"No, no," said Seton. "There's no use in that."

"I stay here," insisted Sental.

"It's no good," answered Seton. "This game that I'm playing is on such a long chance that there's nothing but luck could help me. No man would be any good."

"To guard your back?" said Sental.

"It wouldn't help. Besides, you've nothing to gain by staying. These people mean nothing to you. You have no real battle against El Blanco, either."

Sental raised a hand.

"You have argued enough," said he. "I stay here at the ranch with you. I am no longer a child, but I am as ready

203

to die as another man. I shall stay here; I shall guard your back! We'll talk no more about it."

Seton considered for only a moment, but then, as he saw Sental about to unbar the gate, he surrendered. He said not a word, but together they rode into the corral, and, reaching the pasture gate beyond, they unsaddled the horses and turned them loose in the green field.

Still in silence, they were coming back toward the bunkhouse, where the idle hands, tired from the day's riding, were gathered, smoking, chatting, laughing loudly. Then big Douglas Walters passed them on the way to the barn. He stopped when he sighted the stranger.

"Do you know him?" asked Seton.

"No," said the foreman.

"You ought to know him. He's worth knowing, for that matter. He's Gaspar Sental."

"The devil!" exclaimed Walters, the words bursting involuntarily from his lips.

"Not the devil, but closely related," said Seton. "You've heard of him, then?"

"Heard of him?" said Walters. He grew confused and colored. "I think I have," said he.

Seton stared straight at him.

"I thought you had," said he. "And he's heard of you, also."

"What do you mean by that?" said Walters.

Seton pointed toward the hills.

"Ride after Ortez and catch him if you can," said he. "He'll be able to tell you, I suppose."

He turned on his heel and went on, with his friend, and left the foreman glowering after them. But Walters did not go on toward the barn. Instead, he went back toward the house, walking very slowly, like a man who has received the stunning shock of unexpected bad news.

"Why did you tell him that?" asked Sental. "Why did you show him what you know? He might have told me something worth knowing, if he'd thought that I was down here as a hired murderer to kill you."

"He might have told you something," said Seton, "but I

204

have an odd feeling about this business. I prefer to keep it all in the open. I greatly prefer that. There'll be no more skulking and hiding and ambushing, if I can avoid it. I'll try to get them into the open; and, if I can meet them there, we'll take our chances. I could have kept Walters in the dark for half a day, perhaps. But is it worthwhile? I don't think so. I'm getting impatient. I want to get to grips with the thing and have it ended."

"Be as impatient as you like," said Sental. "God knows that I shall do my best to guard your back, when the fighting begins. Be as impatient as you like, but don't throw yourself away. There's no sense and point in that."

"No," agreed Seton, "there's no point in that. But do you see where I stand? Do you see how I feel about it, man?"

"No. I try to, but I can't."

"Why, I feel as if something I can't see had its hand on my shoulder and were pushing me ahead. What will come of it I don't know. I hardly ask myself, Gaspar. I only feel, now, that I've come to the verge of the cataracts, and that inside of a day I'll either be smashed on the rocks, or else I'll have won through to quiet waters. With you in the bows, I may win through. And that would be quiet water for the two of us, Gaspar."

Sental nodded. But he was smiling faintly.

"Why do you smile, Gaspar?"

"Oh, for nothing."

"You were thinking of El Blanco?"

"Yes," said Sental.

And suddenly they were both silent, striding on side by side toward the bunkhouse, with set, desperate faces.

CHAPTER 38

Two things disturbed Seton that evening, in spite of the troubles which were already on his mind. One was the remarkable courtesy of the other punchers on the place—except Jake Mooney, who moodily sat aloof from everyone. The other was the cold disdain in the eyes of Henry Ash and his daughter when, at the supper table, they avoided the face of Seton as well as they could.

They had finished with him, he was certain. Their faith was so profoundly given to their foreman that they could not consider judging him or balancing him against the truth and the faith of another man, a comparative stranger like Seton.

So the many dreams were flickering. That hope for the rehabilitation of the ranch, with the money of Hooker to develop it, the building of the dam, the establishment of the great reservoir, the arrangement of all the Ash affairs upon a sound basis and, in the end, perhaps the exposure of Walters' frauds—all of these things grew dim and thin before his eyes. He saw that he had been grasping at impossibilities. But that did not make his heart any the less sore. The politeness of the other punchers seemed an even more evident sign.

After supper, he went off with Sental, alone, and they carried their blankets with them.

"What do you think of those fellows?" he asked.

"I think they're like snakes—ready to bite," said Sental. "I would watch them, amigo. We shall watch them together."

He could not understand, at first, why it was necessary for them to sleep away from the bunkhouse, but when Seton explained, he nodded his head.

"This is only for a little while," said Sental. "Then you will ride south with me. We'll find a way to live in my own country—and to be free. Are there not whole towns where you are still remembered, as families remember a father? They know me, also. We will work together. We will be free as the birds in the air. We will have a life, amigo!"

He laughed softly as he said it, but Seton did not answer at once. At length he said:

"You forget, Gaspar."

Sental paused, also.

"True," said he. "I forget!"

They talked no more. Seton led the way through the night to a small copse which grew in a hollow, and there they made down their beds. They sat for a time in the darkness, smoking the last cigarette.

"It may be," said Sental, at last.

"It may be what?"

"You spoke to me, did you not?"

"No," said Seton.

"I thought I heard you say that tomorrow may be the last day."

"Ay, and it may be," said Seton. "But your own brain said it, not I."

"Bah!" murmured Sental. "Do I begin to talk to myself, like an old woman?"

They rolled into their blankets. Seton remained awake for a moment, looking up through the slender branches toward the stars which freckled the sky. Sleep came, showed him the face of El Blanco in a dream, and the dream wakened him abruptly.

He slept again, a very troubled sleep, but sound enough, it appeared. It was very far through the night when the low voice of Sental wakened him.

"What is it?" asked Seton, and sat bolt upright.

"Listen!" said Sental.

And Seton listened, frowning the sleep out of his brain as

well as he could. He was cold. There was no wind blowing, but the damp of the earth had worked into his bones. He was shuddering with it and with the same coldness of the heart which he had felt when he first lay down the evening before.

Far away, he heard the mooing of cattle.

"I hear cattle lowing. I don't hear anything else."

"That's it. The cattle lowing," said Sental, in the same soft voice, as though he were afraid that he might be overheard.

"And what of that?"

"I've been listening to it for half an hour. You are a sound sleeper, amigo. For my part, the fall of a leaf could waken me—on a night such as this."

Seton canted his ear farther to the side and put away all senses except that of hearing, so hard did he concentrate.

"Cattle—moving away—that's all," said he.

"Cattle moving away. That's it," said Sental. "But moving where?"

Seton listened again.

"Why, toward the hills, I suppose," he said, and yawned. "What's the matter with you, Gaspar?"

"Nothing with me. But with the cattle."

"Can't a cow or two ramble in the night without giving you a start?"

"More than one or two," said Sental.

And at that moment, as though to give a further weight and point to his words, out of the distance floated to them a chorus of lowing—a chorus made hollow and dim not only by its distance but by the confused clamor of echoes, which melted all together.

"And going toward the hills—" suggested Sental.

Seton leaped to his feet. At one stroke his brain was cleared.

"Fool—fool—fool!" he said through clenched teeth, to himself. "They were ready to bite. Last night you said it, Gaspar. And now they are at it. They're driving the cattle. I might have guessed it. My bones felt that this was the night. They're running the cattle now for the river, through the passes. And I—"

He pulled on his boots, cursing. Sental, already dressed, was ready and waiting as Seton ran out of the brush.

"Horses!" said Seton, and he led the way at a furious run for the horse pasture and corrals.

They came to the bars.

Beyond lay the bare, level, blank darkness of the empty field. There was not a hummock of shadow to show where a beast was lying down. There was nothing between fence and fence.

"They've swept the corral clean," said Seton. "They've taken the rifles, too, I suppose. But we've got to see."

He led the way to the side of the barn, and, pushing back the door, he lighted a match.

There was not a rifle in the gunroom. Every one was taken. There was not an ammunition belt. All was gone. They had between them two revolvers and a meager supply of cartridges. That was all.

"We have lost the game before we sat down at the table," said Sental, carelessly. "Well, it's better this way."

"It's not your game. It's mine," said Seton. "But it's not lost yet. There's a ghost of a chance. Good-by, Gaspar! If I—"

"Where are you going? What will you do?" cried Sental. "You have no horse—no rifle? There will be a dozen— twenty of them, perhaps—the gun men of this ranch, and the men of El Blanco. They're not lambs to be driven in a herd by one dog barking! They have teeth, amigo. What is this madness you are about to try?"

But Seton turned away from him. There, straight before him, the hills parted in the distance, and the stars gleamed closer to the horizon's verge. Once before Walters had ridden away in that direction through the night. And would not he ride that way again? The easiest, the quickest route for them when driving the cattle, and, in spite of their numbers, perhaps the presence of Seton and Sental together would make them wish to save every scruple of time.

"I go on foot," said Seton. "Stay here, Gaspar. It is not your game. It is mine, and I'm going to try to get a hand in it!"

With that, he leaned forward and sprang away at a long stride. Like other punchers, running was not his forte. But he stuck to a steady gait until he came to the first sharp slope. There he checked himself to a swift walk, and a big man strode up beside him.

It was Sental. Seton gave one glance at the silhouette of the other and then, speaking not a word, he went on up the hillside. But he was glad of Sental. His purpose had seemed an utterly desperate one, to undertake alone. There was a shadow of a chance now, he felt. And, moreover, it warmed his heart to have one friend, ready to live or die with him! Defeat and death would be easier in such company.

Still, they said nothing to each other as they came to the top of the hill and paused there, by silent mutual consent, to take breath.

They had come a good distance from the ranch buildings, but the space they had gone seemed nothing; the ranges of the hills swept up before them like an infinite sea—and they, sailors without a craft to sail!

Out of the higher valleys they heard the lowing of the cows more clearly, now. On even this small eminence, the sound waves traveled to them far more strongly, and the noise jarred on the very heart of Seton.

Now, as he looked back upon his days at the ranch, and at what he had known and guessed of Walters' plans, it seemed to him that he had been a criminal not to shoot down this worse than murderer, this utter traitor to the man and the woman who had placed such trust in him.

Then, closer at hand, he heard cattle giving voice beyond the next line of the hills. The cattle from the northeast section—of course they would be the last to come in. They would make the tail of the drive, and this must be the herd from that district.

He glanced at Sental. The latter could be seen to nod in perfect understanding, and then the two went forward, racing, shoulder to shoulder, neither able to gain a step on the other. Down across the hollow they swept and up the slope beyond, and only when they came to the farther crest did they throw themselves on hands and knees and go forward, so as not to raise their silhouettes against the stars in the sky. Once over the brim, they had something more than mere landscape to look upon. The whole floor of the narrow valley was paved with dimly gleaming horns that seemed to flicker from side to side like small ghosts of flame. And there was the river of broad, sleek backs, and always the clacking of the toes as the spreading hoofs were raised from the ground.

A whole river of wealth was this, flowing on to what? To the hands of freebooters on the southern side of the muddy river that flowed between two lands, on the farther side of the mountains. Seton gritted his teeth. There, at the tail of the crowd, he saw two riders, side by side, and they were not fifty yards away.

CHAPTER 39

He said abruptly to Sental:

"You take the man closest to. I'll take the other one."

"Shoot?"

"No. We'll go down through the brush and try to stick them up. No shooting, if you can help it. There'll be plenty of time for that, later on, if ever we get the horses under us!"

Yes, there would be plenty of chance for shooting later on, once they were mounted. This was not the end of the game. This was only the dim beginning. And, crawling over the lip of the rise, he went swiftly forward, crouching, glad of the size of the brush which gave shelter to a man who was almost standing erect.

He reached the verge of the brush and the bottom of the hollow just as thé last of the cattle streamed past. The rearmost was a young calf which frolicked, throwing up its tail and its heels, a dim, grotesque shadow.

Seton stepped out into the starlight, his gun leveled in his hand.

"We'll make a stop here, boys," said he.

"By God—" cried one of the drivers, under his breath.

"It's Seton!" said the other.

And two pairs of hands shot up into the air. The ponies halted.

"Gainor and Raymond?" asked Seton.

"Yes," they answered.

"What's the game?"

"I dunno," said Raymond, the gambler. "Walters told us to shift this stock in the cool of the night. That's all."

"I didn't think that you'd know anything," said Seton. "Gaspar, keep an eye on that smaller fellow. That's Raymond, and he's as trustworthy as a crazy snake. You boys just loosen up your gun belts and let the guns drop. It's starlight, boys, but don't take any chances. Don't make any crooked moves. I've warned you!"

"Play it straight, Doc," said Gainor. "Don't be a fool!"

A stream of soft, terrible imprecations was flowing from the lips of Doc Raymond, but he followed that good advice and let the gun belt drop.

The two were gathered up by big Gaspar Sental.

"Now step down out of those saddles," said Seton.

"What're you aimin' to do with us, Jimmy?" asked Gainor.

"Give you a walk home. That's all. It's not far back to the ranch—if that's still home to you lads!"

Gainor groaned. But, with Raymond, he dismounted. They stood aside, while Sental quickly "fanned" them, taking an extra gun from each. That would remove the danger of a rear attack delivered by these two as the herd moved off.

"What's your idea, Seton?" asked Raymond. "You ain't fool enough to think, are you, that you can handle what's started tonight?"

"What's started?" asked Seton.

"Shut up, Raymond," said Gainor.

"As if he didn't know!" said Raymond. "Go ahead and run your brains out agin a cliff. It's the best that I wish for you, anyway!"

Seton laughed. One look had showed him that the horses were the pick of the string of each of these punchers. Fast and strong, they would stand the hard riding which he and Sental would have to give them.

"Boys," said he, "I could have plugged you both. It would have been quicker. It would have been safer. Will you tell me what's become of Blood and Bones?"

"Aw, Walters had that runt," said Gainor. "He said that any hoss you picked would have to be a good one. If it was good enough for you, it was good enough for him. There you have it!"

"Good!" said Seton. "I wanted to meet Walters, before. I'm keener to meet him, now."

He sprang into the saddle. The stirrups were exactly the right length, for it was big Gainor's mount. As for Sental, that matchless horseman cared little whether his stirrups were short or long. And they sped off up the side of the valley, working at a slant until they reached the crest of the eastern ridge.

Beneath them they saw the solid droves drifting to the rear, until they came to the end of the hollow. The leading animals were just mounting the rise, and, ahead of them, a solitary rider.

He was the lead man, whose work it was to keep the foremost animals turning into the right gaps and ravines. In time, the beeves would follow his horse as sheep follow the goat. He shouted back at the two shadowy riders.

"Hello? What's up? What's the matter, Gainor?"

"Trouble!" bellowed Seton.

He had recognized the voice of Chet Ray. His own shout was so loud that it certainly could not serve to identify him, and they swept straight down on Ray.

"Is it that damned Seton?" called Ray, when they were

close at hand. "What's he up to now? I've always sworn that I carried the bullets that would finish him!"

"Shove up your hands, Chet," said Seton, thrusting a gun under the nose of that astonished youth. "You get me on another day. Shove 'em up quick, or we'll have to turn you into salt meat."

"It's you! It's you!" muttered the boy, and slowly he raised his hands.

"Turn the head of the herd," said Seton to his companion. "Turn 'em back over the rise. Just turn the leaders and the rest will follow 'em along. Ray," he added, while Sental went to perform this easy task, "you deserve worse than I'm giving you. I'm lightening you of your gun belt and your guns. I ought to lighten you of every pound of flesh and bones that makes you. Now climb off this horse and hoof it."

Chet Ray slid to the ground, throwing his leg over the horn of the saddle, his hands still raised. He said calmly:

"Seton, I don't make you out. You're a crook. I know that. This bluff about going straight makes me sick. It makes all of us sick. And the day'll come when we'll get you. If one of us ain't enough, then we'll get six to turn the trick. Where's Raymond and Gainor?"

"Back there, walking home. Good-by, Chet."

And he spurred away, taking the extra horse on the lead rope. The form of Chet Ray grew dim behind him. Sental, having turned the lead cattle and sent them streaming over the top of the hill, now swept up beside him.

"I'll tell you something, amigo!" he called through the night. "A little mercy is a dangerous thing!"

It started Seton thinking.

What would Sental, left to his own devices, have done in such emergencies as this? Certainly he would not have left three living enemies behind him. Shot them down?

Well, the law never would have called that act murder. How many legal murders were performed, then, inside the limits of the law? There was, in a sense, more actual justice among the hunted men, he felt. Here and there was some cruel devil, like El Blanco, like Douglas Walters; but, on the whole, were not the men outside the law very much the same

214

as those inside it? Only some weakness, some bad chance, some sheer overflowing of the spirits had warped them into strange and wrong courses, and, the start once taken, they flowed down hill, like water, to the great dark ocean of crime.

Sental stretched a long arm before him.

"The dawn, amigo!"

There was neither light nor color in the east or anywhere in the horizon's circle; but the mountains and the hills stood out more sheerly black. They had a more distinct form, and the stars were dwindling and growing old. Yes, the day was coming. And his breath left his body, for a moment. To steal through the night, striking swift blows by starlight here and there at the malefactors—that was one thing. To range under the open eye of the day, discernible at a great distance —that was quite another.

Yet they still had a period of dimness before them. Above all, they still possessed an element of surprise that would work for them. They were supposed to be back there somewhere in the brush, near the ranch. They were supposed to be sleeping, the pair of them, waiting for the sun to rise before they stepped out to the next day—and found the ranch deserted of men, of cattle, of horses. They were supposed to be bound hand and foot by the lack of horses to ride in the pursuit, no matter how early their suspicions might be aroused.

Instead, they were galloping on the trail of danger. God alone could tell how the thing would come out, but a stern, fierce, small hope remained in the heart of Seton.

Grayness increased in the eastern sky, now. The mountains lost some of their blackness. Rocks glinted, high up the slopes. The day was fast coming upon them. He could see the set face of Sental, close beside him. And suddenly it seemed ridiculous to him that they had ridden so far without exchanging a word!

So they came into the upper valley of Benson Creek, and at the same time Sental's horse stumbled, and went dead lame.

It might have been no greater matter than a stone picked

215

up inside the shoe, but they had no time to investigate. Instead, they got Sental on the lead horse and swept on.

They were on the heels of the main herd, now. Before them, as the horses dropped to a walk, straining up some abrupt slope, they could hear the clacking of the hoofs, like dull castanets in the far distance, and they could hear the sounds of the lowing that crowded against the walls of the ravine and swept back to them in heavy billows. It was still too dim a light to note the dust in the air with the eye; but it stung their throats and choked their lungs.

All the wealth of the Henry Ash ranch was pouring up this course to the crest, and, when the crest was reached, it would be streaming down the farther side like water through a flume. No stopping it, then. A very few miles and the cattle would be herded onto Mexican soil, safe from pursuit, safe from recapture.

Seton ground his teeth. After the first success, his hopes had been very high. Now they dwindled, they diminished fast. They had checked off three of the treacherous marauders. They had stopped a fragment of the herd. But the main body of the cattle was pouring before them, climbing the pass to Mexico.

He groaned. He leaned forward, jockeying his horse. And, when he looked back, there was the great horseman, Sental, constantly at his heels, also swayed forward, making the least of his weight to help the struggling horse.

For they were riding without mercy, regardless of lifting or falling slopes. They were pushing toward the brightening light of the day which might well be the last day for both of them. And there was neither fear nor hesitation in either of their hearts.

The day grew yet brighter. They could see the dust cloud which forever unfurled in their faces, and then, as they climbed a ridge, they saw well before them the solid, living mass of the cattle streaming over a farther rise.

CHAPTER 40

Then big Sental reached for his riding companion and clutched his arm.

"We're too late," said he.

"We *can't* be too late, Gaspar!" cried Seton.

"Look!" said Sental. "They're going over the head of the pass now. They're streaking over there away ahead of us."

"No. They're not quite to the top of the grade."

"They will be, twenty minutes before we can ever reach the top of the slope. They're gone from us, old-timer. We never can stop them once they've started shooting down the grade toward the river. They'll scatter. They'll go like hell."

"We'll try," said Seton, grimly.

"Try for what? To collect some lead for ourselves?" suggested Sental. "Be reasonable. If there's anything to gain, I'll work with you to the limit. But there's no use throwing ourselves away. They're heading to the top, or almost the top. We can't get at them, now!"

It was perfectly true.

The day was brightening each moment; and, as the light grew stronger, they could see the details of the higher pass, the rocky pitches that leaned back on either hand, and the dust cloud that streamed above the herd, tinted like smoke above a red fire by the rose and gold of the sunrise.

"I've lost! I've lost!" said Seton, groaning out the words. "I've started too late, and I've lost by ten minutes—twenty minutes! Gaspar, if you'd only waked me up when you first heard the lowing—"

He raised a clenched hand, and then dropped it loosely upon his thigh.

They saw the rear guard of the main herd; three men rode side by side, their rifles balanced across their saddlebows. One of those was Douglas Walters, and twice Seton raised his own rifle to his shoulder, and twice he lowered it again. The man's back was turned; he could not shoot!

In the meantime, the lead animals had mounted to the very top of the pass and would soon be spreading across the more open land beyond, and the last stage of the drive down to the river would begin with the cattle, fresh from the cool march through the night, quite able to gallop the remaining distance almost as fast as a horse could run.

The very head of the column was obscured in the rising fog of the dust-cloud through which the two watchers could penetrate only dimly.

Then, multiplied by the echoes to a cannonade, heavy and distant, from the top of the rise rang out the noise of rifles, many rifles pouring lead down the pass. The sound froze Seton and his friend to ice. They turned their heads and stared at each other.

"Who's there? Who *could* be there?" cried Sental.

"Some mind reader—some enemy of El Blanco! Look, look!"

For the head of the herd had stopped. It swerved, it broadened. Cattle could be seen, emerging from the milling mass, striving to climb up the steep sides of the pass, slipping back, some of them turning head over heels and falling among the horns of the rest. The whole column had halted, and it began to sway from side to side, bunching here, scattering there. Then rose the bellowing of many steers and the more mournful lowing of the cows. Through this heavy storm of sound pierced the shriller cries of men, and, above it, like the beating of hammers against steel, were the ringing reports of the rifles.

The herd turned. The rearmost, as they swung about, were checked for a moment by the three herders, waving their hats, shooting off guns in their faces.

But fresh swarms thrust ahead down the pass. Goaded by

218

the sharp horns from the rear, this gathering mass at last put down their heads and swept forward in a solid phalanx, in a wild stampede. It was no time for anything living to remain there in the throat of the valley with thousands of tons of stamping hoofs and lunging horns bearing down like a wall of water loosened from a broken dam. Whatever miracle had checked the advance, whoever those men were at the crown of the pass, the plans of Douglas Walters and El Blanco were ruined in a single stroke. That flood of cattle would never stop running until they were down the valley and spreading far and wide across the rolling hills and flat lands of the Henry Ash ranch. In an instant the thing was done. The fall of a stone from a sheer height could not have been calculated more clearly.

Seton, with a wave of the hand to Sental, led the way a little down the Benson Valley; but, at the mouth of the first broad ravine that entered the main valley, he turned aside. They rode in a little distance and then reined their horses about.

So great was the relief and the joy in the heart of Seton that he looked instinctively up, to give mute thanks, and saw above him the flaming sky of the sunrise, bounded on either side, like a burning river, by the dark walls of the ravine.

Douglas Walters was done for. He had failed in his great stroke. He had revealed his deviltry without totally ruining Henry Ash. Both Ash and the girl would have to see through him, now. Could they help turning gladly to such a man as Seton himself, with the support of Hooker behind him, and a future not darkened, but brightened by the sense that work would have to be done? They could not help turning to Seton. Their future would be in his hands. And he would make that future as golden bright as the sky above his head!

So he thought. And the roar of bellowing, the crashing of hoofs that approached them, down the valley, was like barbaric music to accompany his dreaming.

He had a feeling that a miracle had been performed, that the hand of God had been put forth to intervene between Walters and El Blanco, and the work they had attempted. But for the human agents who had performed this task—ah, well, he would find a way to show them his gratitude. He would write their names in his mind with letters of fire.

In the meantime, the forefront of that wall of thunder was rapidly speeding toward the mouth of the ravine in which they had taken shelter. It was about to break across it, when six riders on horses which raced at full speed shot into the mouth of the ravine, and immediatly behind them poured the throng of the cattle, heads down, tails flinging up, dust exploding around them and whirling high in the rosy air above.

Six riders—and such a six!

Sental, as he saw them, was already twisting his horse around and throwing himself flat along the back of it. For first of all came El Blanco, his hat off, his silver hair shining; and just behind him was Douglas Walters in person, his face convulsed with a gigantic rage. Tom Innis and Larry Crane were with them, and two others in gay Mexican attire.

If six hand-picked devils had risen out of hell, they could not have startled Seton more than the apparition of these men. He, like Sental, pulled his horse around. As the animal got under way, he heard a screeching cry behind him. Six throats were sending up that shout.

No doubt that Doug Walters and his men yelled at the sight of him, and the Mexicans at the sight of the renegade from their band, for to all those six, here was presented the most glorious opportunity of making amends for the failure of their enterprise.

Looking back, a flying glance, Seton saw the riders coming like six arrows from six mighty bows. Leaning forward to cut the wind more easily, yelling like fiends, they seemed to have a foretaste of triumph and of blood.

He looked back again, as he rounded a corner of the ravine with Sental. He saw that Walters was falling a little to the rear—the short legs of Blood and Bones were not meant to rival such a pace as the rest of the horses sustained. And at the same time, he saw El Blanco drop his reins over the pommel of the saddle, and, guiding and steadying his racing horse by the grip of his knees and the sway of his body only, he jerked out a long rifle from the holster that ran along the saddle, the butt under his leg.

He jerked it out, brought it to his shoulder, and the same instant fired. Seton's horse staggered as though struck by a club. He did not fall instantly, but his rear legs began to go down and trail. In another moment he would drop. Seton prepared to cast himself free and, falling to the ground, keep his rifle with him. If he were not stunned by the shock of the fall, he would make two or three of them pay for his death before they were able to close in over him!

Then he saw Sental reining back strongly to his side. He saw Sental's hand and arm extended to him, and the Mexican's set, grim face. He could not believe it. Only the day before, his murder had been in the mind of Gaspar. Now the other was willing to risk life for him—ay, to invite almost certain death, for how could one horse with a double burden escape from those six deadly greyhounds who raced in the rear?

But he accepted that sacrifice. He simply knew, in a blinding flash of comprehension, that if he refused the proffer, it would make no difference. Sental would face about as Seton's horse fell and fight with him until they both were shot down.

In a sense, it was no sacrifice. The glory of it transcended life and death. In one stroke, it blotted out the transgressions of Gaspar Sental, his plots, his robberies, his slayings. It washed him clean, hand and soul.

And Seton, swinging his left leg over the saddle bow, put the foot in the right stirrup. He caught the strong, extended hand of Sental and leaped. Right behind the crupper he landed. His own horse he felt go down under the thrust of his spring; and, as he struck the animal of Sental, it staggered, but went straight forward with gallant power.

Rifles were crackling. Then they swept about another curve in the ravine, and the pursuit was behind them. They were safe for some few seconds.

Sental turned his head.

"Amigo!"

"Gaspar?"

"I'm going fast. They have me."

"No, no, Gaspar! They haven't hit you?"

"Under the right shoulder."

He saw it then.

It was a patch of red half the size of his palm, but it was spreading. By its location he knew that the wound must be draining the very life of his friend, and the heart of Seton stopped with anguish.

CHAPTER 41

"Gaspar!" he called again.

The Mexican turned his head once more, and Seton saw that the color of his face already had altered, and there was a drawn white look about his features.

"Courage! Steady!" said Seton. "Keep up your heart, Gaspar. Something will happen. The people who are driving the cattle will turn in after this pack of scoundrels—"

"Listen, amigo," said the Mexican. "My brain is fainting. I am going to throw myself from the horse. Ride on. Save yourself. There is the speed and the strength of the wind in him. Ride on. I have no regrets—"

"If you throw yourself down," said Seton, "I'll turn back and fight over you. I swear it by the God who sees us, Gaspar. But make for that nest of rocks. There. Do you see? Make for that. We will fight them off until the noise brings us help. Quick, quick, Gaspar!"

Sental, obediently, as though he knew, as Seton had known before, that the great heart of his companion could not be denied when it was set in its will, turned the head of the horse for the rocks, and in a moment they were among them.

Seton sprang down. He received in his arms the weight of his friend, lunging down toward him. Bullets whistled about them, and, at the sight which proved that Sental had been wounded, an Indian screech of jubilation arose from the six.

Sental lay upon the ground, on his back. Seton struck the horse behind the knees and pulled down upon the bridle reins. By the greatest luck the animal had been well trained, and first it knelt, then lay down so that the rocks sheltered it from the steady hail of bullets. What a storm of lead was sweeping over them! The stones shook under the solid blows. Sprays of lead were flying as the bullets, striking the rocks, dissolved with the heat of their own speed.

"Gaspar?" said Seton.

The Mexican, bracing himself against a stone, was calmly, deliberately slashing away his shirt, laying his right arm and shoulder bare.

"Attend to those others, my dear friend," said Sental. "I am not too far gone. I can take a little care of myself."

"With a high heart, Gaspar!"

"Of course!" said the Mexican.

His pale eyes smiled at Seton.

"We shall live to drink together and laugh at this!"

"We shall, we shall!" said Seton.

He saw the place which the bullet had wounded. The hole was big, purple rimmed, and the blood was dark red as it poured down over the white of the skin. Tears stung the eyes of Seton. He grasped his rifle and turned to take some revenge for the fall of his friend.

But there was not an enemy in sight. The instant that the two had taken to covert, the six who hunted them had fanned out and each man had gone for a separate refuge. From depressions, from rocks, from behind tufts of shrubbery, from out a poplar grove, rifles fired at them. Taking advantage of the unevenness of the ground, the six could retire, advance, or shift from side to side, unseen.

Seton ground his teeth. Once, twice, and again he tried chance shots at a patch of shrubbery, and at the poplar trees. The third exposure of his head and shoulder won him a bullet that chipped a morsel from his ear.

There was nothing to be gained by such blind fighting except his own death, speedily. So he turned to give the necessary help to his companion. Between them, hastily, they made a bandage. It was composed of Seton's own undershirt. That of Sental must not be sacrificed. Its warmth was needed for his drained body.

First, with a handful of thin dust, Seton tried to check the flow of the blood. But through the dust up-welled the stream again. He tried again, and again, holding the dust in place for a good long moment with the palm of his hand.

While he held it, he searched the face of Sental. It was white as stone, but Seton smiled gently, and the eyes of the Mexican never failed to light within and smile in return. Even his lips smiled, but they did not speak. The man was no fool to waste necessary breath, the least scruple of which might, in another moment or two, be the treasure which would save him from death.

When the flow of blood was stanched, at least for the time being, Seton heaped on still more dust, gently, and then made soft pads of cloth, a small one to fit over the mouth of the wound, and a larger one on this and again a third. Over the three, he passed a bandage made of the last strip of his undershirt, and then another made of the outer shirt itself. It was a good, strong bandage, and he drew it reasonably tight.

"Listen to me, Gaspar."

"I hear you."

"Look up at the sky. Lie quietly, no matter what happens. If you stir violently before a doctor comes to you, you are a dead man. Do you understand? You are no better than a dead man!"

"It is true. But look! We are both no better than dead men. Stop him with a bullet if you can, amigo!"

Seton looked, following the eyes of his friend, and on the farther side of the cañon, working up close to the upper brim, he saw a rider come out from a nest of boulders and pass into a screen of shrubs.

It was quite true that both of them were no better than dead men, once that rider gained the upper ground. The way

224

was difficult. From the distance, it looked impossible, but both the horse and the man were capable of making impossibilities matter of fact. The one was Blood and Bones. The other was Douglas Walters.

And Seton, dropping to one knee, his rifle ready, carefully trained it upon the brush into which the rider had gone.

What was the distance? Five hundred? Six hundred yards?

He bit his lip.

The rose and golden glory was not yet gone from the sky. A mere moment had passed since that moment when he had been sitting his saddle and looking up with a bland satisfaction toward the riotous color of the heavens, giving thanks to his Maker out of a full heart. Now he crouched here among the rocks, with his friend close to death, and a more certain death about to threaten them both.

Carefully calculating the distance, as well as he could, though the misty morning light bothered him terribly, he saw Douglas Walters ride into the circle of the sights, and squeezed slowly down on the trigger, a movement of his whole hand, a delicate touch. At that distance a mere breath could cause him to miss.

The rifle exploded. The rider vanished into the brush that grew higher up the slope, and Seton, as he raised the gun for a moment, looked back at Sental.

The Mexican was watching with blank eyes.

"I missed," said Seton. "Too low, I think."

"Yes," said Sental, decisively. "You were too low. The air is not as dim as you think. Give yourself another forty, another fifty yards."

Seton caught in his breath, held it, elevated the sights anew, and once more he was looking at the distant brush. Was it the wind that waved it, or a rider forcing his way through?

Out into the open appeared the rider once more. There was still a little distance to the upper edge. It looked like sheer rising cliff, to Seton, but horse and man went at it, zig-zagging from side to side, rapidly.

The rifle of Seton clanged, the butt kicking back lightly against the padding muscles that covered his shoulder.

But the rider went on.

Had he been hit? He was a bulldog who would go on, anyway.

"Too low! Too low!" said the master marksman, Sental.

And he made a little movement with his left hand, as if to ask for the rifle, and try his own weak hand. Weak though it was, he was unsurpassed in shooting at a distant target. Natural genius and long practice in his native Mexican mountains had given him that talent.

Seton did not challenge the criticism. He elevated the sights yet higher. Not much, for he knew that he was at least very, very close to the mark.

And now, in his course, big Douglas Walters was almost at the brim. Yes, at the very lip of the ravine, Blood and Bones was pawing, his ears laid back and his snake head thrust outward and upward.

And again Seton took the man and the horse bodily into the sights. The horse would be enough. But no, he could not actually fire an aimed bullet at Blood and Bones, that faithful old companion. He remembered the leap across the ravine, and, with pinched lips, desperately, he focused upon the rider alone. He was shooting low, said Sental, but not much too low. Now he worked up the gun until only the head and shoulders of the distant rider were throbbing, swaying, pulsing in the big black circle of the sights. Delicately, but with a hand as steady as stone, he drew the bead.

At that moment there was an outbreak of loud Indian whooping, and the discharge of several rifles, a sustained discharge from repeaters that sent a whirring shower of death pouring over the rocks. That was the brain of El Blanco, of course, striking at the moment his companion tried the high exploit, striking to unsettle the nerves of the marksman who would now make a last attempt to bring down the hero on the cliff.

Was Seton disturbed? He told himself that he was not. A faint, cold smile curved his lips. He felt that he was taking the life of a human being into the curve of his strong forefinger. So he pressed upon the trigger, and the explosion jerked the barrel of the rifle up.

No longer looking through the sights, as though a glass had been removed from his eyes, more clearly but seeming to be in a more distant field, he saw big Douglas Walters still on the horse, and Blood and Bones that instant gained the upper level and started in toward safety with a leap, his tail blowing sidewise in the wind that swept the upper ground.

And Walters, as he rushed triumphàntly into shelter from the rifleman below, took off his sombrero and waved it with a high flourish, mockingly, rejoicingly.

Ay, it was the act of a hero. The heart of Seton was not warmed by it, but he nodded grimly, and told himself that the man was made with nerves of steel. So were they all— all as keen as wildcats, as savage and as fierce. Perhaps it was the very fact that they lived outside the law that gave them this power. In those other days, when his own life was much as theirs, when he was the hunter and the hunted by profession, would he have missed three such chances, even by morning light and at five hundred yards? He told himself that he would not.

But now it seemed that the last door had been closed upon his hopes.

CHAPTER 42

He looked about him as a man about to die, quiet, collected, calm. One thought alone stabbed him with a poison of grief. It was Molly Ash, who would hear the end of him, and never know all the truth. But he swept that thought away, and the weakness that went with it.

The eastern wall of the ravine was all in shadow; the western wall glowed with a golden light. The sky still burned above him, but with a paler and more intolerable fire. Suddenly he felt as though his spirit had become that of a giant, and the whole ravine was his grave, dug specially for him, and that flaming sky laid there as a cover for his soul. So easy was it for Seton to look forward to death with his friend.

He turned with a smile toward Sental. In another moment, Walters would open from the height with a plunging fire against which the low rocks could not afford them the slightest security.

So he turned to Sental, smiling, and he saw that the other had dragged out a revolver and now held the muzzle of it close to his head.

"Amigo," said the Mexican, "you have one last chance for escape. Do you hear? Rouse up the horse, and, as he rises, jump into the saddle and spur him up the valley."

"And leave you here for them to cut to pieces?"

"They will pay no attention to me. Who am I compared to Seton? I'm a morsel. A nothing. They will ride like madmen after you. I shall lie here. The noise of the guns is heard already by those others, those who turned the herd. They will be here soon. Ride, ride, in the name of God, before he begins to shoot."

Seton shook his head.

"Never!" said he. "Ah, Gaspar," said he, "it's a day that has to come. We faced it together in the old days. We face it together again. We have had our dance. We pay now. That is all. I have no regrets. In the whole world," he said, his voice rising and ringing a little, "I know no finer man to have beside me when I die, Gaspar!"

"If you will not leave me while I am living, you will leave me when I am dead," said Sental. "Adios, amigo!"

And he pressed the muzzle of the revolver against his temple.

"Gaspar! For the sake of God!" cried Seton.

"Will you go?"

"Yes. I go now. You make me a sneak and a traitor, Gaspar. God forgive me, but what can I do?"

"Ride! Ride, man, faster than the bullets can follow. Ride this instant!"

Seton argued no longer. He merely nodded and stretched out his hand. Sental grasped it with the last of his strength, and he raised in his eyes and upon his lips a last smile for his friend. They parted in silence.

One jerk upon the reins brought the good horse like a springing deer to its feet. Seton hurled himself into the saddle as the horse already clawed at the earth to get under way. Then, lying stretched low along the back of the gelding, he forced it straight up the neck of the ravine.

A rod, another, another they flew, before a wild, half wailing cry arose behind them. He changed direction sharply to the left, and the first flight of the bullets flew harmlessly in the rear.

A gun rang from above and clipped the rim of his hat. That was Douglas Walters, at last at his post, only to find that his hunted man was shifting ground! What curses must be streaming from the heart of Walters, now!

Back to the right, Seton dodged the horse. The bullets were humming past him. Wild outcries rang down the valley, and something stung him along the right side, like the touch of a bit of ice. It was a mere grazing touch, that was all.

And then the angling wall of the ravine stepped in between him and the pursuers!

Around another and another corner the horse flew. The ground began to rise. Pray God that it would soon climb to a smooth upper level along which he could make a good time —or on which he could meet Douglas Walters, man to man. Bitterly, hungrily he yearned to meet the man. And El Blanco, likewise, must somewhere and some time be reserved for him.

Another turn of the ravine, and there he saw before him a sheer wall, fifty feet high, and knew that his hopes were blasted. It was a box cañon. Over the lip of the terminal wall showered a cool little stream such as might be poured from a water pitcher. It dissolved into a thin spray and spattered on the black, polished face of a rock below. And there, fifty feet above him, would be safety, if only he could reach it!

No horse could climb that wall. But a man could, easily. Up the valley behind him he heard the thunder of the coming riders. It came in waves, deepening and dying as they turned the various bendings of the way. Another rider would now be speeding along the upper rim—big Douglas Walters, on Blood and Bones. He would be coming fast. There was no hope to escape him, except the chance that he might have left Blood and Bones at a distance from the rim of the valley, before he crawled to it to fire from security and bring down the man he hated so.

In any case, swiftly to mount that wall was the only hope of Seton. He kicked off his boots, threw off his hat. Already he was naked to the waist. He thrust one revolver, handle downward, into a side trousers pocket. Then he forced the gelding close up under the wall, stood up in the saddle and, by a strong leap upward, was able to catch hold of a projecting rock-rim.

The force of the leap set him swinging. He thrust out with his right foot and hooked it upon another projection. He hung there parallel with the ground until he could reach a crevice above him, with his left hand.

So, by degrees, he swarmed up the face of the cliff. It was terrible work. His heart raced, and every stroke of it was an alarm bell clanging in his ears. Speed, speed was all that could save him. Speed such as a monkey could show, no other speed would avail him. The immense power of his shoulders and arms, his desperate willingness to take every chance helped him.

He looked down, when he had reached a high ridge. Over the rim of the cañon wall, he could see the rushing horsemen, he could spy the white hair of the great El Blanco. But they did not see him, and they would be too late, too late!

He looked up and saw the uppermost ridge almost at hand; and to the side, hearing the beat of hoofs, he saw something else—Douglas Walters rushing up on Blood and Bones!

The rifle was at the shoulder of Walters. He fired. Right under the place where the other bullet had raked across his ribs, this one ploughed, and thrust an agonizing hand through the whole body and soul of Jimmy Seton.

His revolver was out, but the pain made his hand unsteady, blurred his eyes. He fired, but he knew that the bullet flew wide. A second shot from Walters clipped the hair above his ear. A third would split his skull.

And then, by inspiration, he remembered, and whistled. At the familiar call, Blood and Bones leaped far to the side. The third bullet from Walters' gun flew at random from its muzzle, and the next moment his rifle had fallen to the ground, and he was struggling desperately to keep his place in the saddle.

Seton, at that, sprang up the remaining face of the cliff and drew himself lightly to the flat beyond. Out of the depths of the ravine below him arose a babel of screeching cries, a horrible tumult of disappointed wrath, a humming of bullets, weird and angry messengers that whined harmlessly through the air, well above his head.

He forgot the peril from which he had been saved. He forgot those wild men in the ravine. He forgot the great El Blanco, and poor Sental lying so far away in the nest of rocks—murdered now, perhaps, by the barbarians who had ridden past him—and he remembered only Douglas Walters.

The latter, finding that he could not master the horse, and seeing his enemy come at him, pulled a revolver and leaped from the saddle. Ill luck made him leap just as the horse was rising, so that he shot up into the air. He landed on all fours in grass, but the revolver skidded far away, and Douglas Walters rose with empty hands to face Seton.

Once, twice and again Seton covered him, covered the heaving breast, the sneering mouth, the wrathful, indomitable eyes. Then he threw his own gun aside and leaped in, hand to hand.

It was madness. It was utter madness. The climb up the cliff had sapped his strength. Already the blood from the double wound was a drain on him, and Walters would be fighting for his life. But a red blindness closed like a mist over the eyes of Seton as he sprang at Walters. And Walters, with a roar of thundering joy for the new chance which had been given to him, leaped in at Seton in turn.

A hard-driven right hand caught Seton on the chin and spun him around like a top. A slashing blow stopped his spinning, and strangely cleared his brain. He saw Walters leaning, tearing up from the ground a ragged rock, half imbedded in it.

There was nothing but murder, no fairness in the man's mind. There was the savagery of a beast, nothing human about his soul, or about the face, hideously slavering.

Seton went in again. He went in as the rock was raised for the death-stroke, and smote around it, and reached the point of Walters' big, square-built jaw.

The stone dropped from his hands. The whole weight, the whole swinging power of Seton had been in that stroke. It dulled the eyes of Walters. It made his mouth sag open; it unstrung his knees so that they sagged together, leaning one against the other for support.

It was an instant of darkness. That was all. He was himself again, snarling like a beast, as Seton came in at him savagely. They locked their arms around each other. They heaved and strained, and suddenly Seton heard a dull snapping sound inside his body. His ribs on the right side, already scored across by the rifle ball, had snapped under the terrific pressure to which they were being subjected.

Walters heard it too, felt the side give under his grip, and he uttered a high, whining cry, like a wolf which has buried its fangs close to the heart of the deer.

Then Seton, grim and calm, loosed his left arm, which had been tugging and hauling. With the heel of it he jabbed upward, against the nose of Walters. The face of the latter became a red blur. He jabbed again. The head of Walters jerked back, and as it came down again, the chin jarred on the clenched fist of Seton, as upon a bedded rock. Instantly his arms loosened. He reeled away. Seton followed close, poised for the final stroke—and behold, Douglas Walters vanished before his eyes!

CHAPTER 43

A wild cry rang in the dim ears of Seton.

The cry dropped swiftly away from him. He looked down. There was nothing at his feet. He had a mad feeling of standing on the empty air and below him he could see the men of El Blanco, and El Blanco himself, almost at the top of the same cliff up which Seton had climbed a moment before.

Agile as a cat, the outlaw reached from point to point, swarming up the rock—not a man, but a sheer agent of destruction, a demon, a spirit. And below him, sheer down, a body hurtled through the air. The body of Walters, arms flung wide, face upturned, contorted, still stamped with the undying hate.

The body struck. Actually it rebounded, or seemed to rebound, and turning, lay quietly, face down.

Seton stepped back from the verge of the height. A strange dreaminess had come over him. He felt neither weakness from the loss of blood nor pain from the wound and the crushing of his ribs.

Blood and Bones came to him like a dog, with pricking ears. He rubbed the muzzle of the horse and smiled at it, speaking gentle words. But there was something else that he must do. Trouble was coming upon him. What was it?

Ah, he remembered, now. It was El Blanco. He must get a gun—so he looked about him. But darkness seemed to have succeeded the flare of the early morning. It gathered heavily. It was a fog before his eyes. Only vaguely he could see the gleam of grass before his feet, but no weapons, no guns anywhere. He fumbled at the rifle holster at the side of the saddle.

It was empty!

He kicked through the grass, but nothing touched his toes. "I'm drunk," said Seton. "No," he added, aloud and in a quiet voice. "I'm not drunk. But I'm fainting. El Blanco is coming, and I have to get away from here."

At that, he climbed into the saddle. He let the reins hang loosely. He merely kicked his heels into the flank of the gelding, and Blood and Bones started off at an easy canter, his head turned a little, as though he knew perfectly well that he must take care of this human burden in his saddle, which sat and jounced so loosely.

A voice shouted at the side. It pierced his brain as a needle pierces silk. It was the voice of El Blanco, shouting to him, challenging him, daring him to turn and meet him, face to face. Meet him with what? With empty hands?

He laughed a little, feebly, foolishly.

They struck a steep grade. Bullets were flying about him, again. El Blanco's bullets, for they flew close. They kissed the air at his very cheek. They sang a wild, brief note at his ear and then fled away.

A solid shock struck him. He could not tell where. It was like the blow of a fist. But he knew, vaguely, that it was a bullet that had gone home, a forty-five caliber bullet such as fitted into a Colt's revolver, of the pattern used by the dexterous, cunning hands of El Blanco.

Well, a bullet more, what did it matter?

The grade grew steeper. He could not see the end of it, which was lost in darkness. He topped the grade. He went down a slope sharper than that which he had mounted, and, beneath him, voices yelled, suddenly.

He looked down. As through a suddenly opened window, he saw the bottom of the valley, and in that bottom there were two riders. One was a slender Mexican lad, with a bright, handsome face, and a rifle at his shoulder. The other was familiarly bulky about the shoulders. It was the big body of Jake Mooney. And those were his shoulders, those were his great arms, that was his face.

The rifle?

It was pointed straight up the hill at Seton. He regarded it casually. It was aimed straight at him. At his heart, perhaps. When that curled finger closed, his soul would be snapped in oblivion of darkness or into radiance of eternal light—

But the rifle did not speak. Instead, he saw the hand of Mooney rise, slowly, and it came down like a hammer on the head of his companion.

"Very strange!" said Seton, to himself.

For the Mexican reeled and fell forward in the saddle, stunned. The rifle dropped to the ground, and the half wild horse of that young rider instantly wheeled and bolted down the slope, carrying itself and its burden in the saddle out of view around the first hill-shoulder.

It was gone, and there was only Mooney before him, holding out a hand, calling to him. Suddenly he was at the side of Jake Mooney. He was being shaken.

"My God," he heard Mooney say, "you're shot to pieces. You're dyin' in the saddle. Who done it?"

"El Blanco, I suppose," said Seton, gently. "Nothing much. I'll have a bit of a nap and then go on to—"

He dropped into darkness. Arms received him. The last he remembered was that he had a foot caught in a stirrup, and that Mooney was pulling him hard against it, and that the head of Blood and Bones was turned to him, with bright, kind eyes. A sympathetic animal was a comfort.

He was in utter darkness. His mind stopped. When he wakened from that trance, he heard voices in the vast distance, wind-borne, blowing down upon him. He gathered his wits. The voices came closer. They rushed upon him with lightning speed. They came so fast that they startled him back to consciousness.

Then he sat up, suddenly. His head was perfectly clear. People had not been approaching him rapidly. They were already there. It was only the lifting of the fog from his brain by degrees that had let in the sound upon his intelligence, as the unshuttering of a window, bar by bar, lets in the light upon a room.

They were there, close beside him, two men, locked close together, writhing upon the ground. A big man, vast in bulk, mighty of shoulders, was now on the bottom. Now he twisted on the top of his more slender foe. The big man had a flaming red neck. Like Jake Mooney. Yes, it *was* Jake Mooney. And the slender wildcat beneath—yes, like a wildcat—that was El Blanco.

He swayed to his feet. A rifle was there on the ground. The one which the Mexican had dropped when Mooney's blow stunned him? He swept it into his hands, and, at the same moment, he saw El Blanco beat the heel of a revolver twice into the face of the man above him.

Jake Mooney dropped, a loose bulk, and above him, rising like a flame, laughing in inhuman joy of the battle was El Blanco.

There was one stabbing pain through the side, through the heart of Seton. Then he was cold, calm, clear-minded. All of him was strangely weak, as if from fever. Only his hands were strong, nerveless, sure as they never had been sure before. He held the rifle hip-high, the muzzle pointing down toward the ground. Even El Blanco he would not murder, El Blanco arrested, thus, on the verge of another slaughter.

"Don Pedro," he said.

"You rise from the dead, my friend," said El Blanco. "You rise from the dead like an Indian, all red. But you are going to die again!"

He trembled with his emotion, that El Blanco. An emotion of joy, perhaps. And Seton looked idly, carelessly at him, rather wonderingly.

"Don't you see, El Blanco?" said he. "I've won. I'm going to live. God is with me, and you're dead this instant as surely as you'll be dead a moment from now."

The joy faded from the face of the Mexican. A sort of startled wonder like fear widened his eyes.

Then, through stiffly compressed lips he said: "You fool!" And the muzzle of his revolver tipped upward.

"You'll miss," said Seton, gravely, and, swaying the rifle up at the same time, he fired from the hip.

He heard and felt a bullet go past his face. It was like El Blanco to shoot for the head, even in such a grave case as this. But El Blanco was there no more. Or was that he? That slender man lying on the ground, face upward, smiling, with the wind ruffling the silver of his hair across a red mark in his forehead?

*　　*　　*　　*　　*　　*

When big Jimmy Seton came to himself, out of the sleep into which he fell, it was three full days afterward. He was pretty well stiffened by a swathing of bandages.

He turned his head to one side. There sat Sheriff Bill Perry. And beside him was the banker, Hooker.

"You see?" said Hooker to the sheriff. "He had to live. He's gunna live, all right."

And the grim face of the sheriff smiled, as upon a favorite child.

"You two," said Seton, his brain struck by a sudden light. "You guessed it. You and your men were the ones who blocked the pass—"

"Hush," said a voice on the other side of the bed, "because Señor Sental is sleeping."

He turned his head to the other side. And there sat Molly Ash and her father beside her.

He looked at them as at a picture.

"Gaspar?" he whispered.

"He's pulling through—slowly—slowly. He's going to live, when he knows that you're all right. And you're going to be all right. I always knew it. You *have* to get well."

So said the girl.

He turned his head still farther. On the bed on the opposite side of the room he could see the face of Gaspar Sental, rock-white, fixed and rigid as if in death. But the covers rose softly above his breast.

"And Mooney?" he whispered again.

237

"Oh, there's nothing wrong with him. Listen! That's Jake singing!"

Ay, a great, hoarse, tuneless voice singing in the distance, making no harmony!

He dropped two vast cares from his mind. Comfort like the approach of sleep came softly upon his brain, and he stared at the girl and deeply, deeply into the quiet of her eyes. They did not turn aside. They opened wider; they admitted him; no question of his asking was unanswered.

"Thank God," said Seton, "that it's the end!"

"No," said she. "It's only the beginning."

THE END

Max Brand is the best-known pen name of Frederick Faust, creator of Dr. Kildare, Destry, and many other fictional characters popular with readers and viewers worldwide. Faust wrote for a variety of audiences in many genres. His enormous output, totaling approximately thirty million words or the equivalent of 530 ordinary books, covered nearly every field: crime, fantasy, historical romance, espionage, Westerns, science fiction, adventure, animal stories, love, war, and fashionable society, big business and big medicine. Eighty motion pictures have been based on his work along with many radio and television programs. For good measure he also published four volumes of poetry. Perhaps no other author has reached more people in more different ways.

Born in Seattle in 1892, orphaned early, Faust grew up in the rural San Joaquin Valley of California. At Berkeley he became a student rebel and one-man literary movement, contributing prodigiously to all campus publications. Denied a degree because of unconventional conduct, he embarked on a series of adventures culminating in New York City where, after a period of near starvation, he received simultaneous recognition as a serious poet and successful popular-prose writer. Later, he traveled widely, making his home in New York, then in Florence, and finally in Los Angeles.

Once the United States entered the Second World War, Faust abandoned his lucrative writing career and his work as a screenwriter to serve as a war correspondent with the infantry in Italy, despite his fifty-one years and a bad heart. He was killed during a night attack on a hilltop village held by the German army. New books based on magazine serials or unpublished manuscripts continue to appear. Alive and dead he has averaged a new one every four months for seventy-five years. In the U.S. alone nine publishers issue his work, plus many more in foreign countries. Yet, only recently have the full dimensions of this extraordinarily versatile and prolific writer come to be recognized and his stature as a protean literary figure in the 20th Century acknowledged. His popularity continues to grow throughout the world.